As Long As You Love Me

A Simple Love Story: Book 5

Dana LeCheminant

Cover design copyright © 2020 by Sheridan Bronson
Cover image © 2020 by Torwaistudio/Shutterstock.com
Vinyl element © 2020 by Vecteezy.com

This book is a work of fiction. The characters, names, incidents, places, and dialogue are either products of the author's imagination or are used fictitiously. Any resemblance to actual persons, living or dead, events, or locales, is entirely coincidental.

First Printing: September 2020

ISBN: 978-1-951753-05-4

To my sanity: it was nice knowing you

CHAPTER ONE

"You need me to do what?"

Steve's sigh was loud enough through the speaker phone that it pulled my attention away from my computer screen, which was pretty impressive. "Brennon, I need you to come by the restaurant for a couple of hours," he said. Slowly, as if he was afraid I'd lost the ability to hear properly.

A quick glance at my watch told me it was almost seven, which would explain why my stomach was growling, but hanging out at my best friend's restaurant wasn't necessarily going to solve that problem for me unless he was actually planning on cooking something. "But I thought you were closed tonight."

The Globe was always closed on Thursdays, to give him the chance to prepare for the busy weekends. He wasn't changing things up on me, was he? I shuddered at the thought. The last thing I needed was Steve Evans doing something unexpected.

"We are closed," he replied.

"Then why—"

"I'm trying something new tonight, and it's up to you to make sure I don't end up injured."

Well that was intriguing. Steve was mostly blind, but he was as stubborn as they came and rarely asked for help. Most of the time he didn't need it anyway, but the fact that he was willingly admitting his shortcomings meant he really did need my help. "Where is Lissa tonight?"

1

I asked. Wouldn't his wife have been a better option for something like this?

Steve chuckled. "She doesn't approve."

"Steve, are you doing something dangerous?"

"That all depends on you, my friend. See you in twenty." He hung up before I could make a better argument, leaving me in an uncomfortable silence.

I had never minded silence before, but the last month had left me in a perpetual stillness that served as a blank canvas for my thoughts.

Most of which turned into songs.

"Do *not* start singing," I warned myself then frowned at my screen. I had plenty of work to get done, but it wasn't like I could just leave Steve hanging. If Lissa didn't like what he was doing—why would she let him do it, first of all?—then it was probably a good idea for me to go over there.

Or maybe I could call Matthew… Steve's cousin-in-law saw my best friend more than I did lately, and it wasn't like he had much work to do. He and his wife ran a coffee shop, but I was pretty sure Indie did all the work. Anyway, they closed late in the afternoon, so Matthew probably had plenty of time to go check on Steve.

"Who am I kidding?" I muttered. "Matthew's probably right in the middle of it with him." The two of them had become friends almost the moment they met, and Matthew was literally incapable of being serious. He had turned Steve into even more of a reckless buffoon than he'd been before he lost his sight.

"You're talking to yourself, Brennon," came a voice through my open door.

I tensed. "Jake?"

He poked his head in a moment later and replied, "Yeah?"

"What are you doing here?" It was nearly seven, for crying out loud, and he had gotten here just after I did this morning. AKA ridiculously early. I thought he'd already gone home.

Grinning, he shrugged and said, "Being the best assistant ever. I was just about to grab you some dinner. Salad or steak?" He only waited half a second before he decided, "Steak it is," and turned to go back to his desk.

"Wait!" I called and regretted it because now I couldn't change my mind. I should have just taken a second to think before I opened my mouth.

I knew better than this.

"I'm actually heading to The Globe," I said, cringing. I desperately hoped Steve was trying out a new dish and would need me to taste test things, or I was going to regret making this decision to go to his restaurant. My stomach would regret it.

The grin Jake gave me had me a little worried, since it seemed like he knew something I didn't, but he didn't feel the need to explain himself. "Good idea," he said. "In that case, I'll head out!"

"You know you don't have to be here whenever I am," I said. Seriously, he had been here more than twelve hours. It was one thing for me to work this much—that was just what I did—but it was another for my assistant to be so dedicated when he probably spent half his day searching the city for the best chicken parmesan to order me for lunch. (It was from The Globe, no question.)

"I know," he replied.

Do you? I wondered.

"Unless you need anything else from me, I'll see you tomorrow!" He waited just a moment, in case I changed my mind, and then he was gone.

As was my chance to get a steak just right. I didn't actually know what Jake told the chef at Pico's, but it only ever came out perfect when Jake was the one ordering it. I knew that one from experience.

"Guess I'm helping Steve," I grumbled, though I wasn't actually mad about it. Steve's restaurant was doing so well that I barely got to see him as it was, and weekly dinners with his family just didn't cut it. So even though I still had plenty to do here at the office, I gathered up my keys and switched off my computer screen, and then I made my way through the empty office to the parking garage.

By the time I pulled up outside The Globe, my stomach was trying to eat itself, and I was on the verge of getting grumpy. Jake didn't usually let me go this long without food—he had seen me hangry one too many times—which meant he somehow knew I would be coming here tonight. I just wasn't sure how concerned I needed to be about that fact.

I figured the door would be locked, since the restaurant was closed, but I tried it anyway out of reflex. When it opened without resistance, I paused in surprise. Even more concerning was the chatter of voices inside. Steve was rarely quiet when he was in his kitchen, but this wasn't just one guy singing to fill the silence.

This was *dozens* of people.

"Steve, what have you gotten me into?" I muttered and warily crossed the lobby to step into the main seating area.

I stopped dead. Maybe I didn't get out much, but it seemed a little strange that each table would only have two seats. And those two seats were filled with one man and one woman. My eyes locked on a large banner on the left wall, and though I wanted to be angry, mostly I just felt sick to my stomach as I stared at the printed words:

Dating around the World: Singles' Night at The Globe

"Nope," I said out loud and turned to head right back to my car.

"Where are you going?" Steve said, appearing out of nowhere and blocking the exit. The man may not have been able to see all that well, but if his smirk was to be believed, he knew exactly what my reaction had been. "I thought you were going to help me out."

"You're trying to set me up," I replied. And while I hated the fact that my best friend thought he knew better than me, I was honestly surprised it had taken him this long to even try. He had been blissfully married for a whole month now, and I was pretty sure a married man's first goal was to get his friends married too.

Steve tried hard not to grin. He failed. "Set you up?" he said. "Nah. That involves choosing someone for you. You get to do the fun part." He clapped me on the back and nearly knocked me over.

"I thought you said you needed me to keep you from getting injured."

"I do. I'm waiting for you to punch me in the face for this."

I wanted to. And if I was any sort of fighter, I would. But the woman at the nearest table was not-so-subtly watching me out of the corner of her eye, and punching the host would make her think something was wrong with me.

Why would you care about that?

Because she was pretty, and her blonde curls gave her a softness that reminded me of—

Whoa now. Had I really just been about to compare her to Steve's wife? Something was seriously wrong with me, and not just because the song "Pretty Woman" had just started playing in my head. I had dated Lissa for less than a week before she and Steve fell for each other, and it wasn't like I had ever actually loved her.

Love. I didn't believe in love.

That lie was getting harder and harder to believe.

"So are you going to stand here all night, or are you going to give this a chance?" Steve asked, putting a hand on my shoulder as if to tell me I didn't actually have a choice.

At least Lissa hadn't thought this was a good idea. It was nice to know she was on my side.

Speak of the devil, I thought as my phone buzzed with a text from Lissa herself.

You don't have to stay, she said. *I can pick him up when it's over.*

She'd just given me an easy out, but it shot through me like a challenge. Ever since she and Steve started dating a year and a half ago, Lissa had decided she understood me, and she had acted accordingly. She'd been wrong, of course, but at least I had a good idea of how I should act when around her. But unless she had somehow discovered how hard it was for me to back down from a challenge—I hoped she hadn't—she really thought I didn't have the guts to stick around for some speed dating.

I knew this was a monumentally bad idea, but I had to prove I wasn't a total loss. I could spend a night socializing with strange women.

Ha.

I groaned. "Where do I need to sit?" I asked, trying not to sound like there was nothing in the world I wanted less. Steve was still my best friend, after all, and I didn't want him to think I wasn't grateful that he was thinking of me. I highly doubted he tricked me into coming to this because he wanted to torture me.

At least it wasn't karaoke. He'd tried that once in college, and it hadn't ended well for either of us. He had attempted pulling me up on stage, and I'd fought until we both ended up falling into a bartender with a tray full of drinks.

"I knew you'd come around, man," Steve replied, and he seemed absolutely thrilled that I had agreed. "There should be an open seat for you somewhere…" He glanced around, but it wasn't like he could see anything beyond a few inches, and even then, his vision was questionable.

I quickly searched the room then suppressed another groan. The only empty seat I could see was across from a woman who looked more plastic than human. She was probably nice, but if I had any chance of enjoying myself tonight, I would have to end up across from someone who looked a little more real, like the girl at the next table over who wore hardly any makeup at all.

"I'll find it," I told Steve before he started trying to navigate the field of tables. "Where do you need to be?"

He grinned, and I noticed several women in the audience eyeing him with interest. "I'm on snack duty," he said. Oblivious.

Thank goodness. Taking him by the elbow, I slowly directed him toward the kitchen before he bumped into too many people on the way. "You might want to flash your wedding ring before Lissa has a reason to be jealous," I muttered.

Steve had always been popular, since he had that devil-may-care attitude that had filled his life with daring stunts and adrenaline-pumping activities. Plus, he was obnoxiously handsome, and that may have played a large part in why I befriended him so quickly our freshman year at Stanford. It was easy to hide in the background when there was a guy like Steve Evans to take the spotlight.

Laughing, he pushed his left hand though his curly hair and looked so natural doing it that I wanted to smack him. He was only making things worse. "Lissa jealous?" he asked. "Come on." But he seemed inordinately pleased by the idea and looked over the crowd, as if he could actually see the longing glances coming his way. He had only been married for a month, and he was still in the honeymoon phase. Honestly, I was pretty sure he would never leave it.

As soon as I got him to the kitchen, he settled right in, quickly tying an apron around his waist and gathering up the supplies he would need. For a blind guy, he was right at home in this kitchen, and I was so glad he had found a way to get back to his bright self. For a while, he had been losing his battle with the darkness that came after his accident.

Thank goodness for Lissa. Without her, I probably would have lost my best friend.

But now that Steve was all situated, it was my turn, and it took a whole lot more effort than it should have to walk the little distance to that last seat and sit down. Most of my energy just went to putting on a smile instead of a grimace.

My first table partner looked up from her phone when I sat, and her eyes swept over me. It seemed she liked what she saw, because her phone disappeared into her purse. "Hi," she said and held out a manicured hand. How did women even get anything done with nails like that? "I'm Cherry." She had a deep voice, low and sultry, and it sent a chill down my back.

"Brennon," I said and wondered how long I would have to sit here before we changed tables. What were the rules of tonight's speed dating, anyway? Had the event even started?

"What do you do for work, Brennon?" Cherry asked.

Was Steve going to play host, or had he hired someone else to do that part? Everyone else in the room was either chatting with their table partner or glued to their phones.

"I'm a stockbroker," I said. "You?"

"I'm in between gigs," she replied with a broad smile. *Actress?* "Stockbroker, huh? That must be exciting."

How long had some of these people been sitting here? "If you think spreadsheets are exciting, sure."

"You must make good money doing that."

I stopped looking out over the room and fixed my gaze on Cherry. She didn't necessarily sound greedy, but most people didn't. And yet I knew she was here hoping to meet a rich man who could pay her way through whatever "occupation" she pretended to have. It must have been in the way she said it.

Jokes on you, I wanted to tell her. *I may be well enough off, but I'm not looking for a trophy wife.*

Luckily for me, I had dealt with enough of the rich and powerful that I knew exactly how to act like one of them. "You must be a model," I said and leaned one elbow on the table, trying to look casual and relaxed. That part wasn't exactly easy when I had a whole lot of unplanned conversation ahead of me, but I did my best.

Cherry's smile somehow grew wider. "How did you know? Have you seen one of my ads?"

Bus stop bench ad for hemorrhoid cream? But that was being unfair. "You do remind me of something," I replied with a smile. Like the dress-up dolls I had never actually seen up close because I was an only child and Molly didn't like dolls.

My smile disappeared.

Now why did she have to go and pop into my head like that? I'd been doing so well.

Don't think about your old friend, Brennon. You know that.

Thank the ever-blessed heavens for Steve, who pounded a mallet on a gong and ended the conversation before I made a fool of myself. "It's about that time!" he shouted, doing his best to look like he was actually seeing anything out in the restaurant. "My staff will be bringing around some appetizers pretty soon, but until then, you know the drill. You'll have two minutes to talk before I ring the gong, and then you gentlemen will move on to the next number. Any questions?"

A hand lifted somewhere in the middle, but either Steve couldn't see it, or he ignored it and kept talking.

"I honestly don't care what you talk about as long as both of you get some words in. And please, no making out inside the restaurant. This is a classy place, and I'd like to keep it that way. Move along!" He slammed the mallet against the gong again, and all of the men rose to move to the next table.

Some of them, I noticed, did so reluctantly, while others couldn't wait to talk to someone else. I was of the latter group and gave Cherry a half-hearted smile before moving over to Table #14.

"I don't want to waste any time," my new partner said before I'd even settled in my chair. "I'm Judy. I design floral arrangements. I have two dogs and a parakeet, and I don't like beans because they look weird. If I could go anywhere in the world I would stay right here because San Francisco is the best place I've ever seen and there's nothing quite as nice as home."

I blinked, waited a second to make sure she was done, since there had been no change in speech pattern outside of her suddenly going silent and staring at me, and then I took a deep breath. So she was a talker? Would she rather I be a talker like her, or would she rather dominate the conversation?

"I'm Brennon," I said.

"Have you ever done something like this, Brennon? I'm totally nervous, and it's been a while since I last dated so I'm afraid I'm going to make a total fool of myself or maybe even end up without connecting with anyone at all. Wouldn't that be awful? I think I…"

Was it rude of me to tune her out? Probably not. She was happier talking to herself anyway. Didn't she understand the power of a good conversation? AKA taking a moment to listen?

Steve's gong came none too soon, and as I moved to my next table, I tried to see how close he was to getting food out. I was starving, and that wasn't making it any easier to be personable. He was flying around the kitchen in a cloud of steam, shouting things to his two cooks over the chatter that had already started up again, and I had no idea how he was timing our conversations *and* cooking whatever it was that smelled amazing.

I glanced at my watch as I settled in my new seat, curious.

After I introduced myself to my new partner, Heather, we fell into an uncomfortable silence. There was nothing particularly striking about her—brown hair to her shoulders, almond eyes, a sweet smile—

and I couldn't figure out why someone like her would come to something like this if she wasn't planning to start up a conversation.

"So Heather," I said and glanced down at my watch. Only thirty seconds gone. "How long have you lived in San Francisco?"

She shrugged, only keeping eye contact with me for a second at a time. She was trying, at least, but I was pretty sure she was more uncomfortable than me. That was saying something. "Just a few months," she said.

"And before that?"

Another shrug. "South Dakota."

Did you live in the middle of nowhere and never learn how to talk to people? But that was rude, and I was not someone who could judge a person based on the way they interacted with other people. I was doing okay, so far, but that was only because I was concentrating hard. If anything distracted me, like that thought about Molly, I was—

I cursed under my breath. I should have seen that trap I just laid for myself, but I had stepped right into this pit because I wasn't looking where I was going. Thinking about Molly twice in one night? *Brennon, you're an embarrassment. Get a hold of yourself.*

"I'm sorry," Heather muttered, pulling my attention back to her. "I'm so bad at these things. But my friend made me come." She glanced at a woman a few tables away, who seemed to have realized how miserable her friend was because she sent a commiserating smile our way.

I know the feeling, Heather. At least her friend felt a bit guilty. When I glanced over at Steve, he was whistling cheerily to himself. I glanced at my watch—three minutes. *Someone* forgot he was supposed to be timing these things, and I sent a glare toward the kitchen. He probably thought he was so clever and picked out someone he thought I would get along with, giving me two terrible choices before I got to this one.

Nice try, Steve. Heather was sweet enough, but if we tried to go on a date, the pair of us would probably be bored out of our minds. I knew *I* would be, and this was coming from a guy who watched the stock market fluctuate all day. No, I needed someone I could talk to for hours on end.

Then I could stop talking to myself. That would certainly make my assistant happy.

Steve must have sensed my growing irritation with him, because he grabbed his mallet and signaled for the men to rotate.

Was he ever going to bring me some food?

My next partner was big into sports and promptly shut down when I told her I didn't have a favorite football team.

The woman after that tried to convince me I needed to put on some muscle weight. She wasn't wrong, but then I would have to get a whole new wardrobe. And I really liked my suits.

I arrived at the next table to a heavenly sight: the best bruschetta I had ever seen. It was terribly rude of me, and I would absolutely regret it later when I revisited tonight in my dreams, but I stuffed a whole piece into my mouth and barely suppressed a moan of happiness because I hadn't eaten since lunch. My stomach rumbled as it attacked the tomatoes and bread, and then my face flushed with heat when I realized my new table partner had just watched me devour an appetizer like I had been stranded on a deserted island for weeks.

And she didn't seem to care.

"I've always said this place has the best food in the state," she said with a smile. "I'm glad someone agrees with me."

It was the woman I had noticed at the beginning, the blonde one with the hair like Lissa's. Only this woman's hair was curlier, and as soon as that thought struck me, I knew I was in trouble.

Her hair was just like Molly's.

Dagnabit, Brennon. Again?

"I'm Katie," she said and held out her hand to me.

I was about to return the handshake when I realized I had garlic sauce on my hand. Coughing—and wishing I had never shown up to this stupid event—I wiped my fingers clean on a napkin and took hold of her hand. "Brennon," I said. "Sorry for, uh…"

I couldn't get a read on her. The others had been easy to figure out, but Katie felt just a little too normal. Familiar. It didn't help that her eyes were a bright shade of brown, almost hazel. A bit close to Molly for comfort.

What would a woman like her want from a guy like me?

"Don't be sorry," she said, and I was pretty sure she meant it as she looked me over. "I'm sure the chef would appreciate knowing someone likes his food that much. Do you want mine?"

Yes. "No, you should have it." *But if you don't eat it in the next thirty seconds, it'll be gone.*

"I'm actually allergic to tomatoes."

I refused to acknowledge the thought that tried to creep up. It didn't matter that someone else I knew was also allergic to tomatoes. It wasn't like she was here to shove them all onto my plate so she didn't have to look at them. "If you want, I could, uh…" I cleared my throat. "I could go ask the chef to make you something else so you don't have to go hungry." *Not that bruschetta is much of a meal to begin with.*

Katie waved my offer away, but she did seem pleased by it. "I wouldn't want to bother him."

"Oh, he loves to cook. He'd take it as a personal challenge to make you something even better than this." I said that last part right before stuffing the other bruschetta into my mouth. She'd already seen me do it once, so what could it hurt?

Letting out a gasp, Katie turned to the kitchen as if realizing she was talking to someone totally famous. "I wondered if maybe you knew him," she said, practically in awe. "So how close are you?"

He's married, Katie. Don't even try it. "I've known him for years," I said. Almost half my life, to be exact. "He's the only reason I'm here tonight. If I had known this was speed dating, I wouldn't have come." *Well that's a terrible thing to say to the one person who is tolerable at this thing.*

"You don't think speed dating can be useful?" Katie asked, and she deflated a bit.

Had I really made enough of an impression on her for her to be disappointed? Outside of knowing Steve, she knew nothing about me, and I planned to keep it that way. *Since when did I become such a Scrooge?* Could a person be considered a Scrooge outside of something Christmas-related? I didn't get the chance to ask Katie, because someone else answered her question for me.

"Not when you're Brennon Ashworth."

I turned, alarmed to find Matthew Davenport sitting backwards in a lone chair near the doors to the lobby and leaning on the back of it. Just how long had Steve's cousin-in-law been watching me?

"Sorry?" said Katie, though she examined Matthew with interest.

He's also married, I should have said. *And expecting a baby.* Instead, I just stared at Matthew and wondered why he would be sitting there as if my conversation was prime entertainment.

Matthew chuckled. "You know, Brennon," he said without acknowledging Katie's question, "I'm a little disappointed in you. I bet Steve a hundred bucks you wouldn't last five minutes out here. Now I'm flat broke, thanks to you." Not likely, since the Davenports were one of the wealthiest families in California.

Of course Matthew knew about this whole scheme. I'd been right, and he was smack dab in the middle of Steve's nonsense, as always. If there was one thing I could count on when it came to Matthew Davenport, he had no idea how to be serious, which meant he was probably a terrible influence on my friend.

"How long have you been watching?" I asked through gritted teeth.

He leaned his chin on his arms, laughter in his eyes. "Pretty much all night," he replied. "Katie, you can do better than this guy, no matter how sharply dressed he is. I've never actually seen him wear anything other than a suit, and that's just sad."

How sweet of you to say. I bit back my response, just in case it came out as the lyrics to a ZZ Top song since that had started playing in my head, and I tried to think back on what I might have done or said to this man to make him think he needed to insult me. Granted, his insult was technically almost a compliment, as the Davenports were far too perfect a family to *actually* be mean. But still. I may not have had much hope for actually connecting to someone, but couldn't he have done this when I was talking to Heather? I was sure he would have loved to fill that silence, since he was so enamored by the sound of his own voice.

The gong rang out through the restaurant, but I wasn't feeling particularly social anymore. "You're giving Steve a ride home, right?" I asked Matthew as I got to my feet.

He had the nerve to look insulted. "Of course. What kind of friend do you think I am?"

He did not want me to answer that question. "Katie," I said, "it was nice to meet you."

She smiled, and she looked so much like Lissa that it made my stomach twist in my gut. No, she looked like Molly. *Uh oh.* "You too, Brennon," she said. "Do you want to—"

"Good luck tonight. I hope you find someone." And I rushed from the restaurant before Steve or Matthew could try to call me back.

CHAPTER TWO

I reached the second floor of my building just as my neighbors were unlocking their door to head in, and though a large part of me had had enough socializing for one night, I knew it was too much to hope I could sneak back down the stairs before they saw me.

Seth caught sight of me first—big surprise, since nothing escaped the man—and nudged his wife, Catherine. Was it too much to expect the guy to at least smile instead of chilling my blood with his usual scowl? He had been one of the top assets of the US Government for years, and even though he had taken on a much quieter life by becoming a personal bodyguard, he was still absolutely massive and full of all sorts of talents and skills that made him deadly to anyone who crossed him. I was in constant terror of getting on his bad side.

His wife, on the other hand? She and I used to have all sorts of conversations out in this hallway, and she was the closest thing to a friend I had outside of Steve and his wife.

"Brennon!" Catherine said brightly, and she bounced forward and threw her arms around me. Though always friendly and cheerful, she wasn't often physical, so that part threw me off until she said, "Matthew just told me about what Steve did."

Seth and Catherine Hastings: Steve's brother-in-law and Matthew's cousin, respectively.

I resisted the urge to groan, mostly because Matthew had probably told Catherine all about me making a fool of myself. At least Seth gave me a pitying grimace, so I knew he was definitely on my side with this one. When it came to the Davenport family, it was good to have allies. They were a powerful bunch, both good and bad. Luckily, I only interacted with the good ones.

"What Steve tried to do," I corrected. "It wasn't that bad." Lying to Seth Hastings? *Foolish move, Ashworth.*

"The man's an idiot," Seth muttered, and while that opinion was a bit strong, it wasn't anything more than I expected. I loved Steve, I really did, but when it came to his brother-in-law, he played a dangerous game. Seth had never been all that keen on the idea of his sister marrying my friend, and Steve really liked poking the bear. The bear in this case being a two hundred and fifty-pound ex-Green Beret with a whole lot of pent-up energy and the muscle to do a lot of damage if provoked.

The worst part was Matthew often egged Steve on and made things worse, and I was honestly surprised the two of them were still breathing. For some unfathomable reason, Matthew Davenport truly enjoyed being in the middle of Steve and Seth, and one of these days, he was going to get caught in the crossfire if he didn't wise up and get out of the way.

Catherine scoffed as she slid her hand into Seth's. I was pretty sure she had never been afraid of her husband; he was always soft with her and far more attentive than I would expect from a guy of his background. "Steve's heart was in the right place," she said gently. "I may not be your best friend, Brennon, but even I know you're not going to find the right person for you with something like speed dating."

She was right, but that was because there probably wasn't a right person for me. It wasn't her fault for thinking otherwise.

"Lissa should have stopped him from doing it," Seth said, and I was surprised to hear a bit of anger directed at his sister. "But she always turns a blind eye when it comes to that—"

"Seth!" Catherine scolded and whacked his arm.

He rolled his eyes but had the decency to frown and look moderately apologetic. "Sorry, Ashworth. I know he's your friend."

If I had to guess, he was wondering why that was.

Since the first time I was roped into going to Davenport family dinners, I had done my very best to stay on Seth's good side, just because I'd seen firsthand how easy it was to get a rise out of him. Despite having spent much of his adult life as a soldier, Seth Hastings tended to wear his heart on his sleeve. At least that made him easy to read... Because I'd spent a lot of energy to make it so, he thought I was blissfully normal and level-headed. I liked to think I truly was, but that meant my friendship with the impulsive and almost reckless Steve Evans didn't make sense from the outside.

Wishing it wasn't rude to just walk away from this conversation so I could wind down and go to bed, I fought to find a good explanation for why I had stuck with Steve for fifteen years. These two were the king and queen of lifestyle in Northern California, both of them beautiful and wealthy and altogether good people. I highly doubted they could understand my need to keep Steve in my life.

"He's known me longer than anyone," I said. "And he still sticks around. He may not be the smartest guy sometimes, but he's not someone I want to lose."

The pair of them glanced at each other, sharing some silent conversation I was too tired to try to read, and then Catherine smiled. "Did you at least find anyone interesting tonight?" she asked me.

Not you too.

I shrugged, grabbing my keys out of my pocket so I could start wrapping up this conversation before it got a little too deep into the topic of my love life. "I didn't stay long enough for that," I said and figured a joke here might make for a good getaway. "I'm not big on people trying to throw themselves at me."

Catherine smiled again, but it was a tight smile, as if it masked a tension just beneath the surface. And then, to my horror, I noticed Seth stood just as stiffly as his wife, and I felt like a terrible neighbor for not asking earlier: "How are you guys?" *You're better than this, Brennon, and you know it.*

Seth shrugged one shoulder, but Catherine must have been dying to talk about whatever was bothering her, because she jumped right into it: "Oh, you know, just dealing with my pathetic father."

Well that was interesting, and definitely distracting enough to turn my thoughts somewhere other than my dating history. "What did he do this time?" I asked. Milton Davenport wasn't someone I knew well, but everyone knew he wasn't exactly a good man. He was an even worse father, and Catherine had grown up with all sorts of issues she had to work through because his parenting style was practically non-existent. Catherine Davenport had raised herself.

"He showed up at the Munroes' place," Seth growled. "He was trying to avoid running into me."

Clearly Milton hadn't been paying attention to his daughter or her husband if he didn't know Seth was Adam Munroe's personal body-guard and of course would be at his house. But putting Milton and Seth in the same place at the same time was dangerous. The last time that had happened, Seth had nearly committed murder at his own wed-ding.

I had never been more grateful for my very average, normal parents than when I saw firsthand what kind of man Milton was.

"Why was he here?" I asked. "I thought he was keeping to the East Coast."

"He was," Catherine said with a roll of her eyes. "But apparently he's gotten into some shady things and run himself into the ground, so he came here hoping to get money from Uncle Harris. It's okay, though, because Lanna's dad may be quiet, but he'll hold his ground when he has to."

"It's the lawyer in him," Seth added.

I had never figured out how a man like Harris Davenport, a formi-dable and powerful corporate lawyer, could have ended up with an incurable jokester son like Matthew, particularly because his sister had turned out just fine. Matthew and Lanna couldn't have been more dif-ferent as siblings, and where I tried to avoid him when I could, I really liked being around her. She and her husband, Adam, were quiet, unas-suming, and calm. Pretty much the opposite of Molly.

And that was my cue to go to bed. Clearly I had lost all control over my thoughts if I was comparing Lanna Munroe to *Molly*. There was no reason to bring up my old friend right now.

"I hope your dad doesn't start causing trouble," I said and pushed my key into the lock on my door.

Catherine, however, didn't seem all that convinced, and she let out a huge sigh. "I'm so glad Mom protected my inheritance before she died so he couldn't touch it," she said and leaned into Seth as if hoping for protection from her father and his need for money. "I think at this point, he's more determined to ruin all of us than to get his hands on our cash, but the money would be an added bonus. I just hope he doesn't start taking more drastic measures. He's never lived a frugal life, and I'm not sure he knows how."

I'm not sure you *know how,* I thought, eyeing Catherine's always flaw-less appearance. She and Seth both came from big money, and I doubted they had ever brought lunch to school in a brown paper bag like us mortals. At least they didn't flaunt their wealth like some of my clients, many of whom were among the elites like the Munroes, Hastingses, and Davenports. If this family I'd been pulled into by Steve wasn't the nicest family I'd ever known, I would probably hate them. Sure, I had a nice condo and made decent money, but I would never call myself an elite. Not when I had grown up deep in middle-class suburbia.

"You look tired, Ashworth," Seth said.

I almost wondered if he knew I was sizing up his wife's wardrobe and trying to calculate what her outfit tonight cost, since he had slipped into a bit of a glare and a growl.

I am tired. And I'm not going after your wife. "You know how Thursdays can be," I said, though I had no idea if someone like Seth would have a clue what I meant. His life was perfect. "Plus that speed dating really took a lot out of me. I should probably get to bed. Have a good night."

"You'll find someone," Catherine replied as I moved to my door. "I know you will."

I gave her a smile but said nothing, making my way inside and locking the door behind me. She meant well, just like Steve. But the problem was I had already found someone, and that ship had sailed a long time ago and left me stranded on this deserted island that was my life.

Besides, if my constant comparisons to Molly tonight were any indication, I was as likely to find love as Seth was to be afraid of the dark.

I had the weirdest dream. It was one of those dreams where everything
was just a little bit off, but it all felt right, like dreams always do. We
were in my childhood bedroom, but the dresser was on the wrong
side of the room and the wrong color, and the window looked out over
the ocean even though it should have opened up to a small backyard
with more weeds than grass. The fifteen-year-old girl who sat on the
floor flipping through a magazine was off too, and it took me a second
to figure out why. I had never known Lissa that young, so I wasn't sure
how I knew what she looked like.

"Bren, am I more of a thinker or a feeler?" she asked, and I realized
it wasn't Lissa at all.

It was Molly.

What was she doing here?

She grabbed a pencil as she gazed at the magazine. Her long, curly
blonde hair fell over her shoulders, even though she'd tried to pull it
back into a braid, but she didn't seem to notice. She never did. She
looked up, hazel eyes bright and searching, and I couldn't help but
stare. I hadn't seen her in years. "Well?" she asked.

"Why?" I replied. I wasn't sure what I was doing as I sat on my bed,
but I was annoyed that she would interrupt it. She knew me better than
to do that. Or at least she *had* known me better.

"I want to see who my Backstreet Boys soulmate is."

"It's AJ," I said.

"No it's not." She frowned at the magazine and marked a couple of
answers. "My soulmate is a lot more romantic than that." She leaned
against my leg as it hung off the bed, and her touch sent an electric
shock through me.

The dream shifted, and we were sitting in our high school cafeteria
instead, though Molly was still doing her quiz across the table from
me, while I skimmed through a stock market report. She was eighteen
now, and her hair was shorter but just as ill-behaved. I was thirty, and
my suit felt too tight.

"I'm more of a dog person than a cat person," she said, scribbling her answer. "Don't you think?"

I wanted to tell her she hated dogs, but I was suddenly on the other side of the room with a flash of lightning, a whole crowd of people between us. I shouted her name, and she looked up, a little frown on her lips as if she couldn't understand why I was still talking to her.

"I was right, Brennon," she said, her voice carrying across the room as if she were standing right in front of me. "You're not my soulmate."

And I woke to the dulcet sounds of "As Long as You Love Me" playing on the TV. A glance at my watch told me it was three in the morning, and I fumbled for the remote to turn the music video off before it got stuck in my head, though it was probably already too late. The dream had been so vivid, but it was starting to fade as reality slipped back into focus. Reality and an acute headache, which likely came from falling asleep with my head leaning on the back of the couch.

"Brennon, you idiot," I mumbled and forced myself to my feet so I could get ready for bed. Rain pounded the windows that lined one side of the condo, and a rumble of thunder cut across the steady noise. "You know it's a bad idea to start watching TV after nine."

I had only been living by myself for a month, but talking to myself had become an alarmingly regular habit. I figured it was because I wasn't used to my condo being his silent, but then again Steve hadn't exactly been loud when he lived with me.

"He was always with Lissa anyway," I reminded myself. But now that he was married to Lissa, I didn't even have him as an occasional noise. My home was just silent.

And I hated it.

"Sorry," I said to my suit as I hung it up in the closet. The wrinkles from sleeping in it on the couch were painful to look at, and I knew I'd have to drop it off at the dry cleaners sooner than I'd planned. "I won't do it again." But I'd said that before, and now that my best friend was off and married, I didn't have anyone telling me to go to bed at a decent time. Or at least change before I sat in front of the TV. How had I survived before Steve came to live with me? I hadn't had this problem before.

The answer to that was simple: I hadn't known Lissa before.

"Best not to think too hard on that point," I told myself.

As much as I loved being friends with Lissa, Steve's wife had completely disrupted the careful constancy I had crafted for my life over the last several years, whether or not I let myself acknowledge the fact. For that reason, I was as much afraid of her as I was of her brother, Seth. Of the chaos she brought into my life. That dream was proof, and now more than ever it was clear how much she resembled Molly.

"No," I said out loud as I moved into the bathroom and grabbed my toothbrush. "Lissa has blue eyes."

Big distinction there, buddy.

I had never let myself dwell on the fact that I had first been drawn to Lissa because she looked like the girl I'd grown up with, but it was hard to ignore after a dream like that. Pursuing someone who looked the way she did had been a bad idea from the beginning, and I was so grateful she and Steve had fallen for each other. If they hadn't... Who knew where I'd be now?

As I brushed my teeth methodically and carefully, I considered my reflection. Sure, it was three in the morning, so I was bound to look tired. But the exhaustion in my dim blue eyes was worse than I expected, and I was pretty sure that was because of that dream. It may have been several months since I last dreamed about my childhood best friend, but tonight Molly had been just as disarming as ever. It was too bad I couldn't get mad at Lissa for looking like her, because that would make this a whole lot easier.

Why blame myself when I can just blame someone else?

Really, it was Steve's fault. That whole speed dating thing had been an utter nightmare, and I should have known it would mess with my head like this.

When I finished washing my face, I made my way into my bedroom and sat on the edge of the bed, knowing I would never fall asleep if I didn't stick to routine, though I had little hope for getting any good rest after a dream like that. Plus, I would probably be revisiting my sad attempts at conversation all night, and the evening would likely haunt me for years to come.

Taking a deep breath, I turned to the picture frame that had sat on my nightstand ever since my mom had made me go through my box of old high school things a few years ago. If she had known this particular picture was in there, she probably would have burned it by now, but I was glad it still existed. It was a reminder of why I didn't trust people to be predictable no matter how much I wanted them to be. I could control just about everything in my life, but I couldn't control people. It was why I generally stayed away from them if I could help it.

It was why I told myself I didn't believe in love.

This photo was a testament to what could go wrong if I let people in. It was a story of a lost life, a past immortalized in two smiling faces, that I could never go back to.

"You're gone," I told the eighteen-year-old Molly in the photo. She smiled back at me with laughter in her eyes, probably because my bow tie was crooked. Prom night had been one of the best nights of my life, and she had ruined everything just a couple of weeks later. "You're never coming back," I continued. She kept smiling, and I turned the light off with a sigh, settling against the pillows.

"So why can't I get you out of my head?" I finished.

Fifteen years of trying to forget her, and she was lodged in there as deeply as ever.

As always, the room stayed silent around me.

CHAPTER THREE

I met Molly when I was eight years old, just after she and her dad had moved in next door. It had rained all morning, and despite my mom's warnings that the yard would be too muddy to work on the treehouse, I was determined to do it anyway. I'd only been outside for a few minutes when she came out into her own yard, her curly hair pulled back in a massive ponytail and her clothes too big for her.

She didn't see me as she walked the perimeter of her yard, bouncing her hand along the top of the short wood fence that encircled her yard and separated it from mine, and I couldn't find my voice to say hi or anything. She had such an intense look on her face, the kind of deep in thought look that no eight-year-old had any right to have, and I wanted to know what she was thinking about as she kicked mud around.

Eventually she got close enough to me that I either had to hide behind the little fence and pretend I wasn't there, or say something.

"Hi," I said when she was only a foot from me.

I should have gone with the first option.

She screamed and shoved me. My feet slipped in the mud, and I ended up sprawled flat on my back with a grunt. By the time I sat up, she was already gone, the screen on her back door bouncing shut.

She sat next to me on the bus to school the next day, told me she was sorry for pushing me, and we were inseparable after that.

Twenty-five years later, and I could still remember exactly what she wore that day on the bus.

I got to work at seven the morning after that dream and couldn't help but wonder how I had managed to go almost fifteen years without revisiting my first meeting with Molly. I might not have been able to stop thinking about her entirely, but before now I had kept more specific memories like that at bay. But after that dream, I was afraid the careful walls I had put up over the last decade and a half were crumbling.

Maybe I needed to rethink blaming Lissa for all of this. Even if she was innocent, and the problem ran deeper than that, blaming her would be a lot easier than admitting I had failed in the one thing I promised myself I would do when I was eighteen:

Forget Molly.

Completely.

And move on.

I wandered up to my office with my head still pounding and the thought that it was going to be a very long day. The only thing that gave me the strength to step out of the elevator was the knowledge that my job was utterly and completely controllable. I never had any surprises from my coworkers, and money was easy to track and follow. I rarely dealt with clients face to face, since I didn't need them in front of me to trade their funds, so no matter how exhausted I looked, nobody would need to know. I could get through the day, and everyone would think I was my usual, unchanging self.

Everyone but Jake.

"Whoa, boss," my assistant said when I approached his desk. "Late night?"

I grabbed the cup of coffee he held out to me and chugged half of it, even though it burned my throat. "Whatever you're thinking I did last night," I rasped, "you're wrong."

He grinned. "How was dinner?"

Though I glared at him, since he most definitely knew about the whole speed dating thing and hadn't thought to warn me, his smile didn't change.

"Should I push the meeting with Donovan to nine?"

I was about to remind him that I never delayed appointments with clients, especially important ones like Colin Donovan, but I changed my mind when my headache gave a nasty throb. I definitely needed more than a couple hours of couch sleep. "Yeah," I agreed. "Thanks." Jake looked a little too amused by my state, so I gave him a glare. "Or, you know, just sit there. That's fine too."

His grin grew so wide that I was tempted to threaten to fire him. But then I remembered that I'd tried that before, and he'd just laughed at me. Jake was the best assistant I'd ever had, and he knew it.

"I'm getting you another cup of coffee," he said as he picked up his phone and started dialing Donovan's office. "You look like you need all the help you can get. Hey, Ramesh, it's Jake. Think your boss can find something to do for a couple of hours?"

If I wasn't so tired, I would have given his rolling chair a good kick. "No phone calls until eight," I muttered, even though he was deep in conversation with Donovan's assistant now and talking about some recent video game I knew nothing about. I shut my office door behind me and took a slow, energizing breath. I had a couple of hours to get myself up to function now, and then it was back to business as usual. No weird dreams about girls I hadn't seen in fifteen years and no early 2000s pop songs could throw off my equilibrium so completely that I couldn't return myself to balance. After all, when it came to being predictable, I was king.

I started singing the chorus of "As Long as You Love Me" to myself and flipped on my computer, settling in my chair.

Yeah, it was going to be an incredibly long day.

"You're in a mood today."

I looked up from my computer screen, realizing I had been staring at it for too long and getting lost in thought while the page refreshed. I would have to talk to Jake about our internet problems, because it was really starting to get ridiculous. Eight seconds to load a spreadsheet?

"Sorry," I said and gave my client, Colin Donovan, a smile. "Long day." *Long night, more like*, but I knew how he would take that.

Stop living such a wild life, he would say, and we would laugh a little because Donovan went out with people even less often than I did, though *he* had a good reason for staying at home. He, at least, had his family to go back to.

He was one of my oldest clients, thankfully, so he'd seen me at my good and bad and simply gave me a half-smile that told me he understood. Donovan was one of the few exceptions to my general rule about not meeting with clients in person when I could avoid it. He had become one of the most reliable people I knew, so I didn't have to wonder what he might do or say. He was here because he was going on vacation for the bulk of the summer, just like he did every year. He wanted to make sure I had everything in order with his funds so he didn't come back any poorer than when he left.

I wanted to stop thinking about Molly, because she was seriously messing with my head and making my job harder than it needed to be. How was it she managed to disrupt my life even when I hadn't seen her in years?

Considering I'd been distracted by memories of her all morning, there pretty much wasn't any point in trying not to think about her today. She was in my head, and she wasn't going away. Pretending otherwise would just give me a worse headache.

I took a quick glance at Donovan's file now that it had loaded, though I already knew it well, and I jumped right into explaining my plans for the next couple of months. It wasn't anything different from what I'd been doing the last couple of years, and Donovan wasn't any more worried than he usually was. He trusted me to take care of his money, just like all my clients did.

Predictable. Logical. Simple.

My favorite attributes.

"I'll have my phone on me," Donovan assured me as he left, though the odds of me needing to call him were slim to none. "Don't party too hard while I'm gone."

Thankfully, the meeting restored a bit of balance to my day, and I had a feeling things would be better from here on out. Now that things were more or less back to normal, I settled more comfortably in my chair and went to work. This, alone in my office with nothing but money and spreadsheets to keep me company, was where I could be completely myself.

Pretty much the opposite of speed dating.

As usual, Jake had lunch on my desk almost the instant I realized I was hungry, and I looked up at him wondering how I could have found someone so perfect. "You know me too well," I said, though I really wanted to tell him he was sent from heaven.

Jake laughed as he grabbed a water bottle from his back pocket and tossed it to me. "Yeah," he agreed. "I know you're always hungry."

"I'm not always…" But I stopped myself because he was right.

It was the curse of spending the last couple of years living with the head chef of one of San Francisco's most popular restaurants. Steve was a genius on a stove, and he'd had to practice before his restaurant opened. A lot. I had to admit I had gotten used to eating his attempts, which were always amazing, and I definitely missed that perk. My stomach missed it. My weekly family dinners with the Davenports were not enough to curb my cravings for the man's food.

"Do I pay you enough?" I asked Jake, already knowing the answer.

"Nope," he said, and then he was out the door and back at his desk.

I'd have to bring that up at the next staff meeting, since I had a feeling I wasn't the only guy at *Bay Bridge Investments* who relied heavily on his assistant. I only had so many Warriors tickets to give him before he realized his talents were worth more for him to leave than to stay and help keep my life on a schedule.

A few hours after lunch, I was back to singing that stupid Backstreet Boys song from my dream when Jake knocked on my office door, probably to bring in my dinner, so I called out for him to enter and kept singing.

"Interesting choice," said a man who wasn't Jake.

I jumped to my feet the moment I recognized Jefferson, one of the partners of our firm. I'd spoken to the guy a few times, but he rarely came down to talk to us brokers because he was too busy building up the company and schmoozing new clients. Unlike me, Jefferson was a people person and loved being out and about, chatting and golfing and going out to lunch with people. Even now, he looked like he'd just come off a coastline cruise, which I'd heard was one of his favorite things. His thick silver hair was windswept and enviable.

"Mr. Jefferson," I said quickly and held out my hand for him to shake. My office suddenly felt sweltering, and I desperately hoped my hand wasn't sweaty.

Jefferson's handshake was firm, and he took to examining my office rather than me as he shook. "How long have you been here, Ashworth?" he asked after a moment.

I had to count back the years to answer Jefferson's question, so he probably thought I was a bit slow. "Uh, eleven years, sir."

"Eleven years," he repeated, his eyebrows high. "That's a long time."

I had no idea what he meant by that. "Uh. Yeah. It's a good company."

He started wandering my small office, looking at the few things I had on my shelves. Books and files, mainly, but I had a picture of my parents by the door, as well as a photo of Steve and me just after we graduated Stanford next to my little fern that sat in the window. "You like it here?" he asked, touching one of the fern leaves.

"Of course," I said, though I was a little worried I would start singing out loud again if that song didn't stop playing in my head. I was so focused on Jefferson being here that I could barely focus on holding my tongue. But was he really asking if I liked my job? I was pretty sure I had succeeded in never making anyone suspect that I didn't.

"So why haven't you tried to become a partner?"

Never mind needing to hold my tongue. My words caught in my throat, and I stood there feeling like I was brand new to the company and had no idea what I was doing. Partner? That had been my goal from the beginning, but I figured I was simply mediocre, since no one had ever brought it up with me. Until now, at least.

"Sir?" It was the only word that I could think of that wasn't absolute nonsense.

Jefferson grimaced as he settled in the chair opposite my desk and gestured for me to sit as well. "Janice was right," he muttered. "You are ridiculously proper, aren't you?"

The song was still going, and I got distracted enough that I wasn't sure what he said at first. "Uh."

The grimace turned into an amused smile. "Relax, Ashworth. You're not in trouble."

I couldn't remember the next line of the song. And I didn't know what to say. I tried to take a deep breath, hoping that would knock some sense into me that didn't involve Nick Carter's voice, but everything about this impromptu meeting was too confusing. I just ended up giving myself chest pains as I sat there.

"I didn't think I was," I managed to get out at the same time my head jumped back to the chorus of the song. "I'm just... I'm not sure what you're getting at. Sir," I added, for good measure.

Jefferson let out a chuckle and picked up a book I'd left on my desk with the intent to read but had never given myself the time. It had sat there for months. *The 7 Habits of Highly Effective People.* It was one of Steve's favorites, but I hadn't even opened it after he and Lissa gave it to me for my birthday a couple months ago.

I was pretty sure they'd just given me the exact copy I already owned, since it had the same mark on the long edge of the pages, but whatever. I wasn't going to read it anyway.

And still the Backstreet Boys kept singing.

"Shut up," I growled under my breath.

"You have the best numbers in the entire company," Jefferson said, thankfully distracted as he browsed the book. "You're always here early, always leave late, and I can't even begin to tell you how many potential clients have heard about you and want you as their broker."

The office temperature rose again. "Oh," I said, which sounded ridiculous but was a whole lot better than any of the crooning lyrics running through my head. I decided I should probably say something else, though. "Uh, thank you."

"Which brings me back to the question: Why haven't you tried to make partner?"

Did he really expect me to have an answer to that? Because I didn't. Yes, I wanted to become a partner and have some say in the workings of the firm. Yes, I worked harder than I should in the hopes my efforts would be noticed. But did he want me to say that? To tell him that he and the other company head had spent the last eleven years basically unaware that I existed? *How about I guilt you into giving me the job?*

31

He looked up at me, making eye contact for the first time. He looked older than I remembered, though I was pretty sure he couldn't have been more than fifty. Only twenty years at most separated us, but I felt like we were worlds apart. Kort Jefferson knew exactly what he was doing with his life and what he wanted to have happen and how to reach his goals without worrying about stepping on other people's toes or saying the wrong things. He was confident and charismatic and had everything he could possibly want.

And I…

"You seem like a good kid," he continued, his eyebrows pulling together as my silence continued, "but you can't be afraid to go for what you want. Initiative is more powerful than most people realize."

"Yes," I said a little too quickly. *Smooth.* "I mean, I'll keep that in mind."

He smiled a bit as he rose to his feet and gave my office another little examination as I stood as well, since it felt like that was the sort of thing I was supposed to do in this situation. "You aren't big into stuff, are you, Ashworth?" he said.

"I don't see the point of holding onto things," I said without hesitation. That, at least, I did have a response for, though I kept the second half to myself: *Everything inevitably goes away.* I had learned that particular lesson early on in life.

My comment made his smile widen, and he said, "Sounds like you found the right business," as he headed for the door. "Money never hangs around for long. I'll see you around, Ashworth."

It was for that exact reason I had become a stockbroker. Compared to dealing with people, the stock market was blissfully predictable.

As soon as Jefferson was gone, the last couple of minutes seemed to rush into me and knock me down into my chair. Had he just said…? After eleven years of doing the same thing and no one ever hinting at anything more, I had pretty much decided becoming a partner was out of the question, which was fine. I knew my place, and I was good at what I did. Not everyone could claim that. But Jefferson seemed to *want* me doing more, which was so far from what I expected that I felt pretty dizzy as I sat there.

Or maybe that was because I was hungry.

Reaching across my relatively empty desk, I tapped the intercom button on my phone and said, "Jake?"

"Dinner will be here in an hour, Brennon," he replied immediately.

I definitely didn't pay the kid enough. And until he started working for me three years earlier, I hadn't realized just how valuable it was to have an assistant who recognized the benefit of constancy, just like I had.

Without really meaning to, I muttered some lyrics out loud, though the song was long gone, replaced with a million questions I didn't have answers for.

And I really didn't like that.

CHAPTER FOUR

By the time Jake came into the office with my dinner, my stomach had twisted itself into so many knots that I thought I might hurl.

"But I got you the Maverick," Jack said, holding the burger in front of my face.

I had just spent the last twenty minutes doing everything in my power to not picture my boss's face morphing into Kevin Richardson's—Jefferson didn't even look like the Backstreet Boys—while playing any song I could to drown out the one that had been stuck in my head all day.

The last thing I wanted to do was eat something.

"I'll eat when I get home," I lied and tried to concentrate on my screen. The whole thing was blurry, and suddenly I was wondering if I needed glasses.

"You don't work well when you're hungry," Jake continued.

"I'm not hungry."

He laughed, which made me look up in surprise. One of the things I loved about Jake was knowing he didn't hate me or feel the need to mock my quirks. At least not in front of my face. If he was laughing at me now, it meant I didn't understand him like I thought I did.

"You're always hungry, Brennon," he said, and then he sat down across from me. "Are you still freaking out about Jefferson coming down here?"

"I'm not—" Jake's look cut me off. "Fine," I admitted. "I'm freaking out." Among other things. No matter how hard I tried to stop her, Molly kept popping up in my head and singing along with that stupid song that wouldn't go away. And saying out loud that I was panicking was only making my tension worse. "You didn't happen to listen in on our conversation, did you?"

For the first time ever, I wondered if my assistant was as nosy as the ginger kid down the hall who worked for, one of the other brokers. I didn't know the assistant's name, but I knew he was the one to go to if I needed information on anyone in the building. I'd only used him a couple of times, but the information had been well worth the awkward conversations.

Jake looked completely at ease as he reclined onto the back two legs of his chair and looked out the window. "Of course I listened," he said. "Why do you think I'm such a good assistant?"

Not for the first time, I looked at my assistant and wondered why he was content to do the job that he did instead of, well, literally anything else. He was only twenty-four, but he was dead smart and cheerful and personable and pretty much the exact opposite of me when it came to people. He had looks going for him too, dark-skinned, tall, and muscular, and he had the sort of easy smile women seemed to like. He could be doing anything. Why did he spend all day—literally—sitting at a desk and making sure I didn't go hungry?

You're too good for this, Jake. "So?" I asked, frowning a little and drawing his attention away from the window.

"So it sounds like Jefferson is waiting for you to march upstairs and ask to be made partner," he said, and then he laughed, probably because I was gaping at him. "Wow, Brennon, I thought you were smarter than this."

So did I. "Why wouldn't he just ask if I wanted a promotion?" I wondered out loud. "If he was here to talk about—"

"Initiative," Jake replied. "Exactly as he said."

Could it really be that simple?

"Look," Jake said, dropping his chair back to all four legs on the ground and leaning forward. "You're probably the best boss there is, in any field, but you got issues, man, and I worry about you."

I frowned. "Issues," I repeated. *Thanks.*

He nodded as if he hadn't just said something that was making me dizzy again, as well as slightly irritated.

I rarely felt the need to pull rank on Jake, and I really didn't want to have to remind him that I held his livelihood in my hands.

He looked at me as if it should have been obvious what he was talking about, and it really wasn't. "It's like you're so afraid to stick your foot in the door because you think something will shove it right back out," he said. "What I don't get is how you can completely slay the stock market when it deals with other people's lives but have no guts to go after something you actually want for yourself."

"I have everything I want," I countered.

Jake clearly didn't believe me, and he looked at me like I had just told him I wanted to take up ballet. "Like what?" he asked.

I had better things to do than argue with my assistant, but I wanted to prove to him that I was right so he would stop being so…confrontational? Pushy. Nerve-wracking. "I have a job I love," I said and waved my arm around the office. "I have an amazing condo in the middle of San Francisco. I have two happy and healthy parents who are proud of me and what I've accomplished."

"You also have a best friend who stole your girlfriend and just got married to her," Jake said with a smirk.

"Wow." That one hit me like a ton of bricks, and for a second, I forgot how to breathe. I didn't generally get blindsided so easily, and I had the thought that maybe it wasn't such a good idea to have an assistant who knew me quite so well. Or maybe I needed to stop having weird dreams and freaking out over little things my superiors said.

"How long have you been wanting to say that?" I asked as a headache started to build behind my eyes again. *And where'd you find the guts to actually say it?*

Jake wasn't the least bit chagrined. "Since the wedding," he said.

"That was a month ago." And the whole event was still vivid in my mind, down to the cut of Lissa's dress and the way Steve could barely smile because he was so convinced it was all a dream. He had spent the morning of the wedding in near tears because he wasn't going to be able to see her walking down the aisle—his blindness had been especially bad with all the wedding stress—and I had spent the whole morning assuring him that I would describe everything about her in detail. And I did, wondering the whole time why I didn't have the guts to say no.

I wasn't in love with Lissa, not by a longshot, but that didn't mean I hadn't once pictured her walking down the aisle toward *me*, not Steve. Those imaginings felt like ages ago, like dreams I had had as a young man but forgotten.

"She was never my girlfriend," I said, as much to myself as to Jake. "We went on a couple of dates a year and a half ago. She was always Steve's."

"She was never anyone's," Jake countered, and I had to give him credit for that one, simply because I knew Lissa would hate the idea of belonging to anyone but herself. Still, Jake was toeing the line of what I would allow in a conversation between boss and assistant, and he didn't seem ready to stop talking anytime soon. "You just didn't fight hard enough for her to stay with you," he said. "Didn't I tell you not to spend so much time here at the office? Didn't I say she would probably—"

"I'm done for the day," I said sharply and nearly slammed the power button on my computer monitor to turn it off. I mentally shuddered and resisted the urge to turn it back on to make sure I hadn't broken it. I got to my feet instead, reaching for my wallet and keys in the top drawer of my desk. "Have a good weekend, Jake." I wasn't angry about the topic, since I was totally and completely over Lissa and probably hadn't been in love with her to begin with, but Jake had pushed the line too far. I was tense enough as it was.

I expected him to hear the frustration in my voice and leave, but of course he decided today was a good day to catch me off guard. "Jefferson is still here," he said pointedly. "And you should probably go talk to him before he heads to Brazil on Sunday. He'll be gone until the end of the month."

I stood frozen. "How do you know that?" I asked, though it definitely wasn't the most important question for me to be asking. Besides, I already knew the answer: Jake was a ridiculously good assistant.

Most of the time.

"Better question is are you going to hate yourself for not chasing something you've wanted for years?" he replied.

I counted to ten before letting myself say anything that could potentially come out terribly wrong, and then I sighed. "Why do you suddenly think you know me better than I know myself?" I grumbled as my keys slipped from my grip, back into the drawer.

What would I even say if I went upstairs? *Hey Jefferson, my assistant made me come up here because he thinks I'm a coward. Wanna give me your job?* That would go over well.

Hopping up from the chair, Jake slipped over to the door. "I'm very wise," he said with a smirk, and as he started down the deserted hallway, he turned around and added, "Maybe don't self-sabotage this one, yeah?"

If he wasn't the best assistant I'd ever had, I would have seriously considered firing him for that comment. Self-sabotage? For how much I planned and prepared and did my very best to be as consistent as I possibly could be, how could he think I would mess things up for myself? Better yet, how could he think he had the right to tell me what to do? That was my job.

He thought I wouldn't do it. That was why he said it with a smile, because he was so convinced I would never hop in that elevator and go upstairs and talk to Jefferson about what I needed to do to be made a partner.

"Well," I said out loud, and I jumped because I hadn't realized how silent the office was until I made a noise. Everyone else had already gone home. "Well," I said again, just because the silence was disconcerting, "he doesn't know me as well as he thinks."

And I stepped out of my office, moving toward the elevators at the end of the building while I thought about exactly what I would say to Jefferson.

"Hello, sir," I tried out loud. No, he already thought I was too proper. "Good evening, Mr. Jefferson." Somehow that was worse. "How's it hangin'?" I groaned. "Hi," I said. I would just say *hi. I've been thinking about what we discussed earlier, and...*

I hadn't interacted with Jefferson enough to know how he generally talked or what phrases he used most. I'd never been in this situation before, so I didn't know how formal I needed to be.

"Just sound natural," I told myself. And to my horror the music started up in my head: Aretha Franklin's "A Natural Woman," of all things. "What is wrong with you, Ashworth?" I moaned and dragged my hands down my face.

What would Jefferson do when I brought up the subject? Would he smile? Or would he just roll his eyes because he hadn't been offering me the promotion; he'd just been curious about those of us who might be interested. He probably talked to all the brokers because he was a good boss and knew the importance of knowing his employees.

The elevator hadn't opened, I realized suddenly, because I hadn't pushed the button to bring it to my floor. Sighing, I slammed both the up and down buttons at once because I was so irritated with myself.

"Initiative," I said, reminding myself why I was standing here. "Jefferson likes initiative."

Was that what this was, or was it just stupidity? Jefferson was getting ready to leave the country for a few weeks, and I highly doubted he was eager to have this conversation at seven on a Friday night. He probably just wanted to go home to his… Crap, did he have a family? I had no idea.

The elevator doors finally opened, but just as I was about to step inside, I froze. There stood Jefferson, a look of confusion on his face as he glanced around the empty floor. "You getting on, Ashworth?" he asked, holding out his arm to stop the doors from closing.

This wasn't the plan! I was supposed to have the whole elevator ride up the three floors to his office before I had to start talking. I wasn't supposed to have a 1960s soul ballad running through my head. "Yes," I said before his bemused expression got worse, and I hurried inside.

As the doors shut in front of us and the elevator shuddered into movement, Jefferson seemed to be watching me, though I couldn't bring myself to meet his gaze. "Hi" wouldn't work anymore because we'd pretty much skipped that part already, and I seemed to have forgotten what came after that. So I just stared at my reflection in the shiny metal door and prayed I got lucky. And that the radio in my head would turn off for once. Like that would ever happen.

"I see you're here late," Jefferson said, breaking the silence.

We only had seven floors to go before we hit the lobby. I had to do this fast if I wanted to do it at all. Why was it so hard to just say what I needed to say?

"Yeah," I agreed. *I've been thinking.* "I—"

"You know we don't require overtime, though you're welcome to work it, right?"

I nodded. *I'd probably still work even if you didn't pay me overtime.*

"Don't you have someone at home who would rather have you there instead of here?"

I glanced at him, and I was pretty sure he was trying to remember what he'd seen in my two photographs in my office. "No," I said. "I live alone." And leaving it at that sounded depressing, so I added, "My best friend used to live with me, but he got married a month ago." *I've been thinking, and I've definitely thought about the possibility of becoming a partner.*

"No hot date tonight?" Jefferson continued.

Ha! "Nope."

"Handsome guy like you? Why not?"

I snorted a laugh. I couldn't help it, and when Jefferson raised his eyebrow at me, I shrugged. "Probably because I always work late."

I didn't expect Jefferson to laugh as loud as he did, and he kept laughing until, to my horror, the elevator came to a stop and opened up to the building's lobby. I hadn't even had a chance to say a word about being a partner!

"I like you, Ashworth," Jefferson said as he stepped out. "I hope I see you around more."

What was I supposed to say to that? I couldn't even think of a sound to make let alone a coherent response that wasn't from the song, and I stood there in the elevator, probably gaping at him as he paused when he realized I hadn't followed.

"You coming?" he asked.

"I forgot my keys," I replied. "Gotta…gotta go back up and grab them."

Jefferson gave me what I guessed to be a knowing smile. "Don't work too hard," he said with a wink, and then he was gone.

As the glass doors swung shut behind him, I dropped my face into my hands. "I was hoping I could talk to you about that partnership," I said and let the elevator close on me.

At the rate I was going, I was never going to be anything but a well-liked stockbroker with endlessly unfulfilled ambitions because I couldn't open my mouth and say the words on the tip of my tongue. "That's why I don't date," I muttered.

Among other reasons.

CHAPTER FIVE

Once I'd gotten back up to my office, it seemed stupid to consider the idea of doing more work. It was already 7:15, and the whole building seemed empty apart from me, eerily silent and still. But if I went home, the silence would only continue, more suffocating than in a giant office, but I really didn't have anywhere else to go. My life, in all its conformity, was pretty boring when I got down to it, and the most exciting thing I ever did was the Davenport family dinners on Sundays.

I took the elevator down to the garage, trying to come up with an idea for what to do on my own on a Friday night, and climbed into my Lexus feeling so disoriented by my conversation with Jefferson that I had to sit there and take a few deep breaths before I shifted the car into gear. Maybe I would just go to bed early, since the whole week had been rather exhausting. Yeah, my bed sounded nice, even with the frightening prospect of having another dream set in Memory Lane. Besides, the sooner I went to bed, the sooner the weekend could be over and I could get back to work and routine.

Clearly I didn't pay attention to where I was driving, because when I pulled to a stop against a brightly lit curb, it took me a couple of seconds to realize I was not outside my building. Instead, I had managed to drive myself to The Globe.

Steve's restaurant.

Again?

I muttered a curse under my breath, tempted to just drive off before I got any stupid ideas.

But Steve, as usual, would somehow know I was there and didn't stop by to say hi, and he would kill me the next time he saw me. Outside of oddities like Thursday, which had probably been prompted by Matthew, Steve, at least, was mostly predictable. Most of the time that worked in my favor, but instances like this? Not so much.

Grumbling, I climbed out of my car and made my way to the door. I would just stay long enough to chat with my best friend for a minute, and then I would leave. Easy.

Or maybe not.

Unlike Thursday night, the lobby of The Globe was absolutely packed with people. I shouldn't have been surprised, given the continued publicity the place had gotten in the year since it had opened, but I was. Steve and Lissa had somehow created something wonderful together, and they were thriving because of it. The lobby was so full, in fact, that I could barely get inside the door, and as I stood there smashed up against a couple of women who gave me cold looks, I decided Steve's wrath was probably a price I could afford to pay, since there was no way I would be getting inside the restaurant anytime soon. He would understand that, since he had to know how many people were dying to get a taste of his food.

"Brennon!" came a voice from across the lobby just as I reached behind me for the door.

I groaned inwardly and met the eye of the hostess, Alya. Her smile said, "Come on in," but the rest of the expressions in the lobby—geez, did they all have to stare at me like that?—said, "Don't even think about it."

"I'll wait," I said weakly. *Or go home.*

But Alya's stare hardened, and she pointed at me sharply then down to the spot on the floor next to her. "Unless you want Steve to find out you didn't stick around," she added. "I know I don't."

Steve had been very particular about his choice of hostess, overruling Lissa in the decision because, as he put it, the difference between a good restaurant and a phenomenal one was the person who decided who got a seat and when. He had definitely made a good choice, and Alya was about ready to march over to me in her monstrously high heels and force me inside. I hadn't talked to her much over the last year since the restaurant opened, but I did know she was big into jiu jitsu, so to avoid discovering how good she was at martial arts, I slipped between a fur-clad woman and her Russian mafia-looking husband to make my way into the restaurant.

"Same table as always," Alya said as I passed, and I was pretty sure she smirked at me.

"I should get you fired for giving preference to customers," I grumbled back, but I couldn't help but smile as I made my way through the busy restaurant to the back corner, closest to the kitchen. Even after the speed dating disaster, this restaurant felt like home. Steve and Lissa made it that way, which explained why my subconscious had brought me here. Home meant I wasn't likely to be surprised by anything.

Still, I was pretty sure coming here was a bad idea after the week I'd had. I was tired, not particularly hungry yet, and my head was starting to pound even more than it had at the office.

"Why didn't I just go home?" I said under my breath as I settled at my table, in what looked like the only free chair in the entire place. I was pretty sure it was more packed than usual, which was saying something. Sure, it was a Friday night, but I had a feeling some of these people had been waiting for hours to get a table.

Steve had been a genius when he suggested they only open for dinner five days a week, since I didn't think he would have been able to keep up with so many guests if they were open for more than a few hours a day. They did, however, tend to stay open longer than the posted midnight closing time, just so they could try to feed as many people as they could, which had earned them even more respect from the residents of San Francisco.

The food was the main attraction, obviously, with dishes from around the world that Steve had learned to cook from natives of the countries they came from, but I had a feeling a good portion of the hype was because people loved to watch the master at work. Despite being almost completely blind for the last three and a half years, Steve was an incredible chef and a wonder to watch. With guidance from Lissa and her family, he had figured out how to rely on his other senses and muscle memory to know exactly what he was doing, even if he couldn't fully see it.

And Lissa, genius that *she* was, had designed the kitchen so all the guests in the restaurant could see into it and watch him work his magic. True, he had other cooks helping him, but even someone who had never watched the goings on in a kitchen could see Steve was the primary reason the food was as good as it was. Even now, he was carefully filleting a salmon as if he could see it clear as day and shouting to one of the cooks that he needed a pasta ten minutes ago.

"He's amazing, isn't he?" a soft voice asked beside me, pulling my attention away from the kitchen.

I did my best to smile at Lissa, but with the way my day was going, I wasn't so sure I managed it.

"Of course he is," I said, my voice tight.

Lissa had a way of digging beneath the surface when she talked to me, often to places I didn't want her to go. There was a reason I kept my past in my past, and she had spent the last year and a half since I met her trying to uncover it.

Sitting in the chair opposite me, Lissa folded her arms and apparently decided she needed to stare me down, which was a lot scarier than she realized. After years of fighting her way to the top of the financial world in Boston, she had really perfected her glare and was starting to resemble her Special Forces brother, Seth, a little too much. "What's up, Bren?" she asked.

More than I could say in a night. "Why do you think something's up?" I asked, though it was only delaying the inevitable. Lissa was stubborn, and there was no way I was going to be able to stop my head from repeating "What's New, Pussycat," even though I could barely see the connection my subconscious had made to that song. When I was younger, Molly had made it a game to see how many songs she could get stuck in my head throughout the day because it happened so easily, and I had never grown out of it even after she was gone.

In fact, I was pretty sure it had only gotten worse. Once upon a time they had only been background music, but now those songs seemed to drown everything else out, and I'd broken the volume button so I couldn't turn it down, let alone completely off.

Lissa's stare only intensified. "Talk, Ashworth, or I'll drag Steve away from the fish and tell him you look miserable."

"Please no," I said before I could think of a response that sounded a little more dignified.

I'd taken care of Steve after his blinding accident for nearly a year before Lissa stepped into our lives and did a better job. In less than a month after meeting her, Steve had reversed our roles and had managed to become a weird sort of protector who felt he had to fix my every little problem for me. Hence me needing to be told to go to bed. I'd managed to calm him down and keep his focus on Lissa and the restaurant, but I still had nightmares of him scowling at me from across the condo because he thought I wasn't eating enough vegetables.

I'm a grown man, Steve, I had wanted to tell him so many times. *I'll eat vegetables when I want to eat them.*

If Thursday's trickery was any indication, he definitely didn't think I could take care of myself.

Grinning, Lissa straightened up in her chair and repeated, "What's up?"

I wasn't sure which was worse, telling Lissa my problems or repeating the same line of music over and over again. No, I knew. Lissa was harder to get rid of. Impossible, even. Hence the disequilibrium I'd felt in my life ever since meeting her a year and a half ago. She was almost another Molly. "I'm dealing with something at work," I said. *I'm dealing with my own self-sabotage, according to my assistant.* "It's nothing."

"Bull."

I knew she wouldn't drop it, and I yet again regretted leaving my car. Why didn't I just listen to myself? Probably because I was constantly drowned out by the most annoying songs. *And you have no self-restraint*, I told myself. "I'm working on getting a promotion," I mumbled.

"That's great," she said. "So what's wrong?"

"Nothing's wrong."

"You said that already."

Technically I said, "it's nothing." But I kept that sharp remark to myself. No matter how irritated I was with work and my stupid head and Jake's newfound wisdom, I didn't want to be angry with Lissa. "I'm not sure I'll get it," I said.

"Why not?"

My anger bubbled closer to the surface, so I grabbed the glass of water a waitress had just filled for me and gulped down half of it before I managed to calm down. I'd rarely gotten angry with Lissa before, and I didn't want that to change now. She didn't deserve that from me. It would be easier if I were just honest with her, since she would eventually worm the truth out of me like she always did.

I do have self-restraint, I thought. *Just not with Lissa. Lissa and Molly.*

"I don't think I'm qualified," I said, though I wasn't sure she could hear me over the hum of conversation in the restaurant.

Her frown said it all, and I knew she was about to launch into a rant about how dead wrong I was, so I held up a finger and added, "That's not going to stop me from trying." Assuming I found the guts to stop being a coward and just talked to Jefferson about it…

Man, I was exhausted. As Lissa thought that comment over, I dropped my chin in my hand and contemplated pulling out my phone to order myself a ride instead of driving myself home. Though the idea of what might show up in my dreams wasn't making me want to go home all that much… The chances of another dream like last night were painfully high.

"You should go home and get some sleep, Bren," Lissa said, probably seeing how tired I was.

"I don't want to go home," I replied, and then I winced. That was a whole can of worms Lissa would be more than happy to open. *Think before you speak, Brennon.* That was not a habit I could afford to lose.

"Why don't you want to go home?" she asked, frowning even deeper than before. She knew me too well, which meant she knew that I spent plenty of time at home. Or rather, I had before Steve left, and now things were all wrong.

"The condo is too quiet," I said and looked at her, wishing I hadn't. I hated that she pitied me, and I suspected she still felt bad about the way things had ended between us. Clearly she didn't remember that I'd been the one to let her go, not the other way around. It had been my choice, even though there hadn't really been another option.

It was better for all parties involved that she had ended up with Steve and I had ended up alone.

"You've lived alone before," Lissa pointed out quietly. She wasn't as buoyant as she'd been a minute ago, which made me feel worse. "What's different?"

"I don't know," I said. "It's just…quiet." As annoying as it was how often I had songs stuck in my head, the silence at home had become off-putting and uncomfortable.

"This is why I told you to get a dog," Steve said right behind me.

I jumped, biting back a curse, and turned to him. If he wasn't blind, I would have elbowed him in the gut for sneaking up on me like that. "I don't need a dog," I said, though I couldn't help but smile.

I had had the same conversation with *him* multiple times. Lissa was the one who finally made it happen, and Steve's dog, Captain, had already made his life easier. I, on the other hand, didn't need a dog.

I needed to figure out how to get my life back in order so I stopped getting surprised by things like Jefferson stopping by my office. Before Lissa and her resemblance to Molly threw me off my game, I would have anticipated that happening and been prepared.

"I thought you couldn't wait for me to leave," Steve said, and he reached out his hand toward our table. Lissa took his fingers, pulling him closer so he could wrap his arms around her from behind and fix his unfocused gaze on me. "I thought you loved being alone, so why the sudden loneliness?"

I blamed Molly and that dream, even though this problem had started a month ago. I would never tell him that. I didn't need him feeling guilty for moving out and leaving me alone with my thoughts. "I don't know," I said. "But it's kind of awful."

"So we *definitely* need to find you a girlfriend."

"No," I said at the same time Lissa gently hit his arm to make him stop.

"I told you the speed dating was a bad idea. You know he doesn't believe in love," she reminded him.

I had the sudden urge to duck under the table and vomit, and not just because I was suddenly singing The Darkness's song "I Believe in a Thing Called Love" in my head. I had told Lissa many times since the day I met her that I didn't believe in love, and while I prided myself on being an honest person, that was one lie I would take to my grave. At least with her.

"You keep telling yourself that, love," Steve said and kissed her cheek. "Bren, if you had just stayed last night, we wouldn't be in this situation. I'm finding you a girlfriend so you can stop moping around your lonely condo."

I don't mope.

Much.

"No," I said again, trying to sound firm and unyielding, though that ridiculous song was playing at the back of my mind. I rarely talked to anyone about my love life (or lack of), and somehow today I'd found myself face to face with the nightmare not once but three times. *How about everyone keep themselves out of my business?* "No."

Steve smiled. "Yes."

I felt the blood drain from my face. That was his scheming smile, the one I had seen way too many times during our years at Stanford when he came up with a crazy idea that would have gotten him killed if he wasn't perfect Steve Evans.

"Don't you dare," I warned.

"Too late!" he replied. "Hey Katie, welcome back."

I doubted I could have been any more caught off guard than I was at that moment, and I jumped to my feet so fast that I knocked my chair over. Katie from speed dating stood just a few feet away, and though she glanced at my fallen chair, she managed an easy smile.

"Katie," I said.

"Hello again, Brennon," she replied, wrapping her fingers around the straps of her purse. "Am I interrupting? Steve said you were expecting me."

"I'm just leaving," Lissa said before I could tell Katie she was mistaken, and as Katie watched her get to her feet, I glared at Steve and wished he could see it.

Even if he couldn't see my expression, I was pretty sure he felt my irritation, because he turned a little red and took Lissa's hand. "Help me in the kitchen, love?" he said and let his wife lead him away from the many things I wanted to say to him but never would.

One of these days I might actually punch him in the face, and he would never see it coming.

Don't be ridiculous, Brennon.

"Hi," I said when Katie's gaze returned to me. "Uh, please, have a seat." *Remember when Jefferson said you were too proper? This is what he meant.*

"As long as my chair is a little more stable than yours," Katie said as she sat across from me.

I quickly lifted my chair and slid into it before I somehow managed to knock it over again. "It's been a long week," I said, because that was what people said when they wanted to write off poor behavior. "How have you been?"

Katie's blonde hair was straight today, and her eyes looked browner than they had yesterday. That helped.

She smiled, everything about the gesture simple and easy. She had been hard to read on Thursday, but it wasn't as difficult tonight. Didn't mean it was easy, but at least it was eas*ier*. "Busy," she said. "But that seems to be how everyone is lately."

What had we even talked about during our two minutes during speed dating? Tomatoes and Steve. I knew absolutely nothing about this woman, and I had no idea which store of information I would need to dip into to have a normal conversation with her. She didn't look particularly sporty—thank goodness—nor was there anything about her that screamed any sort of profession, which meant I would have to ask questions.

Yay.

"What is it you do for work, Katie?" I asked, absolutely relieved when a waiter swung by with some menus.

"I'm in accounting," she said, and her eyes drifted down to peruse the menu. "It's not very exciting, I know."

Perhaps not, but it was a topic I could actually contribute to. "I'm in stocks," I replied. "Sounds like we have something in common."

Fancy that. Maybe Steve wasn't *completely* crazy for thinking Katie and I could be a good pairing. How he could have known she was the only person on Thursday worth talking to, I had no idea. He'd been clear on the other side of the restaurant at the time.

But Matthew hadn't.

"Have you had the chilaquiles?" Katie asked, her eyes still locked on the menu.

Had Matthew decided he needed to take an interest in my dating life just like everyone else? That thought was terrifying, because there was no way perfect Matthew Davenport could comprehend how terrible a blind date could be, so he wouldn't see an issue with any of this. Like the rest of his family, he had probably had a fairy-tale love story and had no idea how finding love in the real world worked.

Not like I knew either, but that was beside the point. I wasn't trying to set myself up.

"They're really good," I said, remembering that I was in the middle of a conversation. Thank goodness the radio in my head had taken a commercial break, at least. "Well, everything's good here, which I'm pretty sure you knew already."

She grinned, glancing over her menu at me. "You never know," she said. "Maybe there's a dish your friend just can't make quite right."

I looked over at Steve, who was tossing food in a wok as if he'd been raised in China. "No, I'm pretty sure he's good at everything," I muttered. And I really meant everything. From the day I met him, Steve had done no wrong, and that was never going to change.

"How did you meet Steve, anyway?"

Returning my gaze to Katie, I thought about the best way to answer that question. I was pretty sure she was simply curious, but it was hard to tell with her. "We were college roommates," I said. "And then he lived with me for a while after he lost his sight."

"I can't believe he can do what he does when he can't see," she replied, watching Steve now.

Well, he can see a little... "He's a remarkable man," I said. "His wife is pretty amazing too."

Oops.

That wasn't the best thing to say, something I realized when Katie's eyes narrowed a little. Did that mean she was jealous, or did that mean she thought it strange that I would say something like that about my best friend's wife? Why was she so hard to read?

Clearing her throat, Katie set her menu down and returned her attention to me, even though she didn't seem nearly as happy as she'd been before. Or maybe that was just me projecting all of my stress onto her, since she wasn't the most expressive woman in the world. I never would have thought that would bother me, but it did. Maybe because it was so unlike—

Nope. Don't even go there.

"What kind of accounting do you do?" I asked, maybe a little too quickly but it was okay because it stopped me from thinking about...Molly.

What is wrong with you, Brennon? Focus, man.

Katie shrugged as she said, "I just do in-house work for an art gallery," as if I couldn't possibly have any interest in something like that. Clearly she missed the point when I said we had something in common, and the fact that she worked in an art gallery meant we would have even more to talk about. It was almost perfect, in fact.

"Did you know that Steve is related to Adam Munroe?" I said, knowing that would be exactly what this conversation needed to keep it from completely floundering.

As I expected, Katie perked up. "Adam Munroe. As in *the* Adam Munroe? The art dealer? You're kidding."

I wasn't kidding. In fact, I spent most Sundays at Adam Munroe's house for family dinner because Steve wouldn't let me skip out on it. According to my friend, I needed all the socializing I could get, and there was no better group of people than the Davenport family. It was a combination of three of the most prominent families in California: Davenport, Munroe, and Hastings.

Adam acquired and sold high end art all over the world, and he had been dubbed the "King of Art" because of it. His wife was even a painter, and I doubted anyone who knew art had not heard of them.

"Steve's his cousin, more or less," I said and smiled because Katie had really brightened up. She was easy to please, apparently, which made my job easier. That was nice.

"So you've met him?"

I nearly grinned, which was impressive given the day I'd had. Maybe Katie wasn't all that bad. "A few times," I said. "And he's every bit as admirable as you would think he is."

"You're talking about me, right?" said Steve right behind me, and I jumped. Apparently I'd been more tense than I thought. "Could I interest the pair of you in some appetizers? On the house. Brennon, you're always hungry, so I already know your answer."

Way to make me sound awesome in front of the girl you want me to date. "Nothing with tomatoes," I said, doing my best not to grumble.

Steve frowned as he came to stand at the table's side instead of just out of sight. "But you love tomatoes."

"But Katie is allergic."

"No tomatoes it is."

As soon as Steve was gone—*Shouldn't he have sent a waiter to do that?*—Katie graced me with another soft smile. "You remembered that?" she asked.

Our conversation last night had only been a few minutes long. It wasn't like she'd given me much to remember. "I did," I said, wondering if it was strange for me to remember a detail like that.

Was she going to think I was creepy now? It was only one little fact, and I had a whole store of knowledge about Molly that I couldn't forget no matter how hard I tried. Like how she had always let me have the last bite of ice cream because she thought it was funny how much I savored it.

"That is so refreshing," Katie said, and then silence fell between us.

And as I sat there, searching for a new topic of conversation, I knew I didn't have long before a song popped up to fill the void. Maybe that was why I hated how quiet my condo was now. There was nothing to distract my inner radio, and inevitably one of the songs that started playing made me think of Molly.

I was seriously losing it, and if I didn't stop thinking about my old friend, I was not going to do well on this unplanned date I'd fallen into.

"So have you always wanted to be an accountant?" I asked at the exact same time Katie said, "What made you decide to go into stocks?" Both of us paused, then smiled, and I had never felt so awkward in my life because I was so much better at talking than this, and I knew it.

For some reason, I didn't mind. "You first," I said.

"Yes," she replied. "I have always wanted to be an accountant. Is that weird?"

"Only if it's strange that I used to pretend I was on Wall Street and shouting at the other traders. Molly used to think I was insane whenever I did that."

"Molly?"

Strike one, Ashworth.

"Just an old friend growing up," I said, though I'd lost the energy that I had just started building up and was on the verge of singing "Take Me Out to the Ball Game." I'd have to start at the bottom again, which meant it was time to dip into the classic first date questions that had always served me well on the rare times I actually went on dates. "Did you grow up here in San Francisco?"

Katie smiled. "San Jose. You?"

"San Leandro."

"Have any siblings?"

I shook my head. "Just me. You?"

"Two brothers, both younger."

I paused before asking her about which college she went to, since Steve had returned with a couple of tomato-free salads and a breadbasket, which I was pretty sure wasn't even part of the restaurant's usual appetizer menu. Had he made up a basket just for this particular occasion?

"Might I suggest a specialty of mine, the chilaquiles," he said in the most pretentious manner I'd ever heard, and he bit back laughter when I kicked his foot. This was just like the time he overheard me talking to my mother on the phone about how I had managed to turn all of my white clothes pink when doing laundry freshman year in the classic laundromat blunder. He had found my ineptitude hilarious and bought me every pink thing he could find for the rest of the year, including a pink leopard-print shower curtain and a pair of pink tennis shoes that I still had under my bed because I'd never had the heart to get rid of them.

I would not stand for his games, not when I was trying so hard to make him happy and force at least this one date to go well. "Steve," I said, "your stove's on fire."

"What?!" He turned in alarm, but he quickly figured out my lie and pushed me in the side of the head so I had to catch myself before I fell out of my chair. "Not funny, Bren," he mumbled then wandered back to the kitchen.

I noticed with a smile that he double-checked his massive stove, just in case.

"Sorry about him," I told Katie, and I was glad to see she'd thought the whole exchange was funny, since she grinned back at me as she tore off a piece of bread to eat. "I love the guy, but sometimes he's an idiot."

"I wish I had a fun friend like that," she replied. "All of my friends are accountants."

So she appreciated accountant jokes? It was nice to see she had a sense of humor, though I had no idea how broad it was. "You must have some crazy parties," I said.

"So crazy. Last time one of them pulled a muscle trying to toss a balled-up piece of paper into the garbage can."

"What a riot."

And on we went. It was strange, having a conversation that didn't involve me having to diffuse the ticking time bomb that was Steve and his brother-in-law, or second guessing everything I might say because it would sound boring. Katie actually seemed to appreciate my mundane life, and I could say without a doubt that she would never catch me by surprise because she was exactly what a young and single accountant was supposed to be.

She was predictable.

By the time we finished our meal and she ended the date around nine, since she had a strict bedtime, I was seriously starting to wonder just how Steve—or Matthew, for that matter—had managed to pick the one person in this city who seemed to be exactly what I needed.

CHAPTER SIX

There was something about the restaurant that warped my perception of time. One minute I was sitting there by myself, picking at the remainder of the bread basket and telling myself I should only stay for a few more minutes before I headed home like Katie had, and the next it was almost ten o'clock and Lissa was setting a bowl of pistachio gelato in front of me with a smile before she joined Steve in the kitchen. I'd been sitting in my chair for almost an hour trying to figure out how I had managed to have a half-decent date with a stranger, and I had come up with nothing to explain it, though that could have been because my head was full of cheesy love songs I hadn't listened to in over a decade.

As Lissa tied an apron around her waist, Steve seemed to know she was right behind him and smiled to himself as he sautéed some onions. As soon as his hands were free, he turned and took her up in his arms, kissing her in a way I had never fully managed when I was dating her. I'd gotten close, I had thought, but by that point she was well on her way to falling in love with Steve instead of me because she simply couldn't help rushing into it, since he was one of the best men I knew. My thoughts sang an Elvis song as I watched them, but honestly, I couldn't fault him for falling right back. As much as I wanted to hate him for stealing Lissa from me, it wasn't like she had ever been mine in the first place. Just like Jake had said. Some people were just meant to be together, and Steve and Lissa were living proof of that.

Seriously, they were almost too happy as they stood in that kitchen grinning at each other, though a quick glance at the other guests in the restaurant told me none of them really minded. Apparently a happy chef made better food, and Steve was happier than I had ever seen him in the decade and a half I'd known him.

Lissa was good for him. Just like he was good for her.

Maybe that was what love was supposed to be. Never mind I kept telling myself I didn't believe in love, because I knew as well as anyone that was a downright lie. Seeing what my friend had, and how it had made his life infinitely better, had me wondering if I'd been wrong all this time. Fifteen years of trying to ignore love, and maybe it was staring me right in the face.

Don't get ahead of yourself, Brennon. You know where that leads.

There was absolutely no point in rushing into things with Katie. I was no fool. But neither would I ignore the fact that Katie was the first person in a long time who seemed to appreciate the man I was, not the man I was supposed to be. Even Lissa hadn't managed to do that.

And yet Lissa was one of the few who knew me best, even if she didn't fully understand me like she thought she did. She and Steve were basically my only friends. *Cue the sad violin music,* I thought with a sigh, but what popped into my head instead was a Queen song. "Somebody to Love" had never been one of my favorites, and I rolled my eyes. Maybe, just maybe, if I gave Katie a chance, something could come of it, and I wouldn't have to spend the rest of my life making a fool of myself during first dates.

Ha! Wishful thinking, Ashworth.

Okay, maybe Steve was right about getting a dog. A dog didn't need conversation as long as I gave it food and pet it once in a while. That, I could manage. A relationship with an unpredictable human being? Maybe not. Besides, if I wanted to become a partner at the firm, I couldn't change my habits now, not when Jefferson seemed to approve of the long hours I put in. A relationship would only get in the way of my job, which was my priority right now. Once I had that all figured out, I would have a better chance of making something work.

"Brennon?"

I turned toward the familiar voice on my left, a little too tired to make a connection without a face to go with it. But then I froze, the background radio in my head fizzling out. My heart seemed to stop, and my whole body went numb. It couldn't be...

"Oh my goodness, Bean, it *is* you!" She practically jumped on top of me as she threw her arms around my shoulders and buried my face in blonde curls.

If not for the smell of roses that had followed her ever since she started wearing perfume at thirteen, I would have been convinced it was all just some crazy hallucination. But when my arms wrapped around her and pulled her closer without my say so, there was no way I could tell myself she wasn't real. Not when she felt so real.

"Molly," I gasped when she slipped out of my hold. *But how?*

The universe was laughing at me because there, sitting across from me and grinning as if it hadn't been more than fifteen years since I had seen her or even talked to her, was my childhood best friend.

"I can't believe this," she said.

Neither could I.

"I mean, I haven't been back in California in, like, a decade, and I just chose a random restaurant because I was literally starving, and lo and behold there you are!" She had the same lopsided smile, the kind of smile I'd never seen anyone else do properly. "I'm here doing a piece on restored mansions," she continued as I just sat there and stared, not sure how to react or what to say. "The San Francisco area has some incredible old buildings that have good stories attached, and I'm hoping it'll be a great article with loads of interesting facts and histories."

I had to take a slow, careful breath, knowing if I didn't, I wouldn't get any sound out when I tried to talk. I was still half convinced I was dreaming, and I badly wanted this nightmare to end. "You're a journalist," I said and resisted the urge to pinch myself. Hopefully I didn't sound seventeen again, but there was a buzzing in my ears that was kind of drowning everything out, so I had no idea if I did.

What was happening?

"Photojournalist," she corrected and reached across the table, taking my spoon and helping herself to my gelato just like she would have when we were kids. "I've been over in Asia for years, and you have no idea how good it feels to be back home for a bit. Wait, aren't you allergic to pistachio?"

I was, which was why I hadn't eaten any of the gelato in front of me. But how could she possibly have remembered that? She definitely hadn't been fighting thoughts of me for the last fifteen years. Not like I'd done with her. "How..." My voice cracked, and I coughed then tried again. "How long are you in town?"

In other words, how crucial was it for me to take a much needed—however unexpected—vacation so I could avoid running into her again? I absolutely did not need to feel like I was back in high school. Some things were definitely not worth repeating.

A weird dream was bad enough. The real thing was a nightmare.

Lifting one thin eyebrow, Molly looked at me with her shining hazel eyes and an expression that made me feel like she was going to suggest we do something dangerous or illegal or both. "Depends on how long it takes me to finish this project," she said and leaned forward. "Wanna help?"

For a second, I was pretty sure I'd forgotten how to breathe. No. I absolutely did not want to help. And before I could work up the courage to tell her so, she laughed loud enough that Steve and Lissa both glanced over with interest.

Great.

"I'm kidding," Molly said, wadding up a napkin and throwing it at me. "It's not like a stockbroker would be interested in adventure, is it?"

I wanted this conversation to be over. I wanted this day to be over. I wanted to get as far from my childhood best friend as I possibly could, because if I kept sitting here while she acted like we hadn't spent the last decade and a half without contacting each other once, I was going to explode. How was it possible there wasn't a single song running through my head to distract me when I could barely go three minutes without humming something?

"How did you know I was a stockbroker?" I mumbled then immediately slapped myself in my mind.

Pull yourself together, Brennon. I was more than an idiot who couldn't find his words just because an unexpected girl was in front of him. I was a wealthy trader with an apartment in the same building as Seth and Catherine Hastings, two of California's finest. I had my life together and my ambitions within reach and was one of San Francisco's most eligible bachelors. *Ha!* Maybe I might have been if I could actually talk to people beyond small talk. But I was better than this bumbling fool, and I knew it.

If I could spend twenty minutes joking about how lame accountants were, I could put on a confident face and make small talk with the likes of Molly Piper until I could convince her to leave.

Molly still smirked as she continued to eat my gelato. She looked the same. There was a bit more sharpness to her features brought on by adulthood, but other than that, she was still the round-faced girl with golden curls and nothing but trouble in her eyes that I'd known since I was eight.

"I've been keeping my eye on you, Brennon Ashworth," she said as she pointed the spoon at me.

I set my jaw, sitting up straighter and keeping my expression hard. The sooner I got rid of her, the sooner I could get back to my boring, unchangeable life and the much more important conversation with Jefferson I had to prepare for when he got back.

"Have you now?" I said, trying to mimic the one guy I knew who wasn't intimidated by anything: Seth Hastings. "Seen anything interesting?"

How would Seth sit in this situation? He would look casual but alert, his gaze strong and his arms tense. I tried to do that, though I probably just looked uncomfortable. I doubted my giant neighbor was ever uncomfortable.

"Lots of things have been interesting about you, Brennon," she said.

Oh good. Steve was inching closer, trying to listen in even though he probably had no idea who I was talking to. I had never told him about my friend Molly because there had been no reason to. I left my old life behind and started a new chapter of my life when I got to Stanford, knowing a clean break would make things easier.

Dreams about her didn't count. Those weren't my fault. The daily thoughts of her on the other hand…

Molly followed my gaze and immediately perked up when she caught sight of Steve, which was impressive because she was already as perky as they came. "You know Evans, don't you?" she said.

Of course I knew Steve, and if she really had been keeping tabs on me, she wouldn't need to ask that question. "Why?" I asked. Had she simply heard about the famous blind chef, or was there something more to her question?

"Because," she said, her eyes still on my friend, "that would mean you know his wife."

Excuse me? "A little," I said.

"Did you know she's a Hastings?"

"Technically she was a Montgomery before she married Steve," I growled.

What could possibly be so interesting about Lissa that a photojournalist would be asking questions? Molly needed to leave, and she needed to leave soon, before she butted herself into the lives of my only friends.

Molly waved my comment away impatiently and leaned closer. "That doesn't make her any less a sister to Seth Hastings, does it?"

Ah, so she was here about Seth. That made more sense, though if she thought she had any chance of getting a glimpse of Seth's life, she was about to be very disappointed. Seth Hastings was about as friendly as a grizzly when it came to his personal life, and though it had been a couple of years since he left the Special Forces, that didn't make him any less intimidating. There was a reason I tried to stay out of things whenever Steve and Matthew pushed Seth's buttons.

And Molly would be wise to keep her distance.

"What do you want with Seth?" I asked, hoping I could convince her to stay away from the ex-soldier. For her own safety.

Grinning, Molly shook her head. "His wife, Catherine," she said.

Even more dangerous. Awesome. If Seth knew someone was snooping on Catherine, he'd be even more terrifying. "Molly, I don't think you—"

"She's cousins with Lanna Munroe, right?"

Don't you dare. "Molly."

"I've been exhausting my resources trying to get in contact with the Munroes," she said, putting on her most (and least believable) innocent face. "If I could get pictures of their house, my article would be perfect."

I pulled my eyebrows together, trying to figure out her game. With Molly, there was always a game. It had been that way since the day she moved in next door. "The Munroe mansion? But why would—"

"The Munroes are one of the most famous families on the West Coast, Bren. They rarely throw parties, and since their second baby, no one has set foot inside the place outside of family. Can you imagine what that house looks like on the inside when its occupants are the New King of Art and Lanna freaking Munroe?"

I could imagine it pretty easily.

"Bren, you're close with Lissa Hastings, right?"

My eyes went wide as I realized what she was about to ask me. "No," I said, maybe a little too quickly.

Molly smiled. "You're *really* close, aren't you?"

"She's married to my best friend, Molly."

"Then this should be easy! I just want a few pictures of the house, Brennon. Just to show the world that the Munroes are as incredible as they seem from the outside."

I had to shut this down and fast. "Molly, I can't get you into that house. I don't even know the Munroes!"

"But you dated Lissa," she argued.

Defensive anger flared inside me. "How do you know that?" I growled.

She wasn't deterred. "That makes you practically family."

"Molly." I grit my teeth for a moment, reminding myself that Molly Piper was as stubborn as they came, and persuading her would take more than a simple no. I used to be really good at dissuading her when I needed to, but I'd definitely lost the skill over the last fifteen years. I just had to make sure she understood that going through me was not and never would be a way in to a family who deserved the right to keep their private lives private.

"Molly," I said again, "you're grasping at straws here. I dated the Montgomery girl for less than a week. It's not like the Munroes ever invite me over for Sunday brunch."

"Bren?" Lissa said as she suddenly appeared next to our table. I knew her question meant she was wondering why I looked as angry as I likely did, but her eyes were focused on Molly and a lot colder than I expected from her. Lissa rarely got angry. "Are you done with this?" she continued and pointed to my half-eaten cup of gelato.

I nodded once and kept my eyes on Molly so I could stop her if she tried to say anything stupid.

Lissa made it two steps to the kitchen before she turned back and said, "Hey, Lanna wants me to ask if you're planning on coming to family dinner on Sunday. Steve's making your favorite, and Adam was hoping you could help with the car again."

I almost shouted my frustration to the whole restaurant, barely managing to hold it in. Out of all the things she could have said, that was the worst.

"You know I'll be there," I said, my voice strained, and I refused to look at Molly until Lissa was back in the kitchen and out of earshot.

"Adam?" Molly said, and I reluctantly turned back to her. "As in Adam Munroe?"

I dropped my face into my hands. Why couldn't I have just gone home?

But if I had gone home, I never would have gotten to know Katie a little better. Katie who was so different from Molly that I couldn't believe I had ever compared them even a little bit.

Molly's fingers wrapped around my arm, but I refused to look at her. I knew exactly what would happen if I did, and that was a dangerous idea. "Brennon," she said, "if you take me to that dinner and get me into that house, I will never bother you again. I promise."

"Promise," I said with a dead laugh. "I know how you are with promises."

"Bren." She gently pulled my hands from my face, and I reluctantly opened my eyes.

Yep, she was giving me that look that was impossible to ignore, the one that said she needed me and no one else, that said she would give me the world if I just said yes. It had been fifteen years, but that look was just as potent as ever. No one could make a man feel important like Molly could.

"I need this project to do well, Brennon," she said. "If it doesn't... I'll be ruined. Please." She bit her lip, and I felt my resolve crumbling.

Who was I kidding? My resolve was never there. This was Molly Piper, a girl I had known since I was eight years old. The day I said no to her was the day I was no longer Brennon Ashworth, and she knew it.

But then she spoke probably the only words that could remind me exactly what she was asking: "If anyone can get Lanna Munroe to open her life to the world, you can."

"No." The word came out so low and menacing that I almost thought someone else said it.

Even Molly looked surprised, sitting back in her chair with wide eyes and for once nothing to say. I was pretty sure she had never heard me talk like that, and she had no idea how to react.

Neither did I. Seeing the woman once a week wasn't exactly grounds for wanting to protect her from the likes of Molly Piper, but I did want to. It was probably because Lanna let me into her house every week as if I were part of the family, and I definitely wasn't. I was just the strange neighbor/ex-boyfriend/best friend that tagged along because I had nothing better to do on Sunday nights. But Lanna treated me like I was more than that, and she had no idea how much I appreciated—needed—that. It was almost like she understood me in a way no one else did, even if we hardly ever talked. Like she knew what it felt like to put on a front for everyone and empathized with the life I'd chosen.

After the things I'd been through over the years, that was not something I wanted to lose. Just like I couldn't go without Steve. I didn't hold onto much, but people like those two? I would hold onto them forever if I could, because there was nothing else to keep me from falling apart.

"No?" Molly asked finally.

I barely even breathed. "No," I repeated. "I am not letting you into that house, Molly."

After everything they had done for me over the last year or so, I would never be the reason Lanna and Adam Munroe had more of a public eye on them than they already did. It was more than just their wealth or Adam's prestigious art trade. The two of them had been through a lot, and even if I didn't know the details, I knew they deserved their privacy.

"Brennon, I don't think you—"

"It's good to see you, Molly," I said, hating the taste of the lie on my tongue. It was time for me to go home, and I got to my feet before she could argue. "Good luck with your story."

And even as I walked out of the restaurant without looking back, I was pretty sure that wasn't the last I was going to see of Molly Piper.

So much for predictability. If Molly was back, there was no way of knowing what might happen next. And as I slipped into my car, the music in my head slowly faded back in with the last few lines of that Queen song as if nothing had interrupted Freddie Mercury's search for love.

"Can anybody find me," I muttered.

Apparently Molly could, and that was terrifying.

CHAPTER SEVEN

I called Katie on Saturday morning to invite her to go mini golfing on Monday. I hated golf, and I honestly had no idea if Katie liked it, but it was the first thing I'd thought of, and she seemed excited about the prospect. I wasn't sure if *I* was excited, but that wasn't the point. I needed to prove to myself that I was stronger than Molly. That her suddenly showing up again would have absolutely no effect on the trajectory of my life.

After that phone call, I spent all of Saturday cleaning and blasting music as loud as my ears could stand. I wasn't a messy person, and I generally dusted things off and vacuumed my condo a couple times a week, but I needed something to keep my mind off of Molly before I thought myself into an inescapable hole of anxiety. While I could have gone into the office, that would have only reminded me of the absolute pathetic mess I'd been in the elevator with Jefferson.

So instead I cleaned. From the moment I hung up the phone to the minute I fell into bed that night.

I started in the front room, removing each individual book from the bookshelf and wiping them free of dust. I vacuumed the baseboards, scrubbed the window frames, and mopped the entire floor. I cleaned under the couch cushions and inside the vents, and I even spent an hour organizing the cords to my TV system until everything was labeled and zip-tied together.

From there I moved onto the kitchen, removing everything from the cupboards so I could wipe down each shelf. I disinfected the sink and the refrigerator shelves, and I reorganized my dishes so they stacked better. When I found a tiny piece of glass behind the toaster, I couldn't help but think about the broken wineglass it had come from. Steve had broken it, when Lissa was staying here that first week I met her. He'd been hit by a car, and she was looking after him, and I had been an idiot and worked late on a project that could have waited a few days. Maybe if I hadn't been so stupid, things would have been different.

Maybe *I* would have been different, though I wasn't sure if that was a good thing or a bad thing.

I left the piece of glass where I found it.

After hitting the bathroom, my closet, and the second bedroom, I went to bed feeling rather proud of myself for what I'd accomplished. But as I lay there trying to fall asleep, I couldn't help but start to think again about what sort of mischief Molly was up to and how I could stop her from wrecking the lives of my friends. Okay, technically, I didn't know if she really was up to mischief, but this was the girl who had pushed me in the mud the first time I met her and told me later it was because there was a bee—there wasn't. The girl who spent a summer with her arm in a cast because she thought it would be a good idea to climb the fence behind home plate at the baseball field by our neighborhood—she only made it halfway before she fell. The girl who was once convinced she had seen our two high school math teachers making out under the bleachers after school and ended up suspended for a week after she broadcast her claim over the intercoms the next day—she was right, but that didn't matter.

Molly Piper had spent the entire ten years I knew her getting herself into trouble, and it was hard to believe she'd changed. I just hoped she didn't expect me to get her out of it when she did. I had spent my youth protecting that girl, but I wouldn't do it now. No heroism or praise was worth enduring the pain that grew in my chest whenever I thought about her.

I eventually fell asleep after midnight, knowing it was going to be a long night full of terrible dreams.

I woke sometime later to my dark bedroom, which meant it was still too early for the sun to peek through my blinds, and I felt so tired that

I couldn't comprehend how I even had the strength to open my eyes. I'd been dreaming about something—probably Molly—and I knew I had been tossing and turning because my duvet was completely on the floor, leaving me with only a sheet over me.

A very wet sheet.

For a horrifying moment I thought I had done something I hadn't done since I was six, but then a drop of icy cold something hit me square between the eyes, and I looked up just as another drop hit my cheek.

"What the…"

I reached over and clicked on my lamp.

The whole ceiling was wet. Water pooled and dripped in a few places around the bedroom, and as I sat there trying to figure out what was going on while my heart pounded faster and faster, the walls creaked around me. The dripping intensified. And finally my exhausted brain caught up to the situation and I realized that sitting there in my bed was the worst possible thing I could be doing, and I jumped into action.

I grabbed the photo of Molly and me then my phone and laptop, and for half a second I paused at my closet and wondered if I had time to grab a couple of my favorite suits. But I forced myself out of the bedroom, alarmed to see similar water drips out in the hallway as well.

"What is happening," I gasped, slipping on the wet floor and breaking into a run.

I got halfway to the front door when the ceiling collapsed behind me.

It was surreal. The adrenaline pushed me just out of reach of the falling debris and made everything incredibly vivid as I turned and watched nearly everything I owned get doused by a wave of water and drywall and tile like some crazy moment in a movie I was viewing rather than reality right in front of me. I dropped my laptop, hugged the photograph closer to my chest, and just stood there as water and dust continued to rain into my condo, coating my couch and the TV and the fallen bookshelf that had spilled its contents into the pool of dirty water that ran toward my feet and tickled the tips of my toes where I stood. I looked up and could see the clock on the microwave in the condo above mine, and I stared into the unfamiliar kitchen, trying to understand why it was weird that I could hear the fridge humming over the still-falling water.

And then it hit me, and my legs almost buckled underneath me.

I could have died.

Everything I owned was ruined.

I paid good money for this condo so something like this wouldn't happen, and I could have died.

I barely made it across the hall to Seth and Catherine's condo, and my arm was so weak when I knocked that I was sure they couldn't hear it. But I didn't have the stamina to do it again, so I just stood there, soaking wet in my boxers and a t-shirt, an old photo tight in my arms and my legs shaking, threatening to send me to the ground where I would probably stay forever because my world had just crumbled to pieces.

The door opened before I could try to compose myself, and I found myself face to face with a murderous and shirtless Seth. Geez, did the guy spend his whole life at the gym? He was huge! *Focus, Brennon. Your house just flooded.*

"Uh."

Seth looked ready to tell me exactly what time it was and exactly what he was about to do to me, but then his eyes focused on my open door behind me. I followed his gaze, and though I couldn't see much from the light in the hallway, I could see a pretty decent stream of water cascading into my demolished kitchen.

For the first time since I'd met him, Seth Hastings was speechless, and he had to try a couple of times before he managed to say, "Come on in, Ashworth."

Catherine called the police and the fire department and what sounded like the National Guard, and though I was too tired to hear what she was saying on the phone, even I was intimidated by the way she was giving orders, so I wasn't surprised when what seemed like an entire army showed up to assess the state of my condo. I tried to go out there and explain what had happened, but she put Seth in charge of keeping me in my seat, and I knew better than to try to get around a guy who had not once but three times gone up against the entire defensive team of the 49ers and gotten a touchdown, just to prove he could.

Once his wife closed the door, pretty much locking me in, Seth went to the fridge and started pulling out what looked like enough food to feed said army outside.

"What are you doing?" I asked weakly. He had to be tired, since it was four in the morning, but the man looked like he was about to start singing a cheery tune as he moved about the kitchen.

"Making you breakfast," Seth said without hesitation, and he disappeared into their enormous pantry, emerging a moment later with a sweet potato and some canned veggies.

It was bad enough I was just sitting here while Catherine dealt with my problem for me. "Seth," I said.

"No arguing," he countered immediately then stabbed the potato with a fork a few times before throwing it in the microwave. I was pretty sure he didn't realize how terrifying it was watching him wield that fork so ferociously. "If I don't feed you now, Cat is going to try to cook you something later, and that's something we should probably try to avoid."

I had never seen Seth cook before, probably because Lissa or Steve usually made the family dinners, but he seemed perfectly at ease in the kitchen, which surprised me. He was just as much a rich boy as the rest of his family and had likely grown up with a personal chef, and he didn't exactly look the type to take the time to learn. Maybe there was still a lot to discover about this family, but one dinner a week wouldn't teach me all that much, especially if I spent all my time focused on how to act around them.

They didn't need me getting any deeper in their lives, anyway. Clearly, with how easily Molly had almost wormed her way into their world through me, it was better if I wasn't around them at all.

"Maybe I should go help Catherine," I said, rising from my chair at the table.

Seth didn't even look up as he grabbed some things from the fridge. "If you so much as touch that door, Brennon Ashworth, you'll regret it."

I was too tired not to be curious. "What'll you do to me?"

He glanced at me, and his turquoise eyes were bright as he sent a menacing smile my way. "Want to try it and find out?"

I sat back down.

Fifteen minutes later, during which I may have taken a nap sitting up—I was too out of it to tell—Seth plopped a massive breakfast burrito in front of me and said something in a language I didn't understand but might have been Portuguese. I took a bite before he resorted to scare tactics again, and only then did I realize how absolutely starving I was, and I took as big a second bite as I could manage.

"That's what I thought," Seth said as he sat in the chair opposite me with his own plate of food. "Evans was right; you're always hungry. Though I have no idea where you put it all," he added, giving me a searching look.

"Stress eats most of it," I mumbled, my mouth full of food. But I was too tired to care about decorum at the moment. I also chose to ignore the fact that Steve apparently talked about me when I wasn't there. That by itself was enough to send me into a panic if I thought about it too deeply. I didn't like to be memorable if I could help it.

Seth smirked a little as he watched me eat as if I hadn't eaten in days. "I'm gonna go out on a limb and say you've been a little extra stressed the last couple of days," he said.

I paused, trying to figure out his expression. The problem with being friends with Seth and his family was that so many of them were more perceptive than the average person, and it was nearly impossible to hide things from them. That didn't matter most of the time, since I generally didn't keep secrets from the people I cared about, but I knew that if I didn't try to take hold of this conversation, it was going to go to a place I didn't want to go.

But I had no idea what to say.

"So who was the girl you were talking to at the restaurant?" Seth asked. He didn't leave much room for changing the subject, not with that scowl of his. But who had told him? Lissa or Steve?

Swallowing my food, I shrugged. "Nobody important. Just some girl Steve set me up with."

"How about you give me a real answer. I'm not talking about Katie."

I was usually pretty good about saying what people wanted to hear, but this was different. This wasn't Seth asking casually. It must have been Lissa who told him, since Steve wouldn't have seen anything to be concerned about while he was busy cooking up a storm. For all he knew, I'd been talking to Katie all night.

Did your sister tell you to check up on me? "She was my best friend growing up," I said slowly.

Seth processed that for a moment, maybe trying to get more details from my expression. I was pretty sure I just looked exhausted, so there was little chance of him learning more by looking at me. "How long has it been since you saw her?" he asked.

That wasn't a dangerous question, was it? "Fifteen years," I said. "Just after high school graduation." And hopefully I would never see her again, but that was too much to hope for. Clearly I didn't have control over my life, since I was sitting in Seth Hastings's kitchen and finishing off an incredible breakfast burrito in my boxers while an army surveyed my flooded apartment.

And while Seth looked like he was about to carry on with his interrogation, someone knocked on the door then opened it, and Matthew's voice filled the front room as he announced, "Brennon Ashworth, you are a lucky man." Next thing I knew he was stuffing a coffee cup into my hand and grabbing Seth's uneaten burrito before he sat down at the table with us. It was brave, stealing food from someone like Seth, but to my amazement, Seth didn't seem to mind at all.

Maybe he had made it for Matthew, not for himself. Did Matthew often steal his food? Were the two of them closer than I thought? But why would Seth like someone who bothered him almost as much as Steve did?

I sipped the coffee, but though I knew it had come from his wife's coffee shop and therefore was probably delicious, I was too tired to really taste it. I drank it anyway, hoping it would give me some energy to deal with the current state of my life.

"Why am I lucky?" I asked. I didn't feel lucky.

I was confused and tired and somehow still hungry.

Waiting until he finished chewing, Matthew pointed in the direction of my condo. "That could have killed you," he said. As if I didn't already know. "According to Catherine, your upstairs neighbor is on vacation, and the bathtub faucet was leaking, probably for days. They had to call in a plumber to turn it off 'cause the threads were stripped. The guy must not have noticed the stream the last time he turned off the water, and for some reason the drain was plugged. So how're you handling all this?"

How could the man possibly have this much energy at four in the morning? Better yet, how had he even known to come over? Seth must have told him, and I sat there wondering how I had managed to become connected to this family who clearly took care of their own, no matter what time of day. And what did I do to repay them? Basically nothing.

Thank goodness I hadn't let Molly into their lives.

"I'm processing," I said, knowing I wouldn't be able to get away with saying, "I'm fine," though I wished I could. They probably wouldn't believe that.

Matthew smiled. "Sounds about right. Just know we're here for you, so don't bother trying to do things on your own."

"In other words," Seth added, "don't be an idiot."

Nodding as if his cousin-in-law had said something profound, Matthew took another bite of burrito then said, "My lovely wife was kind enough to give me the day off, so I am at your disposal."

"In other words," Seth added, "you're stuck with him, whether you want him or not."

I liked Matthew. I really did. But I wasn't sure I had the strength to deal with his never-ending positivity, and he was more Steve's friend than he was mine. But I knew better than to argue against the Davenport family, so I chose to stay silent and let Matthew and Seth launch into a sudden comparison of Army stories, all of which involved collapsing roofs.

Molly and I had built a blanket fort once. It spanned the entirety of her living room, and we called it Fluffy Town. It was tall enough for us to stand up in and had a little opening for the TV on one end, and we decided we were going to live there for the whole summer. We stockpiled snacks and built up pillowy mounds for our beds, and we felt like the grand architects of Rome. Two hours into the night, the roof collapsed on us, and we were laughing so hard that it took us twenty minutes to free ourselves from the mound of blankets.

The adult version was not nearly as fun.

An hour after breakfast, Catherine returned and announced it was safe to go into my condo. "But the fastest I could get a repair crew to fix it up for you is in a week, maybe two. Sorry."

"So I'll have to find a place to stay," I said to myself. Thankfully the coffee had helped, so I was slightly more awake now and able to think without it making my head hurt quite so much. I could get a hotel easy enough, though I'd want to make sure it was close to the office so I didn't have to commute too far. Or maybe I would just sleep on the couch in my office to make things easier. There were showers in the building, and...

I looked up to find Matthew, Catherine, and Seth all staring at me like I was crazy. "What?"

Matthew lifted his phone to his ear, already calling someone, and Catherine looked ready to slap me as she said, "You're an idiot if you think we don't already have that figured out," she said.

"It's like you don't know us at all," Matthew added, and I wasn't entirely sure what that meant until he said into the phone, "Hey, Lanna," and I felt my stomach drop.

"No," I said immediately. "There is no way I am taking advantage of the Munroes."

Matthew held up a finger to silence me as he explained the situation to his sister, and without even saying anything about me staying there—had I been wrong to assume?—he smiled after listening for a few seconds then said, "You're the best," and hung up. "Now," he continued, this time directing his words to me, "Lanna is already in the middle of making up one of the guest rooms for you, so if you want to call my dear sister and tell her you won't help make their giant house feel a little less empty, go right ahead."

That was low. "She doesn't really feel that way," I tried to argue. "She's got two kids, and I'll just get in the way."

"First of all," Matthew replied, "Benny likes you better than he likes me, which makes me very upset since I'm his one and only uncle. But he'll be thrilled to have you stay over."

"Second of all," Catherine added, "she's got two kids under the age of five, and I'm pretty sure she would enjoy some adult conversation now and again, which she could get if you were there in the evenings."

"But Adam—"

"Adam has three different gallery shows this week," Seth said. "Not to mention a couple of clients to meet with in the evenings."

I couldn't argue that one, since as his bodyguard, Seth would definitely know the man's schedule. Groaning, I dropped my head onto the table and yet again wished all of this was a terrible dream. But no, it was five in the morning, my house was in shambles, and I was pretty much being blackmailed into accepting the hospitality of people who had no good reason to take me into their family home.

"Fine," I relented, and all three of them looked a little too satisfied by that response. "I'm..." I didn't even know what to do with myself now. "I'm going to go see if there's anything I can save," I muttered and rose, waiting for one of them to try to stop me.

Instead, Matthew got to his feet and gave me a look that said if I tried to tell him not to come, he would remind me that just because he was smaller than Seth, he wasn't any less intimidating if he wanted to be.

CHAPTER EIGHT

I t only took two hours to sort through my water-logged possessions, most of which ended up in large boxes that would be taken to the dump, since there was no way I could save them. Books, movies, electronics, furniture… All of it ruined, and it was a strange feeling watching all of what made me me join the ever-growing pile of junk.

Matthew, as much as I originally wished he would leave me alone, was invaluable. He catalogued everything as I went through it, looking up values and prices to make my insurance claim easier to file. Throughout the morning he kept making jokes about California rain and global warming getting ridiculous and if I had wanted a fresh start, I could have just given him all my stuff instead of destroying it. He even got me to smile a couple of times, which loosened my tight shoulders and made it easier to breathe as the day went on.

Once we'd gone through pretty much everything we could get to in my condo—to my dismay, I couldn't reach my closet and the suits inside, since most of the damage had happened in the hallway leading to the bedroom—Matthew phoned in a second breakfast order then sat on my floor with me as we ate. There was something slightly soothing about sitting in silence and staring at complete and utter destruction. I never could have predicted something like this happening, but instead of adding to my stress, the chaos calmed me down.

If I couldn't control my own home, could I really control anything else in my life? Molly included. Maybe it would be better if I just let go for a bit, at least until this whole condo thing was sorted. Just enjoy the silence instead of avoiding it.

But unfortunately, that silence didn't last long.

"So tell me about this girl of yours," Matthew said. "And I don't mean the nice one. I mean the other one."

Him too? What, had Lissa called a family meeting to discuss my life without me? "She's not mine," I replied. If I sounded curt, Matthew didn't seem to care. "There's not much to tell."

"I don't know about that." But he looked more curious than suspicious, which was nice. "According to Lissa, she certainly seems to like you."

I nodded half-heartedly. "She seems a lot of things," I said. I'd never had a personal conversation like this with the man, and I wasn't sure why he was trying so hard. Matthew Davenport wasn't my family, he wasn't even really a friend, and I doubted he could be serious enough to understand anyway. "She's only in town for a few days," I said, "so I doubt I'll see her again."

"And that's why you've been hugging that picture all morning?"

I glanced down at the frame sitting in my lap. Had I been holding that photograph the whole time? "Oh," I said, not really sure what else I *could* say. Especially when a Nickelback song started playing in my head like some sad flashback montage music.

Matthew smiled, and he seemed to think he had discovered something about me. Whatever he thought he knew, he was wrong. "I know it's none of my business," he said.

Are you sure you know that?

"But I've been noticing the way you look at that thing, and something tells me there's a reason you chose to save that out of all the things you could have grabbed. If you want to talk about it, I can—"

"I don't," I said. I didn't want to talk to people on a good day, and today was definitely not a good day. So before he could push the issue, I gathered up my garbage and added it to the pile of what used to be my stuff. "Thanks for your help, Matt," I said, "but I don't think there's much more you can do here. I'll grab what I can and head over to Adam's. See if I can help get my room ready or something."

Matthew gave me a smile and an assurance that his sister really was excited to have me stay for a bit, and then he left to head back to the coffee shop he shared with his wife.

And while I wished I could collapse onto the couch and take a very long nap, my couch was currently covered in wet plaster and drywall, so that really wasn't an option. Tired, overwhelmed, and still a little bit in shock, I tossed my picture frame of me and Molly and the other few odds and ends that weren't ruined into a small cardboard box.

Just as I reached the door, Seth pushed it open and came into the condo. Which wasn't all that weird, except he had Steve by the shoulder and was guiding him inside as well. "Here," Seth said. "I brought you your idiot."

Steve didn't lose his perfectly calm expression as he took in the scene, probably seeing almost none of it. "I'm his *emotional support* idiot," he muttered. "At least use the politically correct term. Well, Bren, if I had known you were going to redecorate this much, I would have moved out sooner. I didn't want to tell you, but the decor was pretty tacky before."

And for the first time all morning, I laughed.

"Good," Seth grunted then left without another word.

"Give me something to carry and tell me where to go," Steve said brightly, reminding me of the impossibly cool eighteen-year-old kid who had been chilling on his bed when I arrived at my Stanford dorm room my freshman year of college. He had said almost the exact same thing. "Preferably before Seth comes back," he added. "It was bad enough having him show up at the house out of the blue, and I don't need him telling me I'm shirking my best friend duties."

I almost felt like crying as I stood there as if seeing him for the first time in years. After the accident that took his sight, I'd thought I'd lost the happy-go-lucky Steve Evans I had known for more than a decade, and it had been nice to see that Steve again.

"I've only got the one box," I told him, glad that he couldn't see my expression well enough to know how suddenly overwhelmed I was feeling.

"Well," he replied, "easier for me. Lead the way, Bigshot!"

He hadn't called me Bigshot in years, and I couldn't help but smile as we went out to the elevator. "Why did you even start calling me that?" I asked. The name had made an appearance our sophomore year, but I never knew the origin.

Steve shrugged. "It seemed like you needed it at the time. Luckily for me, you grew into the name."

I wasn't so sure about that. I couldn't even talk to my boss without stumbling over my words.

"How bad is the condo, anyway?" he asked when I didn't respond. "I couldn't actually see it, but something definitely felt off."

I could still see it, and we weren't even in the building anymore. The destruction was so vivid in my mind that it was making me tired just thinking about it. "The ceiling in the front room is pretty much gone," I said. "Bedroom's even worse. I think… I think I'm lucky to be alive."

"Brennon?"

Both of us turned at the sound of someone else's voice, and instinctively I shifted the box in my arms so its contents were hidden. "Molly," I said, not even a little bit surprised. Of course she would show up now, of all times, when I was wearing Seth's clothes—which were almost comically big on me—and probably had bits of drywall in my mess of hair.

"Who's Molly?" Steve asked, trying to see past me.

"I'm Molly," she replied with a smile. "You must be Brennon's friend, Steve."

Must be. As if she didn't already know. And Steve was giving me a look that said I was forgetting something, but I wasn't sure what I was supposed to be saying, or even what I *might* say. For once, I had no words stuck just behind my tongue.

"Hi," he said after a moment and stretched his hand out. "You were at the restaurant last night, weren't you? I feel like I've heard your voice."

Raising an eyebrow, Molly reached out and took his hand. "That's pretty impressive. So is it true that when you lose one sense, the others get stronger?"

I nearly dropped my box in horror. What kind of a question was that? The man had lost his primary sense, and she was acting like that wasn't a big deal. What was wrong with her?

But to my surprise, Steve smiled. "It's true that I learned how to pay attention," he said. "So how long have you known Brennon? I don't think he's ever mentioned you."

Can I go crawl in a gutter now?

Molly was looking at me like she was utterly and completely offended by my lack of sharing, even though she knew full well why I wouldn't have told anyone about her. After our last interaction fifteen years ago, I had no reason to keep even the memory of her in my life. Not that I'd done a good job of actually getting rid of her...

"That's surprising," she said with a slight scowl in my direction, "considering how much he talks."

I snorted a laugh as Steve turned to me as if trying to figure out if Molly was joking, though she sounded perfectly serious. It was enough to bring me back to my right mind and convince me that this conversation needed to be over.

"What are you doing here, Molly?" I asked. How did she even know where I lived?

"I asked my question first," Steve replied.

Molly grinned at me, the sort of grin that said she knew she was winning whatever contest she thought we were having. Didn't she realize I didn't play games? Not anymore. "I've known Bean since we were kids," she said.

This time Steve laughed. "Bean?"

"Please don't call me that," I moaned.

"He was the skinniest kid," Molly said, ignoring me completely. "The first time my dad saw him, he said Brennon was nothing more than a bean pole, and the name stuck."

"Only because you made sure it did," I muttered. The box in my arms suddenly felt like it weighed a hundred pounds, so I wandered over to the trunk of my car and slipped it into the back. "Molly, it's good to see you, but I have to get going."

"What's the rush?" Steve said at the same time Molly said, "You've never been a good liar."

I glanced between the two of them, anxiety gnawing at my stomach. Steve was looking a little too interested in continuing the conversation, and unless Molly had radically changed in the last decade and a half, I was pretty sure she was up to something. How could I put a stop to this without making her mad and him suspicious?

"I'm exhausted," I said as I closed the trunk. "I just want to get to the Munroes' and take a nap."

Molly brightened, and my stomach seemed to tie itself into a knot. "As in Adam and Lanna?"

"Are there any other Munroes worth talking about?" Steve asked with a laugh. "Do you know them?"

Stop talking, Steve. This was going to get really dangerous really fast, and there was only so much I could do to keep Molly away from the family without flat out telling Steve that I thought she could have an ulterior motive. Best case scenario, she really did just want to write about the Munroe mansion; worst case, there was something Molly wanted from that family, and she would stop at nothing to get it. Molly was a force of nature.

Molly shook her head then realized a second later that Steve couldn't actually see her doing it. "No," she said with way too much delight in her smile, "but I've been dying to meet them. They seem like the most incredible people, and I'd bet they have incredible stories to tell."

"You should ask Adam about the time he got shot," Steve said brightly.

I grabbed his arm. "It's time to go," I growled, because Molly looked like she was about to grab her phone and start recording.

Thank goodness Steve could hear the panic in my voice, and though I knew he would definitely ask me about it later, at least he understood what I wanted. "Molly," he said, "it was nice to meet you, and I hope we see you around again. But it sounds like Bean here is overdue for his nap, so I should probably get him home."

I had my hand on the door when Molly's words stopped me in my tracks: "You're not going to let him drive looking like that, are you?"

I didn't even have the courage to turn around, because I knew exactly where this was heading.

"Looking like what?" Steve asked. "I know it's easy to forget, but I can't actually see him."

"Right. Well, he looks like he's about to fall asleep standing up. Bren, did you even sleep last night?"

"That would have been hard to do," Steve answered for me, "since his condo kinda flooded."

"What?" Molly glanced at the building, as if she could see my condo from here. "How long before you get it fixed?"

"Also hard to do," Steve replied for me. "He doesn't have a ceiling anymore."

Paling, Molly waited a moment, as if hoping Steve was joking, and then she turned to me with worry in her hazel eyes. She looked just like she had the day I found out my grandma died, and I had to wonder if I really looked that miserable. It was just a condo… It wasn't like my whole life was in that building.

Are you sure about that, Ashworth?

"Are you okay, Brennon?" she asked quietly.

No, I was not okay. And this wasn't something she could fix.

If I slipped into the car and drove off without Steve, what would happen? He was independent enough to get around most of the time, but there was always the chance that he would get hit by a car. Again. Would he survive that happening a third time? I could call Lissa as I drove off and tell her… Tell her what? That I'd left her husband standing on a sidewalk all by himself just because I was too afraid of what a little conversation with Molly could do to my best friend?

She ruins lives, I wanted to tell Steve, but I couldn't. Not when Molly was standing right there. But didn't she deserve to be called out? The last thing she had said to me before she disappeared was that we were not friends and would never have a future in each other's lives.

Why was she trying so hard to shove herself back into my life when I had worked so hard to keep her out of it?

"Steve, just get in the car," I said and turned to make sure he did.

He didn't move. "Now that I think about it," he said, "you do sound pretty tired."

I clenched my jaw. "I'm fine. Besides, it's not like you can drive us."

"I can drive," Molly offered.

I glared at her hard enough that she took a step back. And then I felt bad for that and silently groaned. She was going to fight this, and so was Steve, and I was outnumbered and too tired to win. Molly had backed me into a corner, and now she was going to find out where Adam and Lanna lived. She might even try to sneak a few pictures when we got there.

And I couldn't stop her, though that was nothing new. Somehow I had never had much control over Molly Piper, and she clearly planned to take advantage of that wherever she could. I almost couldn't see the point of fighting it anymore.

Especially when REO Speedwagon started singing in my head.

"Fine," I said, barely whispering, and walked around to the other side of the car to slide into the passenger's seat.

By the time we were on our way, my head was pounding with a headache that wasn't going to go away anytime soon, and I worried that I would fall asleep as I pressed my forehead to the cool glass of the window. Everything about this day was a disaster, and I wanted to go to bed so I could wake up and realize it was all just a terrible dream.

"Remember when you let me drive your car in high school?" Molly asked.

I shut my eyes. San Francisco traffic was bad no matter what time of day it was, and I figured it would be less stressful of a drive if I couldn't see how close we got to death by automobile. "You mean when you crashed it into the police car?" I asked.

Molly laughed as if it were a fond memory, not a nightmare. "I thought your mom was going to kill us when she picked us up from the station, but we were fine!"

"*You* were fine," I corrected. "She grounded me the rest of the year, if you'll recall."

"That's right! And I had to sneak up to your room by climbing the drainpipe. Didn't I bend the pipe at one point?"

How could she be so cavalier about that? "My dad thought that was from me sneaking out and put that lock on my window," I grumbled and turned to look at her expression, even though I didn't really have to see her to know she was grinning. Molly was never unhappy, and that smirk of hers had followed me throughout my childhood and had constantly gotten me into trouble. "Can we stop going down memory lane? Please?"

I just wanted this day to be over so I could get back to routine. If Molly was around, I couldn't do that.

"Definitely not," Steve said behind me. I'd almost forgotten he was there. "I'm actually enjoying this little insight into Brennon Ashworth's mysterious past."

Oh goody.

"So Molly," he said, leaning forward in the back seat and sounding way too excited about what he was about to ask. "You and I seem to know two very different Brennons, so which one is the real one?"

I couldn't help but open my eyes and look over, wondering how Molly would take that. She hadn't talked to me enough to know who I was now, and Steve definitely hadn't ever met the person I'd been back before high school graduation. And I honestly didn't know how I would answer his question if he'd posed it to me. Who was I? It had been so long since I'd been myself that I couldn't even remember.

Had I really forgotten my own identity? I had always felt so certain, and yet all it took was a lighthearted question to make me wonder. I had been wearing so many masks over the last fifteen years that I wasn't sure if I would recognize myself.

That's a frightening concept.

"Well," Molly said as she zoomed around another car that was apparently going too slow, "that has always been the question, hasn't it?"

Has it?

"That's a good point," Steve said. "I guess I've known a few different Brennons."

"I'm sitting right here," I mumbled. I needed a nap. I needed to not be here while they were talking about me. "Maybe we can not have this conversation? That would be nice."

"You know," Steve said, leaning against the side of my seat, "I don't even remember the last time I saw you this tired, and you really talk a lot more when you don't have your filter turned on."

"Have you heard him sing yet?"

The blood drained from my face, leaving me dizzy. Maybe I *had* died beneath my collapsing ceiling, and all of this was my own personal Hell. It certainly wasn't Heaven.

"Brennon sings?" Steve asked with alarm. "Dude." And he punched me in the shoulder, though he missed and half-punched the seat as well.

I was half-tempted to punch him back.

Molly laughed and took a sharp turn. She hadn't even asked for directions, which was concerning, since she was definitely going the right way. "He doesn't sing well," she said—*thanks, Mol*—"but that doesn't stop him. Or at least it didn't."

"I barely even hear the guy talk," Steve replied and punched me again.

"Hey!" I complained then grabbed the door handle when Molly went careening down Adam and Lanna's street. "Molly, can you please slow down? I'd rather not run over any children today."

Thankfully she did as requested, but we were pretty much at the Munroe mansion by that point. "You used to be more fun than this," she said as she pulled onto the long driveway and turned the car off.

I sighed and slipped out of the car, glad that I could finally leave her behind. "Steve, are you coming in?"

He struggled a bit getting out, but as soon as his feet were planted on the gravel, he grinned at me. "I've been given strict orders to stick around as long as I can. Lissa will come get me later so we can go shop for dinner."

I didn't see the point of him staying, since I was most likely going to fall asleep as soon as I got the chance to thank Lanna and Adam for taking me in, but that wasn't my biggest concern at the moment. Not when Molly was marching up to the front door. How had she planned to get herself back to wherever she was staying, anyway?

Easy answer: she hadn't planned. The plan had been to get herself here all along.

"Molly," I said in alarm and hurried over to cut her off, even though that meant leaving Steve to navigate the stairs on his own. "What are you doing?"

"Well you can't spend all day out in the driveway," she said brightly, and she rang the doorbell before I could stop her.

"No," I said, "what are *you* doing? Thanks for driving, but I don't need your help anymore. You can go."

That should have stopped her. It should have made her think about what she was doing. At the very least it should have offended her.

But she just smiled and patted my arm. "You really do look awful," she said just as the front door opened a few inches.

Lanna Munroe looked out, her youngest son trying to get past her leg and crawl out onto the porch, and as soon as she recognized me, her eyes brightened. "Brennon!" she said and opened the door a little wider. Then she looked at Molly and impressively didn't change her expression, even though I was pretty sure she would have heard all about Lissa's experience watching Molly and me at the restaurant.

The Davenports were a lot of things, but they were definitely not a family who kept secrets.

"This is my, uh, Molly," I said and bent down to pick up the toddler trying to escape between his mother's feet. "Molly, this is—"

"Lanna Munroe," Molly said and grasped Lanna's hand as if they were dear friends. "I can't even tell you how long I've been wanting to meet you after seeing some of your paintings."

Turning pink, Lanna seemed to lose her words for a moment before she remembered who she was and opened the door completely. "Come on in," she said sweetly. "Molly, it's nice to meet you."

The baby in my arms touched a finger to my nose in interest then smiled, and I couldn't help but smile back.

"Hiya, Harry," I said.

Then Molly gave me a look that said, "I know what I'm doing," before she reached out and grabbed Harry right out of my arms. "Who's this little guy?" she asked Lanna as the boy stared at her with big blue eyes.

It was bad enough Molly had come with me up to the house, but I really didn't need her getting all friendly with Lanna's kids. "Sorry," I said, though I wasn't sure what I was specifically apologizing for. I couldn't exactly say, "Sorry for Molly."

"I'm a bit of a mess," I continued, "so Molly offered to drive me here." *And it probably would have been safer if I'd let Steve drive.*

Lanna's smile was soft, and she stepped aside to let us in. "Steve, are you coming inside?"

I glanced back in alarm. How had I forgotten he was behind me? Molly was messing with my head. Steve had only just made it to the bottom of the stairs, but the staircase was wide enough that he didn't have a handrail to guide him up, so he was moving pretty slow. What a terrible friend I was...

Sighing, I hurried down and bumped my shoulder with his. "You must be getting old," I said lightly. "My grandpa moves faster up stairs than you do."

Thankfully, Steve grinned and wrapped an arm around my shoulders. It was a playful gesture, but it was also one that helped him know where he was going. Lissa had taught me early on that Steve hated asking for help but often needed it, so we had to find a delicate balance between not making him feel helpless and giving him a way to get around.

"Your grandpa died a decade ago," he said and rolled his eyes. "What if I blame it on being dizzy from Molly's driving?"

"Hey," Molly said in the doorway at the same time I laughed.

"He's got a point," I muttered to her as I led Steve inside. And then, to my utter delight, Harry reached out his hand to me, which made me grin. He was still young enough that we couldn't interact much, but he was quickly turning into one of my favorite people now that his personality was coming out more. "Listen up, Harry," I told the kid as Lanna closed the door behind us. "I noticed you crawling just now. You're just a few days shy of being a year old, and if you don't start walking soon, I'm going to be very disappointed in you."

I followed Lanna and Molly into the sitting room, Steve right behind me, and laughed when Harry made a grumpy face. There was nothing like a kid to distract me from all the stress of life. "Don't look at me like that," I said. "You know it's true. Your brother started walking when he was your age. You're better than this, and you know it."

"You never act like that with me," Steve said and rolled his eyes. "Hey, is Adam around? I was hoping to ask him about something."

"I think he's in his office," Lanna said, though she seemed a little confused. Steve and Adam didn't typically interact much, since their skill sets and interests—and personalities, in particular—were pretty different. "Do you need help finding it?"

"Nah," Steve replied, though he bumped into the wall before he found the right hallway. "If I get lost," he called back, "just know it was because your house is huge."

"Your house is amazing," Molly added, reminding me she was there. Not that I'd really forgotten. It was impossible to ignore her once she was in a room, even if she was quiet. Molly had a way of making her presence known no matter what.

Lanna smiled warmly. So far, she hadn't seemed wary of Molly, but if I sensed even a bit of suspicion, I would personally see to it that my old friend never came back. "Thank you," Lanna said. "My father-in-law did a lot of remodeling before we got married, and my husband has a real knack for decorating."

"So do you," I said. Half of the artwork in the house had been chosen by Lanna, and she'd even painted some of it herself. "Besides," I added when she turned that comforting smile to me, "a house is only as good as the people inside it, so that says a lot about your family."

Lanna turned pink, though I hadn't meant to embarrass her, but then I caught movement out of the corner of my eye and turned just in time to catch a flurry of brown hair before Lanna's oldest son crashed into my legs in an enthusiastic hug.

"Uncle Brenny!" the kid said into my stomach.

I laughed, scooping him up into my arms. "Well," I said, "if it isn't my little twin."

"I'm not little," he said with a pout.

I would have none of that nonsense, so I swung him through the air and brought him over toward the couch where Lanna and Molly had sat. Had he already gotten heavier since the last time I saw him, or was I really that tired? *Stop growing so fast.*

"Why are you here, Uncle Brenny?" he asked once I put him safely back on his feet. "It's not dinner yet."

Harry was still pretty young, but his brother, Benny, was the perfect age. Young enough to be full of innocence, and old enough to have developed a pretty constant personality. *Finally someone I can count on.* I never had to question what I did or said around him because he didn't care.

"I'm actually going to sleep over tonight," I said with a big grin.

As he squealed with excitement, I caught Molly's stare and raised an eyebrow.

"Twin?" she asked as Benny started climbing my arm, signaling me to lift him up onto my shoulders, which I did without complaint. "Uncle Brenny?"

"Yes!" he said happily. "He's Brenny, and I'm Benny!"

"We both have blue eyes," I added and spun in a circle a few times as Benny wrapped one arm around my forehead and whooped with delight.

"And brown hair," he said.

"And we both love grilled cheese."

"Spin again!"

I did, but I stopped after only a couple of rotations because Molly was giving me a look I'd never seen before, which was saying something, considering she had been my best friend for a decade. It wasn't a happy look, but it wasn't a sad look, either. Honestly, I had no way to describe it, so I just stared at her until she realized I was looking and quickly put on a smile.

"That's adorable," she said, bouncing Harry on her knee. "I had no idea you were so good with kids, Bean."

"He's amazing," Lanna replied, though she seemed just as pleased to see her baby sitting happily on Molly's lap. For someone who didn't let people into her life very easily, she was certainly taking a liking to Molly.

That was a bad idea.

Benny tapped the top of my head with his palm then said, "Uncle Brenny, I want to show you my room! I got a new bed, and Dad helped me move everything around."

I frowned. Benny's room was on the third floor, and as much as I loved the kid, my legs were already starting to shake from holding him on my shoulders. After getting basically zero sleep and dealing with my nightmare of a condo, I wasn't sure I had the energy to endure the excited tour, as much as I wished I could.

"I think it's Uncle Brenny's naptime," Molly said before I could formulate an excuse that wouldn't break the kid's heart. "But if you want to show me your room, I would love to see it."

Where did that come from?

"But—"

"Benjamin," Lanna said sternly and lifted Harry out of Molly's arms so she could stand up.

I stood almost dumbstruck, watching as Molly held out her hand to Benny and said, "I'm Uncle Brenny's friend, Molly."

Benny considered her for a moment, and then he took her hand, apparently taking an immediate liking to her just like his mother, and led her out of the room.

Where in the world had Molly gotten so good with kids? I couldn't imagine she spent a lot of time with them being a photojournalist, unless she was one of those photographers who snapped photos of starving kids or orphaned children in war zones. Even then, I couldn't imagine her still being this much her cheerful self if that had been her life for the last decade and a half.

Like me, she was an only child. Her dad had mostly raised her on his own after her mom left them when she was little, and he didn't remarry until we were fifteen, so she hadn't really had any motherly examples in her life outside of my own mom. Maybe that had been enough?

"He's getting so big," I muttered, still a bit distracted by Molly's expression earlier.

"I keep saying I can't wait for him to start kindergarten in September," Lanna said behind me, "but that's a lie."

"He's a great kid," I said, frowning when I looked at her. She looked off, like something was weighing on her mind. It couldn't all be because of Benny growing up, could it? *What's bothering you?* I wanted to ask. *And how can I fix it?* But that was none of my business, so I kept my mouth shut.

"And it really is your naptime," she said with a laugh. "Come on, Brennon. You've had a lot to deal with today, and you look like you're about to fall over."

I felt like there was something I was supposed to tell her, something about Molly, but I was pretty much falling asleep where I stood. If it was important, I would remember.

Lanna led me to one of the guest rooms—there were many—and thankfully it was only up one flight of stairs. After showing me where to find extra towels if I needed them, she gave me a smile and backed out of the room, saying, "I've put some of Adam's clothes in the closet, in case you're tired of wearing Seth."

And I was alone. My phone vibrated a moment later, and I turned it on to find a picture of a dog wearing glasses at a computer with the caption "I have no idea what I'm doing." Was my entire relationship with Katie going to center around accounting jokes now? I was way too tired to come up with some witty response, so I set my phone on the side table and took a deep breath to try to calm my heart as it pounded in my chest. And while I was nervous about letting Molly roam the house with only a preschooler to keep an eye on her, I collapsed onto the ridiculously comfortable bed and promptly fell asleep.

CHAPTER NINE

When I woke, I had absolutely no idea what time it was. The sun was high, but it had definitely been at least a couple of hours since I arrived, which explained why my stomach was growling. My head was still aching from earlier, but at least I wasn't so tired that I could barely keep my thoughts straight. A nap had done me good, and it certainly didn't hurt knowing there was little chance I would wake up to a flooding bathroom overhead.

I was pretty sure I hadn't slept that well all week, and suddenly I was feeling like myself again. Even with Steve's question about who the real Brennon was. It was probably because of how calming this place was. Adam and Lanna seemed to fill the house with their peaceful personalities, so I lay in the exquisite bed for a few minutes, just taking the time to breathe a bit before all my stress came back.

Eventually, I decided I should probably take a shower. I could feel dust in places I would really rather not be dusty, and I was pretty sure I smelled like old bathwater. It was a miracle Benny hadn't commented on it when he was on my shoulders.

Grabbing some clothes that were more my size, I took a shower just long enough to make sure I didn't have any more plaster in my hair. Since it was nearly one o'clock, I hurried and dressed so I could see if Lanna needed help with anything before I'd been here for too long. I knew the Munroes wouldn't bat an eye at helping me out while my condo was fixed, but I had every intention of finding ways to pay them back for their hospitality.

The house was pretty quiet, which was unusual. Although, I was really only here for the weekly dinners, during which Seth and Steve usually had an unspoken contest to see who could control the conversation the longest and just ended up shouting arguments over some ridiculous topic. Anything was quiet compared to that. Still, I wandered the whole second floor and half of the ground floor before I even heard voices.

I paused outside the door, trying to remember which room this was. There were too many to keep track, but based on the male voices coming from inside, I ventured a guess that it was Adam's home office. I would have to thank him for letting me stay here—assuming he knew about that already—but just as I was about to knock, I heard Seth's distinctly low voice.

"We have to make the sale on the down low, remember."

I froze with my hand halfway to the door.

"I'm not an idiot, Seth," Adam said, and he sounded frustrated. "I just don't know the best way to keep things off the books. I'm not sure what we've been doing has been working."

"Cash? You deal with cash all the time."

"It's not like I go around carrying briefcases of amounts this large. You've been working for me long enough to know that."

"Working *with*," Seth corrected. "Don't worry, Adam; we'll think of something."

"What do you think that's about?" someone whispered behind me.

I nearly jumped out of my skin and let my thoughts linger on the weirdness of that phrase—*jumped out of my skin*—for only a second before I glared at Molly. I grabbed her by the arm and shuffled her away from the office before Seth heard us, and then I asked, "What are you doing?"

She frowned, her eyes still on the office door as if she was still trying to listen in. "Same thing as you, apparently."

We were still too close to the office. If we kept talking, I knew Seth would somehow realize we were there and threaten us into admitting we were eavesdropping. "I wasn't eavesdropping," I said as I led Molly even farther down the hall, just in case.

Molly snorted. "I didn't say you were," she said, though her eyes betrayed her thoughts. She had never been all that good at lying to me.

"Why were *you* listening?" I demanded. "What goes on behind closed doors is none of your business."

"Bean," she said, rolling her eyes. "This is really rich coming from the guy who decided to listen in on his parents when they were discussing your family vacation so you could hint them in the right direction."

"I was ten," I growled. Way too young to be faulted for wanting to go to Disneyland over camping in Yosemite. "And whether or not I was listening is beside the point. You're a stranger to this family, Molly. Why are you still here?"

She should have left hours ago.

Shrugging, she turned back toward the office yet again, her shrewd eyes revealing too many thoughts running through her brilliant mind for me to feel comfortable about what she heard. "You have to admit," she said slowly, "it kinda sounds like there's something shady going on, doesn't it?"

"I don't know what you're talking about." But what I really wanted to say was, *Say another word about this family, and I will end your beloved career.* Though that did seem a bit extreme...

"You heard the same thing I did," she said.

"I heard half a conversation that wasn't meant to be overheard at all, let alone heard out of context," I replied. "We have no idea what they were talking about."

"Maybe we can figure it out at dinner tonight," she said. But she couldn't have said that, because that would mean she had been invited to dinner. Molly was a lot of things, but she wasn't the sort of person who would just show up at a family dinner without someone telling her to come.

"You're coming to dinner?" I asked, and I was pretty sure I sounded terrified. I didn't care. There was absolutely no way that could end well.

Molly smiled so sweetly that it made me sick to my stomach. It was the kind of smile she always got whenever she was convinced she was about to get something really good. "Lanna invited me," she said. "She's the kindest person I've ever met, and her kids are the cutest! Benny reminds me a lot of you, and I'll bet you're glad to finally have a sorta nephew."

The world was spinning around me. I was going to fall over, or pass out, or start shouting because my tired brain didn't know how to process all of this. "Why are you here?" I whispered and ran my hand down my face. I hadn't shaved since Friday morning, I realized, and I probably looked horrible.

"I told you," Molly said. "I'm working on a story."

At this point, there was no reason for me to hold my tongue. I'd never watched what I said around Molly, and she didn't deserve my filter anyway. "No, why are you *here*? Right here. In front of me. Pretending that everything is normal. This isn't normal, Mol. *We're* not normal."

That killed her smile, and she hunched up a little smaller as she took a step back. "Brennon…"

"You can't pretend we're friends when you made it clear that we weren't," I said and walked the last little bit to the front door. Thankfully, Molly followed me, and she stepped out onto the porch when I opened the door for her. "I can't stop you from coming back for dinner tonight," I said, "but please don't. I don't know what you're doing here, but I don't want you to hurt this family. They're the best thing that's ever happened to me, and that includes you."

I shut the door in her face before I could see how hurt she was by that last comment, and then I fell against the door.

Had I actually taken a nap? It didn't feel like it. It felt like I could sleep for a full day and still be tired, and I knew without a doubt that was all because of Molly. Yeah, okay, my condo was in shambles, but I could deal with that. I could deal with the stuff happening at work, especially since Jefferson would be gone until the end of the month. I could even deal with a hundred accounting jokes if that was what it took to keep a tentative relationship with Katie going. But Molly? I had never been able to deal with her. She was a force of nature.

Chaos personified.

And once upon a time, I had loved that about her.

"Brennon?"

I jumped and looked up to find Seth and Adam standing on the other side of the entryway, both of them clearly confused as they watched me. Had they figured out I was listening at the door? *I wasn't eavesdropping.* "Hi," I said.

Seth raised an eyebrow. "Is there any particular reason you're blocking the doorway, Ashworth?"

I swallowed. He wasn't even trying to be intimidating, and he was terrifying. "Molly was here."

"I knew that already," Adam said, and he couldn't seem to decide if he should smile or frown. I was almost surprised he had any expression at all, given how little emotion the man showed most of the time I was around him. "Your friend seems nice."

Oh heavens, she talked to you? What had Molly said to these people? I shouldn't have left her alone, especially knowing why she was really here. Had she been sneaking pictures on her phone the whole time she was in the house? Were the Munroes suddenly going to end up on the internet for the whole world to exploit?

"You okay, Brennon?" Seth asked.

Of course I'm not okay. "I'm fine," I breathed. I had to shift the conversation before it totally got out of my control. "Adam, thanks for letting me stay here. How can I—"

"If you say 'repay you'," Adam said with a roll of his eyes, "I'm going to take offense to that. You should know me better by now."

I swallowed the rest of my sentence. "Thank you," I repeated instead. *And when did you learn how to talk back to people?* The man hardly talked at all most of the time.

"Catherine should be home soon, so I'm going to head out," Seth said, clapping his hand on Adam's back then coming toward me, since I still blocked the door. Though I moved out of the way, Seth wrapped his arm around me and leaned close. "Anything you want to tell me, Ashworth?" he asked quietly.

I very nearly told him everything Molly had said about what we heard through the office door, simply because Seth was terrifying, but I told myself I was being ridiculous and Molly was wrong, so there was no point. There was nothing weird going on. I shook my head, hoping Seth believed me. "It's just been a long day," I said.

That got Seth to relax a little bit, which made me suddenly aware that I had been so tense that my arms were starting to ache. "Yeah, I'm not jealous of your day," he said then slipped out the door with a wave and a, "See you tonight!"

"Lunch should be ready, and you're not allowed to refuse it," Adam said after that.

I reluctantly followed him to the dining room and chose a seat next to Benny, who immediately told me that now that I'd had my nap, he was going to show me his new room.

Somehow the rest of Sunday flew by. I spent an hour on the phone with the contractor who would be overseeing the repairs to my condo, and that strangely felt enough like work that I almost forgot I was sitting in Adam's office and not mine. As soon as I had determined everything would go smoothly, I agreed to read some books with Benny, since he had learned to read out loud with his dad and was really excited about it. I even called Katie again and talked with her for almost an hour, though I had no idea what either of us said. I needed something to distract me from Molly, and she did the trick nicely.

Before I knew it, I heard familiar shouts coming from the kitchen that meant Steve had arrived and had already forgotten he wasn't in his restaurant and the only people he had to give orders to were Adam and Lissa.

And when I was halfway to the kitchen to see if I could help, I remembered that Molly was going to be here tonight. I stopped dead in the middle of the hallway and wondered if I could somehow find a way to sabotage dinner and make the family cancel. *These are the Davenports*, I reminded myself as I slowly made my way to the front doors so I could wait for Molly on the steps and hopefully intercept whatever plan she might have concocted. *It'll take more than a misplaced chicken breast to shut them down.*

Seth and Catherine arrived twenty minutes later, and though they both greeted me warmly, I could barely find the energy to reply. The closer it got to six o'clock, the closer it got to potential disaster, and the more I tensed up. I had no idea what to expect from tonight, and that was worse than thinking about my poor condo.

It didn't help that Molly was late. Not that I was surprised. I stood at the bottom of the stairs leading to the house, hoping she had forgotten entirely. After all the kindness and compassion Steve's new family had shown me, I could barely stomach the idea of bringing someone into their lives I wasn't sure I could trust. I had almost called Molly three times—I only had her number because she had given it to Lanna—but my fingers had never been able to push the button and connect the call.

A car pulled up into the long driveway, but instead of a cab, I recognized Matthew's Range Rover. He parked right behind Catherine's QX80 then hurried out of the car so he could get to the passenger door before Indie could open it herself. He hadn't noticed me yet, or he probably wouldn't have leaned in and kissed his wife quite as deeply as he did before helping her out of the car.

Or maybe he had noticed me, and he just didn't care.

"Brennon!" Matthew said happily as he walked arm in arm with Indie up the stairs. "Glad you could make it!" He paused at the top of the stairs and whispered something to his wife, and then he waited until she'd gone through the front door before bouncing back down to me. "You do know you have to go inside if you want to eat, right? You didn't get hit in the head with your ceiling, did you?"

Are you incapable of having a serious conversation? I wondered silently. I would never ask him that, but I really was curious. I doubted the guy would have any advice for me in this particular situation. Even if I told him my suspicions that Molly was up to something more than what she said, I doubted he would believe me. As much as he loved his family, Matthew wasn't exactly the type to help out a stranger.

You're not a stranger, I told myself, but it wasn't like I could call myself Matthew's friend, either.

No, better to pretend everything was fine and I wasn't freaking out. I smiled a little, looking out over the street for any sign of an approaching car. "I'm actually, uh, I have someone coming."

Mischief brought him a step closer, and I instinctually moved up one step to keep the high ground. Not like I could actually compete against the man, but still…

"Brennon Ashworth bringing a date to family dinner?" he said. "No way."

"She's not a…" I stopped myself, swallowing my words. I didn't have the energy to try to explain. "Technically," I said instead, "Lanna invited her."

"I'm guessing it's not Katie coming tonight," he said with a smirk. "It's the other one."

Why had I not thought to invite Katie tonight? Sure, that was absolutely crossing a line and basically the equivalent of bringing her to the yearly family reunion, but she could have served as a buffer between Molly and me. Would that have been worth accelerating our little relationship? I had no idea.

When I said nothing, Matthew raised an eyebrow. "Well, you certainly seem thrilled about the idea of her coming. I thought you said she was a friend."

Had I said that? *I don't know what I would call her.* "I'm just worried," I admitted, since I figured he would keep trying to find the reason I couldn't even muster up a believable smile.

He liked to think he was smart enough to know everything that was going on with a person, which was probably how he managed to push so many buttons on the people around him, particularly Seth. Steve had *definitely* gotten worse thanks to Matthew.

Folding his arms, Matthew looked ready to dive into this conversation. "Worried about what?" he asked. "Should I be keeping this friend of yours away from my family?" A few years ago, he had been Adam's bodyguard until Seth replaced him, and I could see that side of him coming out as he watched me.

I'd never really been afraid of Matthew before, but suddenly I was thinking there might be a chance he could change that if he tried hard enough.

Did I want him to keep Molly away from his family, though?

Yes please. "I don't think she's dangerous," I said. *Not yet, at least.* "But I don't know if it's a good idea to mix her in with the group. She's..." How could I even put a word to what she was?

Matthew chuckled a little and shook his head, relaxing again. "We're all something, Ashworth. We took you in, didn't we? See you inside."

They *had* taken me in. And that was what made this whole thing even worse. If Molly did something to hurt this family, it would be my fault. They would blame me for ruining their lives, and I would go back to being completely alone, and my already miserable life would be even more miserable.

Had I completely lied to Jake when I said I had everything I could want? Clearly I was better at lying than I thought, but I wasn't sure that was a good thing.

"Whose cat died?" Molly asked right behind me.

I nearly jumped a foot in the air, sliding down the step and landing hard at the bottom of the staircase, amazingly upright. "Molly! Where did you come from?" No car had come up the driveway, and there was no way she'd gotten here earlier without me knowing about it.

Snickering, Molly slipped her arm through mine and nudged me toward the house, though I could hardly walk with my heart racing as it was. "I walked, Einstein."

"Walked? But—"

"Are you going to take me inside the house or not?"

"Wait." I pulled her to a stop before she could reach for the door-knob. "Molly, I'm not sure about this." My entire relationship with the Davenports rested on the chance that Molly really was here just to tell a story. There was no predictability factor here, and I wasn't much for gambling. Not with stakes this high.

Smiling wide, Molly took both my hands and seemed to glow in the late evening sunlight. I couldn't help but think how pretty she was, her blonde curls bouncing at her shoulders and her eyes sparkling and so much life in her. She'd always been beautiful—something I had first realized when basketball captain Bobby Fenton asked her to the junior high school Spring Fling dance—but time had only made it stronger.

"Bren," she said gently, "I'm not here to write some exposé on the Munroes. What would I even write? They're perfect! I just want to feature the house. I've already talked to Lanna about it, and she's fine with the idea as long as I let her approve the story before I send it to my editor. And I'm planning on talking to Adam about it tonight. You can trust me."

Can I?

The front door opened before I could form any sort of argument to talk myself out of letting her inside, and both of us turned to find the world's favorite princess grinning at us. "Matthew said you were still out here," Catherine said as she took in the scene.

Geez, she'd been spending too much time with her husband, and the sharp gaze she fixed on us seemed to sear right through my defenses. I had always liked Catherine, but ever since she had started interning with an undisclosed intelligence agency, her observation skills—and interrogation skills, apparently—had seemed to grow exponentially. I felt like that glare of hers could see through anything.

Whatever she saw, she wasn't all that pleased. *Interesting.* "Who's your friend, Brennon?" she asked without opening the door any wider. Apparently Catherine was suddenly the deciding factor on whether or not Molly even got into her cousin's house. Did Lanna know? Either way, maybe this wouldn't be as bad as I thought if Catherine decided not to let Molly inside.

I wanted to trust Molly, I really did, but experience had taught me that was impossible, no matter what she said. Besides, I really didn't want her in my life any longer than necessary. Things had gotten chaotic enough, in my opinion.

"Cat, this is my friend, Molly Piper. Molly, this is Catherine—"

"Davenport," Molly gasped, her eyes wide. "Oh my gosh, you're even prettier than in pictures!"

Catherine's lips turned up in a smug grin. Once upon a time she would have gone full diva after hearing a comment like that, but dating Seth had humbled her quite a lot. Now, instead of being featured in the tabloids, she was climbing the political ladder and becoming famous for her merits instead of just her beauty and her money.

"It's Hastings now," she said, and her cheeks turned a little pink like they often did when she remembered who she married, even though it had been a year and a half since she did. "So how do you know Molly?" she asked me.

Molly twisted around to my side and slipped her fingers between mine. I stared at them because I was so not prepared for her to do that. Out of all the things I had anticipated her doing, that was not even remotely on the list. I thought I had spent enough time preparing myself for this dinner with Molly; apparently I had not. And without meaning to, I looked up at Catherine as if I was begging her to help me deal with this sudden event.

"Oh, we go way back," Molly said.

Catherine narrowed her eyes a little, looking down at our hands. "I was asking Brennon, but okay. So you're here for dinner?" She asked that question like a challenge, and Molly responded with a flash of competitive fire in her eyes.

Huh. Catherine versus Molly would be an interesting match and definitely less dangerous than Steve against Seth. Or maybe not. Catherine could be every bit as intimidating as her husband. And now probably wasn't the best time for a showdown, anyway. I had to step in before Molly made things worse.

"Lanna invited her," I said quietly. I knew that would be exactly what it took to get Molly in the house, but at the moment I was thinking that was preferable to a full-on battle. With the way Molly was standing up straighter, I had a feeling she was getting ready to show just how confident she could be.

Catherine was the queen of confidence; Molly could probably do even better.

Molly moved a little closer to me, something Catherine definitely noticed and didn't like, and then she put on her sweetest smile. "I gave Bean here a ride this morning," she said, "and your cousin was kind enough to invite me over. I couldn't resist spending more time with Brennon, and besides, how many people can say they've had dinner with the likes of Catherine and Seth Hastings?"

I nearly dropped my face in my hands, knowing that last comment would be the thing to keep Molly from ever getting within a mile of the house ever again. Catherine hated the spotlight when it came from strangers.

But to my surprise, Catherine smiled a little and opened the door wide. "Only because you put my name before Seth's," she said and threw a grin my way that clearly said she liked the girl I'd brought with me.

'Brought' being a loose term in this instance.

As exhausting as the unknown was, it would be interesting to see how long that amiability would last. "After you," I said then followed Catherine and Molly into the Munroes' mansion.

I really did love this house. Working in the middle of San Francisco hadn't made habitation easy, since I had no desire to commute into the city every day, not when I could see the lines of cars on the bridge from my office window. Places like these weren't far from downtown, but no matter how well off I liked to think I was, my fortune was nowhere near enough to afford a place like this. People like the Davenports and their relations—all these people who had adopted me into their family—were in an entirely different league than me, and the house showed it. It put my condo to shame.

What condo?

I had a feeling it would be hard to go back to my simple life after spending a few days here at the mansion. A condo by myself wasn't exactly a home.

"I know that look," Molly said, looking back at me.

I blinked, pulling my eyebrows together. "What look?"

I didn't have a look. I was just walking. But now that Molly had said something, even Catherine was gazing back with interest, her eyes much too knowing for someone who before these dinners was just an across-the-hall neighbor I ran into every once in a while.

"I don't have a look, Molly."

But she grinned and took my hand again, sending my stomach twisting into painful knots. Why did I agree to let her come? *Oh right, I didn't.* This was a terrible idea. There were too many variables. Too many things that could go wrong.

"You always have a look, Bean," she said. "You miss home, don't you?"

My first instinct was to laugh, but I pushed that down real quick. Maybe it was better to let her think she had me all figured out. "Well yeah," I said. "I only have the time to visit once a month or so because of work. But that's not—"

"How's Susan doing with her foot surgery?" Molly asked.

I pulled her to a full stop in the middle of the doorway, gesturing with my head for Catherine to keep heading for the dining room. I wouldn't keep the family waiting much longer, but I wasn't about to walk in there after hearing a question like that.

"How do you know about my mom's surgery?" I snapped. It was one thing for her to keep tabs on me; checking up on my parents was another thing entirely.

She shrugged, though I was pretty sure I'd thrown her off with my sudden anger because she tugged a little to try to free her hand with no luck. "We're internet friends," she said. "I thought you knew that."

My mom wasn't even friends with *me* online. Besides, my mom *hated* Molly. She told me so often. There was no way Mom had told Molly anything about her surgery. Not directly.

That was a conversation for another time, though. Taking a slow breath and making sure I didn't grit my teeth, I pulled her just a little closer so I could get my point across without being overheard. "I don't know why you're here," I said, "but you need to stop."

She frowned. "Stop what?"

"All of this. My mom, the cheery questions, pretending we're still friends."

Whatever I expected her to do, it wasn't to start crying. Tears welled up in her eyes, and she twisted her hand until she freed herself and was able to take a step away from me, toward the dining room. "What do you mean, we're not friends? Bean, you're my *best* friend."

"It's been fifteen years," I growled.

"I've been working. Traveling. It's not like I could—"

"The last time I saw you, Molly, you said—"

She suddenly rushed forward and threw her arms around me, holding me so tight it almost hurt to breathe. And while I knew it wasn't enough to fix my anger, I couldn't find my words. Not when she still fit so perfectly against me like she used to. Not when her tears soaked into my shirt. Not when that smell of roses hit my nose like a shock to my system and broke down my defenses. I wrapped my arms around her shoulders and shut my eyes tight because there was nothing else I could do.

I was powerless against this girl, and she knew it.

"I'm sorry," she whispered into my chest. "I know what I said. I'm so sorry."

I could still see her at the top of that lighthouse when we were eighteen years old and had the whole world in front of us. I could still hear the exact way she said the words. *I don't want you in my life anymore*, she'd said, leaving no room for argument. *My future doesn't have you in it.*

Going to dinner like this was a terrible idea. Catherine would be back, or maybe Matthew would come looking, or heaven forbid Lanna get it into her head that she needed to set out and make things right. If she saw Molly crying, it would all be over. Molly would take my place at dinner, and I'd be stuck looking in from the windows like some street urchin who had nothing to eat but scraps from the garbage.

"We should go," I said. "This isn't—"

"I can't go," she argued and pulled away. "Brennon, you don't understand."

"You want pictures of the house, I know. Another time, maybe." *Or never.*

"No."

"Molly."

"If I don't write this article, I'm done for," she said, grabbing my arm so tight that I recoiled from the pain of it.

I stared at her. That was real fear in her eyes. "What does that—"

She put her hand on my cheek, her thumb over my mouth as she stared at me like I was the only person in the world who could save her from some unknown horror. "I know it sounds crazy, and you don't understand, but this article is the only thing I have. And without the Munroe house, it won't... Please don't send me away, Brennon. I'm begging you. Please."

If I hadn't frozen the moment she touched me, I might have been able to get away before that final whispered 'please' undid me. But just like it used to, Molly's hand held me motionless, which meant the only thing that could possibly come out of my mouth was, "Okay."

I needed to get my life back on track and stop moaning about stupid things before I fell apart, but apparently that would not happen to-night. I was just glad there were no songs playing in my head at the moment, because then I would be completely out of control.

"Oh, Bren, you're the best!" Leaning up and kissing my cheek, Molly took hold of my hand again and pulled me to the dining room so I could subject the whole family to potential disaster.

I'm such a good friend.

Everyone was sitting at the table when we walked in, their eyes locked on the pair of us as their conversations died almost immediately. I figured it would be a good idea to make introductions quickly, before any of them surprised me with a question I wouldn't be able to answer easily.

"Everyone," I said, suddenly unsure of how something like this should go, "this is my old friend, Molly."

The dining room echoed with a chorus of, "Hi, Molly."

This isn't Alcoholics Anonymous.

"Molly," I continued, though I was having a hard time not picturing what this particular group would do in an AA meeting. Steve and Matthew would probably send everyone else straight back to the bottle. "This is Adam Munroe." Though apparently they had already met.

Adam sat at the head of the table, closest to the door, and he had to crane his neck to see us. As always, he gave us a nod of his head without saying anything. The fact that Adam wasn't much of a talker was probably the only thing I had in common with the guy.

"This is Catherine, as you know," I continued.

Catherine grinned on Adam's left. "And Seth, her husband."

Seth scowled at Molly, but I figured I could blame his bad mood on the fact that Steve was sitting directly across from him and had probably already said something stupid.

Why do you always have to poke the bear, Steve?

I moved onto Lanna at the other end of the table. "You met Lanna," I said to Molly.

And I was surprised she was on the opposite end of the table from Adam instead of next to him, like she usually was. Lanna smiled politely but seemed a little distracted. I'd have to ask her about that later, because for how often she made the world better for those around her, maybe this time the fixer needed some fixing. She deserved some advice or sympathy, whatever I could give her. It was the least I could do after she took me in like she had.

"That's Indie," I said, pointing, "and her husband, Matthew. They're Davenports."

Matthew looked at Molly with interest, and Indie was friendly enough as she lifted a hand to wave.

"And you know Steve already, and his wife, Lissa, who was at the restaurant."

Steve gave a friendly grin. To my alarm, Lissa looked as unhappy as her brother Seth as she looked up at Molly, though I was pretty sure she was trying to hide it.

Lissa was the one who had told everyone about Molly in the first place. Did she know something I didn't? It was too much to think she might actually be jealous, because that was just ridiculous, but she definitely wasn't as friendly toward Molly as she usually would have been with anyone else. I could lie to myself and think Lissa secretly wanted me to get together with Katie, but I highly doubted my best friend's wife cared that much about who I dated.

"Well," Matthew said, "Indie is starving, so…" He laughed when his wife smacked his arm, but it was enough to remind me that dinner was waiting on us, so I pulled Molly to our chairs and sat down, determined to do everything I could to make this dinner go as smoothly as possible.

Forget awkward first dates; this was the true test of everything I had become.

CHAPTER TEN

Just a few minutes into dinner, which had been pretty calm as we all enjoyed Steve's incredible food, I started to relax. Maybe it wouldn't be as much of a disaster as I'd thought, and Molly seemed perfectly content to sit on my left and act the part of shy and demure house guest while soft conversations buzzed around us. I wasn't all that thrilled about ending up next to Seth, especially with Steve right across from him, but maybe this odd peace would continue. Maybe dinner would end without incident and I could push Molly out of the house and my life before anything went wrong.

But, of course, Steve couldn't let that happen. Not when he was in such a prime position to annoy his brother-in-law. I missed the first part of their conversation, but it didn't take long to discover the reason Seth practically bent his fork in his fist as he glowered at Steve.

"I think I'd be really good at it," Steve said, and his lopsided grin said he knew exactly how close he was to pushing Seth over the edge.

"Good at what?" asked Indie in curiosity. I didn't blame her, since a blind man could only take up so many new hobbies without putting in some real effort.

Matthew pretty much lounged in his seat, leaning on one chair arm and looking like he had never been more entertained when he answered, "He's thinking of taking up archery."

I nearly choked on the bite of potato I'd just put into my mouth, and not just because that was a horrible idea. No, I choked because, across the table, Lissa was giving me a look that said I had better intervene.

What do you expect me to do? I was way too busy trying to ignore the fact that Molly sat close enough that I could smell her perfume every time I took a breath. Besides, it wasn't like I had any control over Steve. No one did. He was very much like Molly in that regard.

"Such an idiot," Seth grumbled at the same time Lissa turned to her husband and said, "I thought that was a joke."

"I dunno," Steve replied, clearly loving Seth's growing irritation. "Maybe I have a sixth sense and could be really good at it."

Seth opened his mouth to growl a response, but Lanna beat him to it: "You're welcome to use the backyard here," she said. "There's plenty of room in case this sixth sense of yours isn't what you think it is. So, Molly." Those last two words immediately pulled all attention to the girl at my side, jokes and insults forgotten because these people were incapable of pretending they weren't entirely enthralled by the idea of me bringing someone to family dinner.

I didn't bring her, I wished I could say. *She forced her way in.* If anyone, I would have brought Katie because she was painfully normal and didn't bring chaos wherever she went. At least, I couldn't imagine her creating chaos. An accountant could only get so wild.

"We didn't get much of a chance to talk this morning," Lanna continued. "How do you know Brennon?"

Molly's smile was the kind that could get the teacher to think it hadn't been her who set off the smoke alarm in Chemistry because she'd been burning her assignment in her boredom. I wished I didn't know her better, or I might have believed her innocence. "We've been friends since we were kids," she said sweetly. "My dad and I moved in next door to Brennon's family in San Leandro, and he was so nice to me and made sure I wasn't the weird new kid."

Lanna smiled just as sweetly as Molly spoke. "That sounds like Brennon," she said, and then she added, "I never knew our neighbors."

"I did," Matthew said with a grimace. "You weren't missing anything."

"Are those the ones who called the cops and got you arrested when they saw you climbing the back wall after you snuck out?" his wife asked him.

Lanna's eyes went wide. "You got arrested?" she gasped. "When? And why does Indie know that and I don't?"

Matthew waved her comment away and quickly said, "I don't keep secrets from Indie, and we were talking about Molly and Brennon, not me."

Though she didn't push the issue, Lanna clearly didn't like that response, and she sat back in her chair with a little frown. If I'd been sitting next to her instead of Molly, I would have patted her arm or something, though I wouldn't have the first idea what to say. As much as I liked Lanna, I'd never been good at comforting people, and telling her that her brother was an idiot wouldn't make her feel any better.

She probably knew that part already.

"So Molly, you must know all the dirty little secrets about this guy," Matthew continued, a little red in the face. Hopefully that meant he knew his mistake in word choice to his sister. I couldn't know for sure, because his words cued that song by The All-American Rejects that was popular in middle school. "Brennon hardly tells us anything about himself."

For a reason. "There isn't anything to tell," I mumbled, though I'd almost sung a line from the song instead and knew I needed to be careful. I could see Molly fighting a grin, and I was pretty sure she knew exactly what was running through my head. I was a completely different person from who I was when she knew me before, but some things apparently never changed.

"I doubt that's true," Seth growled next to me, and a shiver ran through me. He may have been nice to me most of the time, but that didn't mean he liked me. I was still Steve's best friend, after all.

Apparently, Molly didn't find anything frightening about Seth, because she smiled at him. "There's a lot I could say about Bean," she said, "but I'm sure you know the best parts of him. I wouldn't want to ruin your perception of him just because I knew him before he grew up."

Well that was…unexpected. Which really shouldn't have surprised me, because nothing Molly did was predictable. Was that why she had never really answered Steve's question in the car? *Which Brennon is the real Brennon?* Had she actually realized how much I'd changed? I certainly hoped so, because that would mean she didn't expect me to be the guy she used to know. I wasn't sure I even remembered who that guy was. Whoever he was, he had crashed and burned, and it was a bad idea to try to get him back.

"We do like Brennon," Catherine said and gave me a warm smile.

I smiled back, though I wasn't sure what to say.

"And what about you, Molly?" Indie asked. "What's your story?"

Both Lissa and Steve leaned a little closer to hear, and I couldn't help but do the same thing. What would she say? Who had she become over the last fifteen years? If she was exactly the same as she had been, was that good or bad? I had no idea.

"I'm a photojournalist," Molly said. "Started at a little independent magazine right out of high school, and then I found a job with a European travel agency for a few years. I've been in Asia for the last six years following more political stories, and it's really nice to be home."

Was it my imagination—probably—or had Seth gotten even more tense than before?

"What part of Asia?" Adam asked with interest.

"All over," Molly replied. "And I mean, literally all over. Everywhere from Syria to Cambodia and in between."

Seth and Catherine exchanged looks, and I wished I wasn't sitting next to them so I could see what their expressions looked like. Silence wasn't exactly illuminating for whatever they might be thinking.

Adam, on the other hand, sat up a little and looked even more intrigued by Molly. "That sounds like a fairly dangerous job," he said, his eyebrows high.

But Molly smiled and shrugged the comment off, as if following political escapades in war-torn countries was as common a job as a stockbroker. She'd never been afraid of anything when we were young, and apparently that hadn't changed. "There were moments," she said.

"But nothing will ever compare to the time Brennon and I got stuck in the middle of Mexico on a school trip."

I felt the color drain from my face and leave me dizzy, and that dizziness only got worse when Molly gave me a grin that said she wasn't about to finish that story nicely. With the way the family was looking at me, they weren't going to let it go, so I would have to fill them in unless I wanted Molly to make it sound a hundred times worse than it had been.

I really liked these people, but that didn't mean I found it any easier to talk to them than to the rest of the world. Coughing a little, I sipped my water and tried to find the best way to tell the story without making it sound like some high adventure. "We were down near Guanajuato for a humanitarian trip," I said, horrified when my voice squeaked a little. I swallowed and took a deep breath.

"We were building a school," I said, and thankfully my voice stayed steady this time, "and Molly and I were painting one of the outside walls while most of the others finished the floors inside. I must have accidentally brushed Molly with my paintbrush, because she—"

"Whoa," Molly said and grabbed my arm. "You absolutely did that on purpose. I watched you!"

I coughed again, but her playfulness felt so familiar that when I looked at her, I didn't feel quite as unsettled as I had since she showed up at the restaurant. This was the Molly I knew.

"Okay," I admitted and even smiled a little. "I painted her arm on purpose. So she decided to paint me back, and before we knew it, we were both covered in white paint and were chasing each other down the streets."

"This was, like, sunset," Molly added.

"Afternoon," I corrected, "but it did start getting dark before we realized how far we'd run."

"Like I said. Sunset."

I narrowed my eyes at her, and she grinned. "By the time we got back to the school," I said, and now I was talking to Molly instead of anyone else, "the rest of our classmates were gone. They'd already hopped on the bus and headed back to the hotel."

"I know what you're thinking," Molly said, and she was talking right back at me. "How could anyone possibly drive away without realizing they were missing the most handsome and charming kid in the class?"

"You mean how could they drive away in the silence that exists wherever you're not?" I shot back. "Anyway, Molly had the brilliant idea to walk back to our hotel, and—"

"That was your idea," she said.

I frowned. "No, it wasn't."

"Yes," she replied. "You said, 'By the time they realize we're still out here, we could be most of the way back.' And then you grabbed my hand and started walking."

"Fine. But it wasn't a bad idea."

"Only you had no idea where the hotel was."

"Sure I did," I said. "I just got a little...disoriented."

"Lost."

"Do you want me to tell the story or not?"

Molly's smile was as innocent as they came, and I nearly laughed at the sight.

"You know that never works on me," I said, and before she could argue, I continued, "We got about halfway across town when we ran into a group of men—"

"Gang."

"—who spoke enough English to tell us we were going the wrong way, and they offered us a ride, since it was pretty much dark at that point. I didn't think it was a good idea, but Molly was complaining about walking so much, so we agreed."

Molly grabbed my hand, her hazel eyes wide. "You forgot the best part!" she said. "One of the guys most definitely had a rifle."

"That wasn't a rifle," I said.

"Yeah it was."

I rolled my eyes. "It was clearly a shotgun."

"Because that's so much better."

"There's a difference, Mol."

"Whatever you say, Bean."

And then, as if I'd been hit in the gut with a shotgun shell, I remembered where I was. I froze, feeling eight pairs of eyes on me, and suddenly the room was spinning around me. All of the Davenports were watching me, not just to hear the story but with expressions of wonder and confusion because there was a high chance most of them had never heard me speak so much before. My tongue sat heavy in my mouth, and I couldn't look at Molly anymore because she'd caught the change that came over me and looked like she was about to ask if I was okay.

"We, uh..." I swallowed. It was like I had forgotten how words worked. "We got in the back of their, uh, truck, and..."

Molly slowly put her hand on my arm under the table, all of her playfulness gone as she watched me. What did she see? I had no idea. But she looked worried. Or sad. Or something.

"We made it about a block before we realized they were taking us *out* of town, not *into* town where our hotel was," she said quietly. Her energy was gone, just like mine. "We were thinking about jumping from the truck and making a run for it, but the universe decided we didn't need to be sold into the slave trade because the gang was stopped by the police just a couple blocks later, and we were able to explain our situation and make it back to the hotel, where our teachers were about ready to die of horror because someone had finally noticed we weren't with them."

There was a moment of silence—I was positive everyone else had noticed the change come over me as well—but then Steve mercifully said, "Brennon, you idiot."

Nervous laughter echoed the sentiment around the table. "You're really lucky," Indie said, and Matthew nodded beside her.

"Like I said," Molly replied, "scary. I didn't run into anything like that in Asia. At least not up close, though I saw a few nightmares through my camera. Especially in Laos."

Seth's glass suddenly shattered in his hand, making all of us jump.

"Sorry," he said immediately, wrapping a napkin around his bleeding hand while Catherine looked at him with evident concern in her eyes and put her hand on his shoulder. He didn't even seem to feel the pain in his palm, even though there was enough blood soaking through the napkin that I felt queasy. "Held it a little too tight," he grunted. His fingers were shaking, which wasn't exactly comforting because I was pretty sure it had nothing to do with the slices he'd just cut through his skin.

Everyone else seemed too shocked to know what to say, but eventually Lanna rose to her feet and said, "We should have a first aid kit around here somewhere."

At almost the same time, Matthew said, "I do that all the time."

And Catherine said, "We should probably get that looked at," while Adam was almost to his feet, ready to help.

To my bewilderment, Lissa was looking at me instead of her bleeding brother.

"I'm fine," Seth said, but his wife was already guiding him out of his chair, and he wasn't arguing.

"Sorry, Lanna," Catherine said as they went. "Steve, thanks for dinner. It was amazing."

Without saying anything, Steve waved his hand, his eyebrows pulled low as he stared unfocused at his plate. What was wrong with *him*?

The room grew quiet again, Lanna still on her feet and no one sure what to say, apparently. I didn't know how, but it was Molly's fault. It had to be. Outside of the Steve/Seth nonsense, these family dinners were generally light and cheery, and I'd never seen Seth so…whatever that was. Molly had thrown herself into their lives, and now the whole family was tense.

And Molly just sat there as if she had no idea she was to blame and was simply confused by what had just happened.

"He must be extra tense lately," Lissa said, frowning. There was more to it than that, but it felt like a secret none of the family were willing to share.

"Probably Uncle Milton showing up the other day," Lanna replied, though I knew it was to cover up the real reason. "That would make anyone tense."

Molly took hold of my hand, her fingers tight, and when I met her gaze, there was something in her eyes that held my attention. What was she hiding from me? It was something she wanted me to know. Just as I was about to ask what it was, she shook her head ever so slightly then said to the table in general, "I hope he'll be okay."

"He's had worse," Matthew muttered, meeting Adam's gaze.

The whole table was full of unspoken conversations, apparently, and this was far worse than speed dating. This family was always so light and happy that I had no idea what to do when suddenly they weren't.

Thankfully, Steve broke the silence as he stood and said, "Hey Brennon, can I ask you something? It's, uh, money-related."

If that was really the case, I doubted Lissa would have kept frowning like that, but I could tell Steve was really eager to have this conversation, whatever it was about, because he went straight for the door without wavering. He was always better at navigating when he was focused on other things.

"You okay?" I asked as soon as we were out in the hallway. "Is the restaurant—"

"You like Katie, right?"

I stared at him. "What?" I knew he didn't actually want to talk about money, but I had not considered he would be asking me about my date the other night.

"You had a good time with her on Friday, right?"

Shrugging, I let my eyes wander the many photos Lanna and Adam had put up in this hallway. I'd always wondered why they took so many, but I'd never been brave enough to ask. Maybe they just wanted to preserve as much as they could. The exact opposite of me.

"Katie's great," I said. "Exactly the sort of person I should be with."

But Steve frowned, as if I had just said what he absolutely did not want to hear. He was the one who had pushed the two of us together, so shouldn't he have been rooting for her? "You talked about accounting for half an hour, Brennon."

"So? It's something we have in common."

Folding his arms, Steve took a deep breath and seemed to be doing his very best to get a good look at me. I had no idea what he saw, and I hoped he couldn't tell how absolutely confused I was by this whole conversation. "You've never been much of a talker," he said. It was more of a question than a statement, though he nodded to confirm it himself. "And I always thought that meant you were shy."

I am shy. But those words stuck in my throat.

"But you were never shy with Lissa," he continued, and he started to pace the hallway, impressively avoiding both me and the massive decorative vase nearby. "In fact, when you were around Lissa, you were pretty much a different person."

Where was he going with this? If I snuck back into the dining room, would he even notice I'd left? I was tempted to try it, just to see, but I forced myself to stay put because Brennon Ashworth was never rude.

"Do you remember what I told you that night in the hospital?"

"You mean when I conceded defeat?" I muttered then froze because that thought was *not* supposed to come out of my mouth. Of course he was referring to the night I had backed down and let Lissa fall in love with him instead of me, but what I should have said was, *The night you told me how much you loved her.* It had never been a battle for Lissa's heart. Or, I would never admit to that.

You just did, Ashworth.

Steve pointed at me. "That," he said, his voice sharp. "That's what I'm talking about."

I winced. "What are you talking about?"

"Your whole dinner date with Katie was the most boring thing I've ever heard, and I am honestly amazed either of you stayed awake for it."

I frowned. While I could admit I had been doing my best to keep my focus on Katie, I hadn't noticed him hanging around. I would have to try to get a table that wasn't right next to the kitchen next time I went there...

But first things first. I must have been more tired than I thought, because I had no idea how any of these things were related. "Steve, you're not making any sense."

Groaning, he ran his hands down his face and kept pacing, only this time he bumped into my shoulder as he passed. "Sorry, Bren, I'm just... There's something... I need to go to bed," he finished with a sigh.

He did look tired. Ever since he met Lissa, he'd worked hard to stay healthy and keep up his energy, but it almost looked like something was wearing on him. How late had they kept The Globe open last night? Having an indeterminate closing time probably wasn't good for him.

"You're different with Molly," he added as he headed for the dining room again. "And I'm not sure that's a bad thing."

He returned a moment later with Lissa in tow, which meant the family dinner was probably over. And though I could tell he wanted to keep talking, he also clearly needed to get to bed, since he held tight to his wife's hand and let her lead him, which he didn't often do.

But then Lissa paused, her frown focused on me and making me wish I could be anywhere but in this house. "Do you think you can get back to the car on your own, Steve? I need to talk to Brennon for a second."

Well this is concerning.

Steve seemed to understand what she wanted to talk to me about, since he nodded and kissed Lissa's cheek before making his way to the front door with one hand on the wall. It wasn't like he didn't trust me, but he rarely left me alone with Lissa. Just in case. And I didn't blame him for that one, considering I had dated her first.

Folding my arms, I ran through a list of possible scenarios in my head as Lissa seemed to sort through her own thoughts, but it was pretty easy to figure out where this conversation was going to go.

Lissa was, generally, a happy person. Her optimism was one of the things I loved about her, and I was pretty sure very little could dampen her spirits. So the fact that she frowned now, even with the other strangeness with the rest of the family, made me nervous.

"So," she said after a longer pause than I was comfortable with. "You've known Molly a long time?"

What was it with this family and Molly? "Since I was eight," I said.

"Why have you never talked about her?"

I really wished I could know the reason behind that question. It would change how I answered it, and not knowing meant I could get myself into dangerous territory. Was she worried about me? She didn't need to be. I liked to think I could handle Molly, though maybe that was a stupid frame of mind. Was she jealous? That was way out of the question, given the way she looked at Steve at any given moment. Did she distrust Molly? She had a right to, though there was no specific reason I could offer for her to do so.

Lissa looked up at me, her concern growing.

"I haven't seen her since high school," I said. "We..." How to put it? "We had a falling out."

"Like a breakup?" Lissa asked.

My answer came out harsher than I meant it to: "We would have had to date to break up." And Molly and I hadn't dated. At all.

"Oh." She seemed appeased a bit, if not completely at ease. "You're different around her," she said.

I put my hands in my pockets. Of all the things she could have said, that one tightened my chest the most. It was bad enough that Steve had noticed too, but Lissa wasn't going to drop the issue until I said something.

"Different how?" I said. I needed to know so I could fix it. Stay predictable. *Someone* had to be.

Shrugging, Lissa glanced down the hall, toward the front door. "I should go," she said, and her voice was as soft as her touch when she placed her fingers on my arm.

But her touch made me shiver, and I pulled away.

"Tell Molly it was nice to meet her," she said.

Molly. My panic returning, I had to force myself not to run back to the dining room, and I could only imagine what was happening inside. At best, Molly was telling stories about me that belied my carefully constructed persona. At worst...

Breathless, I stumbled back into the room with an apology on my tongue.

"How's Steve?" Matthew asked, and he had a smile on his face as he leaned onto the back two legs of his chair. It reminded me so much of Jake, which reminded me of the disaster that was the current state of my job, which somehow reminded me of my condo, so I had to take in the rest of the room before I could formulate an answer.

Give myself a moment to think.

Indie was talking to Lanna, her hands on her pregnant belly. Molly was talking to Adam, who looked... Well, the best I could describe it was confused. But overall, everything seemed to still be in one piece, and the room even felt warmer than it had been before I followed Lissa. The tension was gone.

"So the original foundation is still here?" Molly was asking. She had her phone out, probably recording Adam's response for her story. "That's incredible. And I know a lot of the house has changed, but I think readers will be more interested in what you've turned the place into. You are the King of Art, after all, and people are curious about what happens behind these walls."

Maybe I just imagined it, but I was pretty sure Molly sent me a glance that was supposed to say something along the lines of, "Listen carefully." What was she up to?

"Steve's fine," I muttered to Matthew and stepped a little closer to Molly, just in case I had to intervene.

"I'm not so sure we're all that exciting," Adam said with a half-smile. "You'll feature more of the house than my family, right?"

Molly put a hand on his arm. "Of course. The piece is on several houses in the area, so I only have so much room anyway."

"You look exhausted, Brennon," Matthew said, pulling my attention back to him. He was looking at me like he was hoping to figure out why I was so tired just by staring at me. Maybe that worked with other people, but I tried to never be that easy to read. Besides, he knew exactly why I was tired.

"I am exhausted," I said quietly. "That happens when your condo gets destroyed in the middle of the night."

Lifting his hands as if I'd pointed a gun at him, Matthew smirked and said, "Easy there, Ashworth. It was just a comment."

I must have sounded a lot more irritated than I'd meant to. Or maybe Matthew just liked to think he knew me as well as he knew his family. "Sorry," I said, though I wasn't sure I meant it. "It's been a stressful weekend."

"Tell me about it," he replied and put his arm around Indie. "This one keeps me up half the night moving around."

Indie smacked him. "I do not."

"Sure you do."

"Well if I do," she replied, "it's your fault. This baby is getting way too big for me to get comfortable."

And if I had to guess, Matthew was thrilled about the idea of his child coming soon. He smiled at his wife with the kind of smile I hadn't seen in years outside of this family in front of me. It was a smile that was nothing but pure joy. What did that feel like?

Without meaning to, I looked up at Molly and found her watching me. She had smiled like that once upon a time, and I had thought that meant she cared for me the same way I cared for her.

I couldn't have been more wrong.

"I should probably get to bed," I said quickly. "I've got a lot of work to do tomorrow. Molly, don't you have somewhere to be?"

She didn't, and she knew that I knew that, but she nodded and clasped Lanna's arm before coming over to my side and slipping her hand in mine. It wasn't the first time she'd done it, but this time felt different. This time there were several witnesses, witnesses who all exchanged glances after looking down at my hand entwined with Molly's.

"I'll walk you to the door," I told Molly because that was what I was supposed to say in this situation. Not because I wanted to extend my time with her.

The moment we were out the door, I twisted my hand free and stuffed both into my pockets as I went down the stairs. I didn't have to say anything because I knew Molly would explain. She knew exactly why I was upset. I could hide from everyone around me—just not Molly.

"I know what you're thinking," she said when we hit the bottom of the stairs.

"Enlighten me," I growled. I could still feel her fingers around mine, like she'd left a burning mark behind. It wasn't that she held my hand. She'd done that all the time in high school, and I'd never known anyone more physically affectionate than Molly no matter who she was with. It was the way she did it, the things it implied.

It was bad enough letting Molly into my friends' lives, and I was not about to make them believe a lie too.

"They don't trust me, Bren," she said.

Imagine that. "And why does holding my hand fix that?"

She frowned. "Because they trust you."

"We're not a couple, Molly. I won't let them think we are."

"I know that."

"Do you?"

She let out a huff and sat down on the steps. "Brennon, I know you think I am here for some sinister reason, but I did not come here to hurt you. You have to believe me."

I curled my fingers into a fist, trying to get rid of the sensation of her touch. I had always been good at reading people—at least I liked to think I had—and once upon a time I had known Molly so well that she didn't have to say anything for me to know what was going through her mind. Taking a deep breath, I tried to remind myself of that girl, the one I knew before she completely destroyed my life as I knew it.

"Mol," I said quietly and slowly lowered myself down to sit next to her. "This family is one of the few good things I have in my life. They expect certain things from me, and you are not one of those things. I want to believe you won't hurt them, but if I'm wrong…" I sighed. As much as I wanted to trust her, I couldn't find it in myself. "As soon as you get your story," I said, "you need to leave. Disappear. That shouldn't be too hard for you."

And though I knew it was rude, I jumped up and walked back up to the house without looking back.

"Something's going on with them," Molly said right as I reached the door, freezing me in my tracks. "After what we heard this afternoon, I think—"

"Goodnight, Molly," I said, but when I got inside, I paused in the entryway. Seth and Adam were acting strange. Lanna seemed more stressed than usual. Matthew was keeping secrets. I didn't want to think Molly was right, but…

"This is the Davenports you're talking about," I muttered and rolled my eyes before heading to my guest room to go to bed early. "Of course Molly isn't right."

So why had everything felt off tonight? I didn't have any answers, and I fell into bed determined to forget about that question. It was the least I could do after the family went to so much trouble to help me out. But as I lay there in the darkness, my fingers still tingling from Molly's touch, I worried my carefully normal life was doomed to be a thing of the past.

CHAPTER ELEVEN

I woke early Monday morning with a feeling I hadn't felt in more than a decade: I didn't want to go to work.

I lay in the ridiculously comfortable bed in the Munroe guest room, staring up at the dark ceiling and trying to find the motivation to get up and get ready to head to the office. But my body didn't seem to want to obey my thoughts, or maybe I wasn't trying all that hard, and I glanced at my phone sitting on the nightstand next to me. It was almost six o'clock already, and on a normal day, I would have already been heading to my car.

"Nothing about the last few days has been normal," I muttered and grabbed my phone.

I texted Jake and told him that I had to take care of my condo and wouldn't make it into the office today. He responded only a couple of minutes later, which was impressive for a guy who actually had a night-life.

No worries, he said. *I'll take care of everything.*

Let me know if you have any questions, I replied then settled back into the bed.

I honestly couldn't remember the last time I had taken a day off. Even when I got sick, I usually just locked myself into my office and kept the lights off while I worked. The idea of taking a vacation was almost laughable, and I filled my weekends up with more work. The fact that I was tempted to just lie here for several more hours had me worried about my mental sanity.

"It's Molly's fault," I said out loud. *Always Molly's fault.*

I couldn't just sit here forever, though, so I forced myself to sit up. Maybe I would check on my condo, like I'd told Jake I was doing. Maybe I would see if Lanna needed any help with the kids or the house. "Maybe I'll get myself some new suits," I said when my eyes landed on the stack of Adam's clothes in the open closet. It wasn't like he dressed poorly, but we weren't exactly the same size. He was broader in the shoulders, which made me feel weak and sickly when his shirts hung so loose.

And I missed my suits.

That was what I would do. Stop by the tailor, maybe check out a furniture store or two, and try to get my life back to normal. The problem was I was worried normal would be impossible until Molly was gone, and it was impossible to know how long before she was. Molly was too unpredictable, and I was probably going to end this whole ordeal with an ulcer.

First things first, though: I needed breakfast.

The house was dark and quiet as I ventured out, which made sense given the early hour. But as I crept down the hallway, being as silent as I could so I didn't wake anyone, my feet paused outside Adam's office yet again.

The light was on.

I knew I should just keep walking, but Molly's voice slipped into my head and told me it was my duty to stay and listen. "That's ridiculous," I whispered, and I knew it, but if by some bizarre turn of events Molly found out I passed up an opportunity like this, she'd kill me. She'd call me boring and too trusting and blind to the possibility that not everything about this perfect family was as perfect as it seemed.

I shouldn't have cared what Molly would think of me. But I did.

Leaning toward the door until I caught a voice, I held my breath and listened.

"Probably not a good idea," someone said. It sounded like Adam. He was quiet for a moment, and then he said, "Matt, I am not going to tell my wife I bought a painting but not tell her what it is. That's the worst cover I've ever heard." Another pause. "I've already lied to her more times than I'm comfortable with."

He must have been talking to Matthew on the phone, and the tension in his voice kept me in place. Adam was always so calm.

"Like I told Seth, we have to keep this off the books or she'll find out. Do you have any better ideas?" He paused. "Not that," he practically growled. "I'd like to hear you say something like that to Indie and see how you feel then. We are getting ourselves in too deep with this one, Matt. We need to finish this. I know. As soon as we can, or we're all dead men."

The room was silent after that, and it took me longer than I would have liked to realize Adam must have hung up the phone. And if his conversation was over, there was a high chance he was going to leave his office. And find me standing there.

Without bothering to stay so quiet, I hurried the rest of the way to the front door and slipped out, my heart racing and my mind reeling as it tried to process what I'd just heard. I really didn't want to think Molly was right, but—

"You're up early!"

I slipped on the front steps, which were damp from a morning drizzle, and landed hard on my backside right in front of Molly, who stood there grinning at me. "What..." I didn't even bother finishing that question as I stared at the rest of the steps below me, trying to process everything.

She understood me anyway. "I wanted to stop by and see how you're doing," she explained, "but it didn't take me as long to walk here as I expected. I was just going to sit on the steps and wait, but then you appeared."

Was Adam getting himself into trouble and dragging Seth and Matthew down with him? But that was ridiculous. Adam was perfect.

"Brennon, you okay?"

I looked up. *No, I'm not okay.* My condo was destroyed and my dream job was hanging just out of reach and the one family I thought

I could count on was acting so completely out of character that I felt like I'd entered another universe.

"I'm hungry," I said. That was the only problem I could solve on my own right now.

"You're always hungry," Molly said and sat herself down on the steps next to me.

And that was when I noticed the bag she held, the bag that smelled like it was full of all my favorite fried breakfast foods. I stared at that bag and failed to keep myself from wondering if she'd brought that for me.

She laughed and dumped the bag into my lap. "You think I'd forget how grumpy you can be when you don't eat?" she asked. She also handed me a toothbrush, the same kind I'd been using since I was in high school. Where had she found one? I could only get them online. "I know you better than anyone, Bean."

The alarming part was that she was right. I hadn't seen her for a decade and a half, and she still knew me. More than Steve or my parents ever had. The toothbrush alone told me that, and I sat there on the steps of the house of people who weren't even really my friends, suddenly feeling like I'd been lying to them since the moment I met them. I had been wearing a mask—several of them—and it was starting to suffocate me.

"What's wrong?" Molly asked. "Wait, eat a sandwich, and then tell me."

I smiled. Or I tried to, but nothing felt real anymore. Had my whole life been a lie? Who I was, what I had become, was carefully constructed so I could control at least one aspect of my life, but over the last several days I hadn't even had that control over myself, let alone anything else. Who I was had been dictated by whoever I was around. I wasn't even sure I could say I was happy with the way my life was, and that thought made me nauseous to the point that I had to move the food before the smell of it made me sick.

"What happened to me, Molly?" I moaned and dropped my face into my hands.

Her arm stretched across my shoulders in a hug that made me tense. "You've had a rough couple of days," she said. "No one expects you to be all put together all the time."

I wished that were true, but that was exactly what the world expected of me. "What would you know? You've been on the other side of the world for half your life."

"Maybe," she said, "but that doesn't mean over there they don't have their own problems. People are all the same, Bren."

"No they're not," I argued. "People are unpredictable. You think you know what they'll say, and then they turn around and tell you everything you believed was a lie."

I hadn't meant to get angry. Not after she so thoughtfully brought me a toothbrush. And breakfast. But the reason I hadn't seen her in fifteen years hadn't changed, and I was desperate to understand *something* about the world.

Frowning, she pulled her arm away. "Now why'd you have to go and bring that up?" she asked, as if the turn in conversation had ruined her good mood. Maybe it had.

Personally, I was already in an awful mood, so I didn't care about bringing up touchy subjects. I'd been wanting to have this conversation for fifteen years.

"You left, Mol." I sat up straight, hoping the confident pose would make me feel more confident. "You told me you had never planned to go to Stanford, that you didn't see a future with us as friends, that there was no point in keeping in touch because you were leaving and never coming back. You left me."

"Bren…"

I sighed, rolling my tense shoulders. "What are you doing here, Molly?" I asked.

"I'm here to write a story about the Munroe house." And then, because she could see I didn't believe her, she added, "I promise. I know what I said to you at graduation, and I know how I must have hurt you, but I'm telling the truth. I have to write this story, and you have to believe me."

I expected to feel something as she pleaded with me. That was how it used to be, and everything this girl did used to evoke in me such a strong emotional response that it was impossible to argue with her. But that connection had broken while I sat there on the steps, and I had no idea what had done it. I feared it was just building inside me, the tension growing until the moment when I snapped and lost all sense of control.

"Why?" I asked, concerned by how cold I sounded. "There are other stories out there. Why is this one so important?"

She would have her argument ready, just like always, and she would do everything in her power to defend herself because she'd always been so good at shifting the blame and keeping any responsibility off of her own shoulders.

But she surprised me yet again. "I can't tell you that."

I stood so quickly that I got dizzy for a second, but I wanted to be higher than her, just so she would understand how important this was. "You can't tell me? Mol, do you have any idea how sketchy that sounds?" *How horrifying and dangerous that sounds?* I couldn't protect her if I didn't know what I was up against.

Though she didn't move or change in any way, she seemed to have gotten smaller as she looked up at me. There wasn't any fear in her eyes like there had been last night, but then again Molly had always been fearless, so I had probably imagined it last night. She had once scoped out a gang in our neighborhood when we were sixteen and collected enough evidence to tip off the cops about a drug deal, even though she could have been caught a dozen times. I wasn't sure anything would ever scare her.

"Brennon, I know exactly how that sounds, but you have to trust me. I don't want you to get hurt, so I can't tell you. Can you trust me? Please?"

I didn't know what I could do, but I did know I couldn't just stand there anymore. I had to move before my brain started overthinking things. Without a word, I turned and started heading down the street. Maybe I'd just walk into the city, since I had the whole day to kill anyway.

Molly followed, just as I knew she would, but she stayed half a step behind me. That would help. If I couldn't see her, I couldn't read her face and see her lies if she said them. "Bren," she said, "do you believe me?"

I waited a full block before I spoke, but I didn't trust myself to say anything more than, "I don't know." After another block, I added, "If this didn't involve the Munroes, maybe it would be easier." I couldn't control Molly, but at least I could try to protect that family. "I won't let anything happen to them."

"I don't want to hurt that family," she said, and it sounded like the truth.

The neighborhood opened up to a much busier street that led, as I knew, right into the city. When was the last time I'd walked farther than from my car to Steve's restaurant when the parking was bad? I had no idea. I didn't have time for walking.

And I missed it.

Molly and I used to walk all the time. It started when we were twelve, the day Molly's cat got hit by a car. She had climbed up to my window late that night and said she couldn't sleep, so we walked around the neighborhood all night and talked about all the fun times we had had with that cat. We did the same thing a week later when I failed an English paper and was too scared to tell my parents about it. Molly had spent the whole walk telling me that I could be brave because one little paper wasn't going to spell the end of my future and a sixth grader didn't need to be good at English yet anyway.

Whenever one of us needed to talk through something, we had done it while walking because then it felt like we could actually do something about it instead of being stuck in place. Our walks were when we had nothing to hide. When we could say what was on our minds without being judged. When we could figure out what it meant to be human. Those walks had gotten me through the stress of the SATs and Molly through her dad getting remarried and both of us over bad dates and lost chances.

I hadn't walked like this since Molly left.

"Brennon, where are you going?"

"Anywhere you aren't," I muttered, too quiet for her to hear. "You don't have to follow me."

"I'm pretty sure you're still hungry," she said.

I was, and now that I was moving, I could feel my stomach twisting in complaint. But I wasn't about to admit that, not when it would only make her think she'd won some argument we hadn't actually had.

How was it she could so easily turn my day into a living nightmare? It wasn't even seven yet, and her footsteps just behind me felt like some terrible beast was stalking me, waiting for the moment to strike and unleash all hell.

"What happened to you?" she asked and picked up her pace so she could turn and face me, walking backward along the sidewalk. She knew I would stop her from running into anything. "You used to be so happy all the time, and now it's like you've turned into some Scrooge. You were so personable when we were younger, and now it barely seems like you're nice to your friends. Where's the Brennon Ashworth cheeriness I used to love?"

She wanted me to be cheery and personable? I could do that. I could be anything she wanted me to be if it would get her to go away and stop messing up my already messed up life. If I knew anything about myself, I knew it would take a lot more than a nudge or two to change what I'd become. Steve had been trying for years, and I'd been fighting right back. I would *not* be the person I used to be, because the old Brennon Ashworth was dangerous.

The old Brennon got himself hurt.

I put on a smile and snatched the bag of food out of her hands, pulling out a fried hash brown patty and taking a massive bite. "I've just had some stressful days this week," I said, keeping my voice light and easy. "Sorry I've been so moody. You keep catching me at bad times, I guess."

She didn't believe me. She frowned as she kept walking backward and looked ready to keep pushing her point.

I had to be a better actor. I lost the smile, but I kept the same tone of voice as I said, "Seriously, Mol, with my condo and some things going on at work, I've just been on edge. You can ask the Davenports; I've never been moody with them."

And that had been by design. If I was moody, they would think they had to fix me, and I definitely didn't want that.

Spinning back around so she was at my side again, Molly slipped her hands into her pockets and waited a moment before she spoke again. "I'm sorry about that whole eavesdropping thing the other day," she said. "I shouldn't just assume something is going on with the Davenports. They seem like good people."

Immediately my mind jumped back to what I'd heard that morning. They *were* good people. I knew that without question. But that didn't mean something strange wasn't going on, something I didn't like the sound of.

Molly grabbed my arm, pulling me to a stop. "You saw something," she said, her eyes going wide. "No, you *heard* something. What was it?"

I so badly wanted to lie and say she was dead wrong. But this was Molly. Molly who knew I couldn't lie to save my life and who knew I hated secrets more than anything and who knew that if I had any doubts that they would stick with me until I had definitive proof they were unfounded.

I clenched my jaw, determined not to say anything.

Apparently I didn't have to. She could read me like a book. "It's not just Adam and Seth involved, is it? Who? Catherine? Matthew? It's Matthew, isn't it?"

"Molly," I said, practically begging. "It's none of your business, so please stop trying to—"

"If you're staying with that family," she argued, "then that could make you an accomplice, whatever it is. You could get into trouble, and that makes it my business."

I needed to start walking again before she started making sense. "Mol, there's nothing going on." *There's definitely something going on.* I just didn't know what.

"I know you don't believe that, so why do you keep lying to yourself?"

"Even if I did have suspicions," I said, and I felt sick just thinking about it, "that doesn't mean I have any right to pry into their lives. None of this involves me, and it certainly doesn't involve you."

Molly tried to stop me from walking again, but I pulled out of her grip and picked up my pace. I had to get away from her as soon as I possibly could, but I couldn't think of a good way to get rid of her without straight up asking her to leave me alone. And I didn't know why I couldn't get those words onto my tongue. Speaking my mind to her hadn't been hard before. What changed?

"Brennon," she said and hurried to catch up to me, "I know you think you're not involved in this, but you're staying in their house. If something bad were to happen…"

"You said that already." Why did I think walking was a good idea? This city was way too big.

"Hey." Molly took hold of my hand again, this time keeping me in place as I tried my best not to think about something bad about to go down. "Do you remember Lily Gonzales?"

The name was familiar, but I had to search long-buried memories to remember. "That girl in ninth grade science?" What could this possibly have to do with the Davenports?

Molly nodded. "Remember when she started acting weird?"

Lily had moved to our school partway through the year, and I hadn't really interacted with her much except in class. She'd been a pretty happy person, though quiet, and she was probably the smartest kid in class. But around Christmas, she had stopped talking to anyone, and I had beaten her grade on a test by almost ten percent. When I'd mentioned my surprise to Molly, she had told me she noticed Lily staring off into space a lot.

"You decided to talk to her about what was going on," Molly said quietly, and she wrapped her other hand around mine so she held it with both of hers.

I stared at our hands clasped together, frowning as the memory seemed to fill my senses. "Her sister had just been sent to Afghanistan or something," I muttered. Lily had barely been able to talk about it.

"She was worried she wouldn't come home. And you said we should go to the arcade to get her mind off of it."

That night had turned out to be one of my favorites that year, and it wasn't long after that that I'd realized how much I loved Molly and the way she could bring happiness into anyone's life.

"Lily still emails me sometimes," Molly said. "Tells me about her sister and where she's stationed. And she asks about you sometimes."

I cocked my head. "Me?" Why would she care about me when Molly had been the one to cheer her up?

Moving slowly, as if worried she might scare me, Molly leaned up on her toes and kissed my cheek, leaving a burning spot in my skin. "You notice people, Brennon. If you hadn't talked to her and found out what was happening, she would have suffered in silence. Sometimes people have to talk about their problems, but they won't do it unless you ask. Maybe the Davenports are the same way."

All of that was about the Davenports? My stomach twisted, and I didn't know if it was because I thought something was really going on with the family or because I suddenly felt like I wasn't standing close enough to Molly for a conversation like this. This was sharing secrets, things we couldn't let the rest of the world hear.

No matter which was true, I didn't like the anxiety building inside me, so I pulled myself away from her and waited a moment to see if the distance fixed my uneasiness.

Not really.

I had a horrible feeling both Molly and the Davenports were to blame.

It was probably a good idea if I carried on with my day, before she convinced me this thing with the Davenports was another Lily Gonzales situation.

Whatever it was, it wasn't something the two of us could fix with a trip to the local arcade.

I needed to get out of here.

Grabbing my phone, I quickly ordered myself a ride then settled myself against a wall to wait, which apparently was not what Molly expected me to do because she stared at me, completely confused.

"What are you doing?" she asked.

I grabbed a breakfast sandwich from the bag of food and un-wrapped it. "I'm waiting," I said. "I thought that was obvious."

Folding her arms, she still stood there like I was acting strange, which really didn't make any sense because I was acting exactly how she wanted me to act. "Don't you have somewhere to be?"

"My tailor doesn't open until eight," I said with a shrug. Actually, I was pretty sure I could get him to let me in earlier, since I was about to bring him a whole lot of business, but Molly didn't need to know that. For some reason, I wanted to keep her on her toes. If she wasn't going to be predictable, why should I be?

"Don't you have to work or something?" she asked next.

"I'm taking the day off." The sandwich was delicious, and I was thrilled to find another in the bag. I really was starving, and I wasn't sure how I would have lasted long enough if Molly hadn't brought me something to eat.

"But you never take days off."

I narrowed my eyes at her, and she did her very best to look inno-cent. Her best, however, wasn't good enough, and I could see right through her. She was fully convinced about what she'd just said, which meant she either knew me better than I wanted, or she had done some digging into my life.

Neither was all that comforting.

Thankfully, I didn't have to comment on her knowledge of my life-style, because a car pulled up to the curb in front of me. "Ashworth?" asked the driver through the open window.

"Have a good day, Molly," I said as I slid into the backseat. I prob-ably shouldn't have left it at that, though, so before I closed the door, I added, "And there's nothing going on with the Davenports. Please forget about whatever you think you know."

As the car pulled away, I glanced back and found her watching me with a look of pure sadness on her face. And as much as I wished I could pretend I hadn't seen it, I knew I was going to spend the whole rest of the day wondering why she thought she had to pretend to be happy when she was around me. She'd never done that before.

Once I had a whole lineup of suits added to my tailor's workload—a task that took several hours because we were both particular about the fabrics and cuts and stitching—and I'd had a long perusal of the nearest furniture store, I was hungry again. Fried food, as tasty as it was, had the unfortunate quality of not lasting long, and I had skipped right over lunch as I tried to reassemble my life.

There were any number of places I could go to grab a bite, but with this whole Molly business and my worries about what Adam and the others were getting themselves into, I wanted to go somewhere familiar.

The Globe looked dark, no lights on in the lobby, but it was nearing opening time. Surely Steve had to be somewhere inside, so I knocked on the door and hoped I wouldn't be inconveniencing him by interrupting his prep time. I badly needed my friend, and he was probably the only person who wasn't too close to the family to be able to offer up an honest opinion. It wasn't like I could ask Matthew what he and his brother-in-law were hiding.

But when the door opened to let me in, it was Lissa on the other side. "Hey, Bren," she said and smiled wide. "Come on in."

I usually enjoyed talking to Lissa, but I wasn't sure she would be able to help in this instance. From what I'd heard, at least Adam and Matthew were keeping things from their wives, and I didn't want to make things worse by bringing it to Lissa's attention. Besides, Lissa's expression was a lot dimmer than I liked, which meant she was already dealing with something.

I silently prayed her issues weren't related to the rest of the Davenports.

"How are you handling everything?" she asked as she led me back toward the kitchen.

I'm not. But this felt like a pretty safe topic, so I decided to roll with it. "I'm fine. Catherine did all the heavy lifting, and Lanna and Adam have been great." *Even though I'm taking advantage of your family, and I don't deserve their help.* Well that was getting too deep into things I didn't want to think about. I needed to change the subject. "Is Steve around?"

The restaurant was seriously *silent*, which rarely happened when Steve was around. On top of his urge to hum or sing when things got too quiet (and constantly getting songs stuck in my head when we lived together), he had a tendency to run into things unless he was focusing really hard on something other than where he was going, which meant his life was almost never silent.

Lissa frowned, her eyes on the door. "I don't know where he is, actually. He said he had something to take care of, but he should have been back by now."

As always, my stomach flipped as I tried not to picture Steve in mortal peril. In the three and a half years since the accident that took his sight, I'd seen him nearly die three times, and it was not an experience I wanted to repeat yet again. "Oh," I said, trying not to sound as worried as I felt. "I'm sure he's fine."

"Well, he won't be when he finally shows up," Lissa replied. I'd never really seen her angry before, and yet there she was, growling her words like they tasted bad in her mouth. "If he would just answer his phone, I wouldn't have a problem." Then she looked at me and put on a fake smile. "I need you to distract me."

"What?" That was the whole reason *I* was here, and I really didn't know if I could even help her when I was already distracted myself. Where would Steve have gone without telling Lissa?

"Distract me," she repeated.

"How?"

"Tell me about Molly."

My heart disappeared entirely. *That's not why I'm here.* "I already told you—"

"Tell me what really happened." Lissa's gaze was so intense that I sank into a chair, unable to keep standing. What did she expect me to say? Sitting next to me, she sighed and added, "You're in love with her, aren't you?"

"No," I said. There was no need to even hesitate.

"But you were."

"Yes." That admission made my mouth so dry that I was afraid I wouldn't be able to keep talking. How had Lissa made it so easy to say when I'd been lying to myself about it for years?

"Tell me," she urged.

I didn't want to, but I did. Apparently I was no better at saying no to Lissa than I was to Molly. Was I really surprised? No.

"I was fifteen when I realized it," I said, though it suddenly hurt to breathe. My chest was so tight I thought I might implode. I had never told anyone about this. "We were doing homework in our treehouse in my backyard, and she was sitting there eating licorice and doing algebra while she swung her leg over the edge, and it just hit me. I was desperately in love with this girl, and I was way too scared to do anything about it."

Just like I was too scared to look at Lissa after telling her this. What would she think of me? The guy who had spent the entire time he knew her telling her he didn't believe in love had fallen hopelessly head over heels when he was a teenager, too young to even know what love was.

"Did you ever tell her?" Lissa asked. Her voice was so soft that I couldn't catch any hint at what her emotion might be, and that not knowing was worse than I could have imagined.

So I looked up, shocked to find tears in her blue eyes. "I…" I swallowed, wishing I could say or do something—anything—to help her smile again. But that was not something I was capable of. Not since I'd given her up. "No," I lied. "I never told her."

And to my utter relief, the door to the restaurant opened, and Lissa's attention was immediately pulled away from me and to her husband as he stumbled inside.

"Where have you been?" she asked before he'd even made it halfway into the room.

I was pretty sure Steve could hardly see anything today, since he turned his head away from Lissa so his ear was focused on her rather than his eyes. "Am I that late?" he asked, a little breathless. "What time is it?" He reached his hand out, knowing she would hurry forward to grab it and lead him the rest of the way to the kitchen, and he smiled the moment their fingers met. "Hey, beautiful."

"Don't," Lissa said and leaned away from the kiss he tried to give her. *Interesting.* "I was worried about you, and you didn't answer your phone."

Reaching into his pocket, he pulled said phone out and showed her the blank screen. "Dead."

"You're about to be dead if you don't find a good excuse for being this late. We open in less than an hour!"

"Lissa."

"You're lucky Brennon came and distracted me."

Steve immediately tensed, and his unfocused eyes searched the restaurant in vain to find me. "Bren?"

"Over here," I said. "Are you going to tell your wife where you were, or...?"

He may not have known exactly where I was sitting, but he managed to hit me with a good scowl anyway. "I was helping your brother with something," he told Lissa then pulled away from her hold to walk the rest of the way to the kitchen so he could get ready. "He must not have been paying attention to the time, or he would have dropped me off sooner."

Lissa wasn't the only one who stared at Steve in bewilderment. Steve and Seth maybe had moments where they weren't bickering, but I was pretty sure they had never willingly spent time together by themselves. The idea of the two of them doing anything near each other, let alone actually together, made about as much sense as me quitting my job to go into acting.

Lissa took a wary step toward the kitchen but couldn't seem to get any closer than that. "Is that really what you were doing?" she asked, and her voice was timid and small.

Halfway through tying an apron around his waist, Steve paused and turned his face in her direction. He seemed to know exactly where she was standing, and he looked about ready to fall apart as he realized his own wife was quite possibly thinking the worst. "Have I ever lied to you?" he asked. Lissa shook her head, and though he couldn't see it, Steve smiled. "I'm not about to start now. I was helping Seth, and he was just as frustrated with me as ever. You can ask him about it, but I promise you don't need to. I love you, Lissa. That's not going to change."

She looked about ready to collapse as tears filled her eyes. I had a feeling my friend wouldn't like it, but I hurried over and took her hand anyway, guiding her to the nearest chair. We sat for a moment in silence, watching Steve take stock of everything in the kitchen and make sure his equipment was where it should be so he could work.

"You must think I'm terrible," Lissa whispered after a moment. She was so quiet I could barely hear her.

Lissa? Terrible? *Never.* "Why?"

She sniffed then froze when Steve paused and focused in our direction. She obviously didn't want him to know she was crying, but she couldn't seem to find anything to say to cover it.

I wasn't sure I had any ideas either. *Steve might be getting involved in something dangerous.* That wouldn't help anyone. *You're too paranoid.* Definitely not. I needed to say something that would get the focus off of them.

Just as I was about to open my mouth and say the first thing that came out, Lissa beat me to it: "So are you going to go out with Katie again?"

Yes, that was a safe topic. Somehow. "Tonight, actually."

"She seemed really nice. A lot like you."

She was nice, and she was a lot like me. That should have been perfect, but Steve wasn't wrong when he said our conversation on Friday had been boring at best. Boring, but easy, and right now easy was exactly what I needed.

"She's a very stable option," I said, knowing how dry that sounded.

"How romantic."

I glared at her sarcasm, glad to see her smiling at me. This conversation was exactly what *she* needed, and I was happy to be of use when everything else I had done the last few days had only thrown the world into chaos around me.

"You do remember that our best date was a game of Monopoly, right?" I said.

"And look at how well that turned out for us."

Well this is awkward. We fell into silence, and I couldn't help but wonder what she was thinking about. We'd never really talked about the week that we dated—I'd never really wanted to—but that didn't mean I didn't still occasionally think about the hypothetical what might have been if she hadn't fallen for Steve. Things had been easy with Lissa, and I'd thought that meant we were supposed to be together.

What an idiot. Nothing good had come from something being easy, especially when it came to my relationships.

Eventually, Lissa turned her gaze to Steve in the kitchen, and she frowned. "Do you think he's hiding something from me, Bren?" she asked in a whisper.

Yes. "Steve wouldn't do that," I said. Neither would Adam. Or Seth. Or Matthew. And yet…

Molly had never pursued something she didn't think was real, and I couldn't imagine that part of her changing, not when her whole job as a journalist revolved around gathering the truth. Could she possibly be right?

Lissa took a deep breath and nodded, probably trying to reassure herself. "You're right," she said and got to her feet to go help Steve. "Are you staying for dinner?"

It was strange seeing the restaurant empty like this, but I knew within the hour they'd have each and every table full. "Will you have room for me?" I asked. It was, after all, one of the reasons I'd even come here, but I wasn't sure I wanted to stay now that I was thinking Steve might be in on the scheme with the other Davenport men. I never would have thought Steve would do something shady, but based on how worried Lissa was, I couldn't stop thinking about it now.

My best friend was lying to his wife, and I hated that.

Lissa smiled. "We always have room for you, Brennon."

I believed her, but I couldn't for the life of me figure out why it was true. What had I done to make them want me around as much as they did?

CHAPTER TWELVE

K atie met me outside the fun center that evening and greeted me with a handshake. It was a million times better than a hug, since I really didn't know this woman and physical contact was so not my thing, but now I had Lissa and Steve in my head again. Seriously, who greeted a second—technically third—date with a handshake? Katie did, apparently, but I suspected that was because she was nervous.

Why she would be nervous to go on a date with someone like me, I had no idea. But at least she was getting easier to read, it seemed, so I would be worried less about how she might react to anything that could happen over the next two hours.

"How was your weekend?" I asked her as we got in line to rent our equipment.

She wrapped one hand around the strap of her purse, and her eyes traveled the little putt-putt course instead of looking at me. Normally I hated constant eye contact, and it was one of the reasons it had almost gotten easier to be Steve's friend because he couldn't actually see me most of the time. Similarly, Katie looking elsewhere was nice. It put me at ease and made me feel like I was less under scrutiny.

Clearly she was good for me, and Steve was absolutely wrong.

"Oh, same old," she said and watched a little kid try eight times to get his ball into the hole three inches away. "What about yours?"

My apartment flooded. Molly came back. I made things weird with a sort-of ex-girlfriend. "Nothing exciting," I said. "So, do you enjoy golfing?"

"I'm not sure if this actually counts as golfing, but I do, actually."
She flashed me a simple smile then returned to watching equally unco-
ordinated children and adults attempt to get a hole-in-one. "I go with
my brothers all the time."

Well, I definitely didn't expect that, and I raised an eyebrow. "Really? How long have you been doing that?"

"Since I was a kid. There's a chance I may have won a tournament
or two."

"So you're going to sweep me under the rug tonight, is what you're
telling me."

"Unless you sweep me off my feet first," she replied, her cheeks
turning pink.

My face burned to match, which was ridiculous because I had no
reason to be embarrassed by someone flirting with me. It wasn't like it
never happened. Not that I was vain enough to think women were
often interested in me, but high school had been full of girls hoping I
would ask them to the dance, and Molly had constantly tried to convince me to take one of them.

She had always done that with a sadness in her eyes, and I had always hoped that meant she felt for me what I felt for her.

Boy, had I been wrong.

"I've always enjoyed sweeping," I said, because that was the sort of
thing a guy on a third date should say. "I might be out of practice,
though."

Catching me by surprise, Katie stepped close and slid her arm
through mine. I did my very best not to tense up, which was my usual
reaction to physical affection. "Well," she said, "now's as good a time
as any."

I smiled. "I think you're right."

It was our turn next in line, so I got us a pair of clubs and a couple
of balls—red for me, yellow for Katie—and we headed to the first
hole. We jumped right into playing without continuing our conversation, which was perfectly fine by me because I'd started singing some
Bing Crosby song in my head that my dad used to listen to. Sure, it was
about golf, but that didn't mean I wanted to accidentally sing one of
the few lyrics I actually knew.

The first hole was supposed to be the easiest one, but Katie beat me by seven strokes.

"Maybe you should loosen your grip," she suggested when we got to the next hole. She wrapped her fingers around my wrist just as I was about to putt, and I froze. "Golf is all about the wrist."

She beat me by ten strokes on the second hole.

"So what kind of stock work do you do, Brennon?" Katie asked on the third hole, apparently giving up on improving my technique. Was I that bad of a student?

Her question should have been an easy one to answer, but my mind went blank. Was there a different kind of trading than what I did? "The usual kind," I said then grimaced when Katie tried not to smile. "I mean, I'm a broker for individual clients here in the city." *Keep it together, man.*

"Do you have any investing advice?"

I had plenty, and I practically breathed a sigh of relief because if I was good at anything, it was advising people on the stock market. I could talk about the market all day—and I usually did. So for three holes I told her the same things I told all of my clients, and the evening started to feel a little more normal. I could do this. Maybe I wasn't great at dating, but Katie made it easy, and I almost thought tonight had some potential to lead somewhere if I just kept putting in the effort to keep conversation moving.

If only Molly could see me now.

In an effort to get back a sense of normalcy, I borrowed one of Adam's suits and headed into the office the next morning. The familiarity of the place as I stepped through the lobby doors was so comforting that I had to stop and stand there for a second to take it all in. From the shiny white tiles to the wood-paneled wall behind the front desk to the faint smell of polish and cleaning supplies that always seemed to come from the janitor's closet over by the elevators, this was home.

"Hi, Mr. Ashworth!" said our secretary who had sat at the desk since before I'd started working here. "Where were you yesterday?"

I hadn't realized someone like her would even notice, when she saw so many people walk in and out of the building. Besides, I was often here before her and left long after. I smiled a little, but I had no idea what to tell her. I didn't exactly want the whole building to know my apartment had turned into a flood zone.

"I, uh, I had something come up."

"Well," she said, her wrinkled smile warm and inviting, "we're glad you're back." Her attention turned to a woman who approached her desk, so I figured it was time to move on.

I got into the elevator with several other brokers and one of the marketing guys I didn't know by name but had seen at weekly meetings, and I tried not to panic. I preferred solo elevator trips, and my last ride with Jefferson hadn't exactly gone well. Most of the guys were silent, though, which was nice.

At least, it was nice until someone tapped my shoulder. "Hey, Ashworth, are you sick or something?"

I turned to find another broker, Lance Roberts, standing behind me. "What?" I asked.

"I'm pretty sure I've never seen you not come into the office. What gives?"

Just how many people paid attention to me without me knowing about it? I thought I'd kept my head down. "I had something come up," I said again. My stomach twisted a little as I noticed most of the elevator paying attention to me now. How was it taking so long to get to the seventh floor?

"You're crazy for still working from home," Roberts continued.

"What?"

"I definitely wouldn't be that dedicated."

The elevator finally opened, and I only moved because I was pretty much pushed by the other brokers, and I wandered in the direction of my office trying to figure out what Roberts meant by that. I hadn't even checked my email since Friday night.

"Uh, Jake?" I said as I approached his desk. I was surprised to see him deep in one of my files, as if he expected me not to show up again.

He glanced up. "Hey, boss. Coffee?" He held up a cup and continued reading what was on his screen.

I took the coffee, still absolutely confused.

"You have a couple messages. I'll forward those over to your computer for you."

Was he not as off balance as I was?

Finally he paused, giving me his whole focus and looking at me as if I were covered in mud. "Something wrong, Brennon?" he asked. "Nice suit."

I swallowed. It was probably better to be specific, rather than tell him I had no idea what was going on. "Why does Roberts think I've been working from home?"

Before Jake could answer, the phone on his desk started ringing, and he picked it up and said, "Mr. Ashworth's office. Oh hi, Mr. Donovan. Yeah, he finished that report yesterday, and I was just about to send it to you. Don't even worry, Mr. Donovan. Brennon knows how important this is, so he made it his top priority. Sure thing. Goodbye."

I felt like I'd just entered the Twilight Zone. I knew my assistant was good, but this was bordering on frightening. "What report did Donovan need?" I asked, my voice just a breath of air.

Jake clicked around on his computer and pulled up a document that contained a detailed analysis on a certain company. If I didn't know the company was an unfamiliar one, I would have thought that report was one I'd done myself.

"Uh, Jake? Did you do that?"

For the first time that morning, he seemed a little unsure. "I'm pretty sure I did it right," he said. "I've seen enough of yours that I just followed the same format."

I sank onto the edge of his desk, unable to stand. "Why the heck are you just an assistant?"

He grinned sheepishly. "You've been here so long that you probably don't know how hard it is to get a job like yours. I'm shamelessly using you to give myself a boost in the right direction."

"But why give me all the credit for work you're clearly doing?" I asked.

"If you get promoted," he replied easily, "I get promoted. It's not that complicated. I'm going to have you look over this report quick, though, before I send it over to Donovan's assistant. Just in case." And he gave me a look that was easier to read than I expected.

My own assistant was giving me an order to get to work. And though he may have been right, I stayed where I was and thought back on the last several days. Jake hadn't just stepped up while I was gone. This had started before my apartment collapsed, before Molly had interrupted my schedule, before I started feeling so out of control.

"Why did this start?" I asked. Jake's frown was worrisome, so I clarified: "I'm not complaining, and you are doing a phenomenal job and will absolutely be rewarded for it, but something must have sparked this little change of you pushing me to step up with you."

Leaning back in his chair, Jake looked completely at ease again. "I was talking to someone the other day," he said, "and she had some good thoughts. Brought some things to my attention. It's amazing what you can learn about your life when you get an outside perspective." And then he gave me a grin that made me completely uneasy because I had no idea what it might mean. "You should try it sometime, Brennon."

I left his desk and shut my office door behind me, almost wishing I'd stayed home one more day. Still, I couldn't expect Jake to do *all* my work for me, so I sat at my desk, opened up the file he had just sent me, and within seconds, there was a familiar energy building up inside me.

No matter how bad I was with people, I was good at this.

By the time lunchtime rolled around, I was finally feeling like myself again, and I had almost forgotten about the chaos that was my life until Jake poked his head into the office and said, "You just got a call from the company fixing your condo, and they said it might take more than a couple of weeks."

My blood ran cold, and not just because I was reminded about the fact that I was very much homeless at the moment. There was no way I could trespass on the Munroes' hospitality for that long, no matter what they said. They had been too kind to me already, and whatever was going on with that family was not something I wanted to get in the way of.

There is nothing going on, Brennon.

"Oh," I said.

Jake watched me warily. "I could call them back and tell them that's unacceptable," he offered.

No, they were probably already working as hard as they could, and I counted myself lucky that they were able to fix it at all. I shook my head, but I couldn't seem to find my voice.

"You also got a call from a woman named Molly," he added. "She told me not to bother you but to have you give her a ring when you're done. I'm assuming she meant call her, not...you know..."

I laughed before I could stop myself. "There is no way I would ever give Molly an actual ring," I muttered. I had learned my lesson when it came to her. "Was there anything else?" I asked.

"Nope. You've got a light workload today. Want me to grab you some lunch?" He glanced down at his phone then grinned, clearly distracted by whatever had just popped up. That wasn't like him, since he was always so dedicated to his job, so I had a pretty good guess what his happiness was about.

"Doing something fun today?" I asked.

He broke into an even wider grin. "Got a date," he said.

I matched his smile, and I silently prayed this kid had good things come into his life. He definitely deserved them. "Why don't you take off early today," I told him. "Go have some fun. I'll probably head out soon anyway and check on my condo, so I'll see you tomorrow."

"Sweet! Thanks, boss."

As soon as he was gone, I wandered back into my office and sat down. I could easily have found some more work to do, like I often did when I had nothing better to do, but I didn't want the sweetness of being back to the routine of work to sour because I pushed it a little too hard.

And I was feeling pretty good, so I pulled out my phone and called the number Jake left for Molly. It helped that it was the same number she had given Lanna, since I had been half-afraid everything about her now was fake, even if she'd given me no real reason to think that. No one else suspected her of nefarious motives. Why should I?

She answered after two rings. "Brennon! How's work so far?"

It was such a normal question that it felt strange coming from someone like her. *Normal. Relieving.* "Fine."

"Well you sure sound excited."

Somehow, she managed to put me in a bad mood with that single sentence. "Why did you call, Molly?" Suddenly exhausted, I sank a little deeper in my chair and wished I had just decided to do more work.

She didn't answer for a second, and when she did, I could hear her hesitation. "Okay, don't cut me off until I've finished telling you this."

I really didn't like the sound of that. "Mol."

"I was just over at the Munroes' house."

"Molly, don't even—"

"Promise me you'll just hear me out before you shut me down, okay?"

I sighed, but it wasn't a lot to ask. Though I had a good idea where she was going with this, I figured I could at least listen. "Why were you at the Munroes'?"

"I was taking my photos for the story," she said, definitely brighter now. "And Lanna was an absolute gem."

That was because Lanna was quite possibly the kindest soul on the planet, but I kept my mouth shut.

"But just as I was leaving, I accidentally"—I rolled my eyes as she spoke—"overheard Lanna talking to Adam, and it didn't sound good."

I sat up a little straighter.

"Lanna thinks Adam is hiding something from her, and he was doing everything he could to avoid the subject, and I know they're your friends, Brennon, so I thought you should know in case there's more to this than you think."

Hiding something? That much was true. But I wouldn't have thought it was anything serious. As far as I knew, Lanna and Adam had the most transparent relationship I'd ever seen. Their whole family was like that.

Or, at least, it had been.

"Bren?"

I coughed, trying to gather my thoughts before they split off on multiple conspiracy theories. "What?"

"As I'm sure you know, they're throwing a birthday party for the baby, Harrison, tonight," she said. "I'm not about to invite myself to something like that, but maybe you can find out what's going on tonight."

I shook my head, though it wasn't like she could see that. "Mol, I know it's been a while, but I'm pretty sure you know what I'm like now. If I try asking prying questions like that, I'm either going to stick my foot in my mouth or make things worse. I don't want them to think I'm up to something, and they'll do that the minute I start talking." And only after I said it did I realize I probably should have denied there was anything going on at all.

"You're talking just fine right now," she said, and I could pretty much hear her frown.

I sighed. "This is different. You're you."

"And you're still you, Bean. You can talk your way out of anything."

Well that was just ridiculous. That was her talent, not mine. "Molly."

"I'm serious! Do you remember that time in middle school when I broke my finger punching Hank Dory in the face, and you convinced the principal that I tripped into him? You even got my dad to believe you."

She had already gotten in trouble for sneaking around the teacher's lounge when she thought some kids were stealing test answers, and another infraction that week would have gotten her suspended. And since she had punched Hank because he pushed me into the lockers, I couldn't just let her take the punishment. "Mol, this is different," I said. "I can't pretend to—"

"Bren, I only told you about this because I'm worried about you. If you think nothing's going on, then nothing's going on."

It was hard to tell on the phone, but it almost sounded like she meant that. So why would she have pursued the idea in the first place?

She was not the type of person to just change her mind about something. Unless I was wrong, and I didn't think I was, she wanted a confirmation just as little as I did.

"You mean too much to me to get caught up in something dangerous," she said. "Just think about it, okay?" And then she hung up.

But before I *could* think about it, my phone started to ring, and I stared at Katie's name for a second, almost too caught up in my thoughts to remember who she was until I was already answering the phone. "Katie."

"Hey Brennon, how's your day been?" She sounded so formal, but it wasn't like she was talking any differently. She sounded like... Well, she sounded like me.

You can talk your way out of anything.

I swallowed. "F-fine," I said, and shook my head to clear it of thoughts I didn't want to think. "Yours?"

"Fine. I know it's last-minute, but are you free for lunch?"

I said yes before I even realized what she'd asked, which must have meant that I really did want to go to lunch with her, even if I didn't immediately think so. I was just tired still from the weekend, probably, and Molly had gotten my mind working too hard.

The Davenports weren't doing anything suspicious. They wouldn't. It was all just a misunderstanding.

"Great," Katie said. "Meet me there?" She told me the name of the restaurant, and I must have agreed because she ended the phone call with a "See you soon!" and hung up.

If Lanna thought Adam was keeping something from her...

Grabbing my keys, I slowly made my way to the elevator and down to the parking garage, hardly aware of where I was going. I knew I had to smother the suspicions that were quickly building up inside me, but I didn't know how. The worry in Molly's voice hadn't helped anything, but Katie deserved more than only a portion of my attention.

Besides, things were easy with Katie, and I hoped she could distract me well enough that I could forget about all of this nonsense, at least for today.

I played my music loud enough on the drive over that I had an Ed Sheeran song stuck in my head—poor choice of artist for the situation, maybe, but it was a catchy song—and I managed a passable smile when I approached Katie, who sat at one of the outdoor tables and waved when she saw me.

"This place looks fun," I said as I joined her. "I love sitting outside."

"Me too," she replied. "I spend so much time in the office that it's nice to get fresh air whenever I can."

Something about that struck me as familiar, and I fought against a frown as I tried to remember where I'd heard a comment like that before. It wouldn't have been Steve, or Lissa, or any of the Davenports for that matter, and I basically didn't talk to anyone else.

What a sad, lonely life. It wasn't all that bad, but it was no wonder it felt strange to interact with someone other than my usual suspects.

Don't call them suspects.

"Do you have any recommendations on what to order?" I asked. "I'm hoping you personally know the chef and can give me the inside scoop."

"I can't claim a connection like that," she replied, "but the Kung Pao Chicken is pretty good."

Another wave of weirdness. It was almost like Katie was reminding me of someone, though I couldn't figure out who. I hoped she was right about the chicken, though, because that sounded delicious. Jake got me Kung Pao at least once a week, maybe more.

"Or the burger," she added, "though it's not nearly as good as the Maverick across town. You haven't had a burger until you've had the Maverick."

Oh crap, she's me.

I had said pretty much the exact same thing to Lissa once upon a time. Same with getting outside because I spent so much time at work. I must have missed it before, but now that I was looking for it, I could see her watching me just like I watched her, as if she was analyzing the right thing to say for the situation. There wasn't a lot of emotion in her face, and she was always so pleasant. Almost painfully so. She was a duplicate of me in so many ways.

And I knew exactly how boring of a person I was, which was great for some people, but...

It's great for you, Brennon. Katie was exactly the person who could keep me on track to being steady and stable and the guy who didn't get his heart broken by a wild card who couldn't be contained.

"I love the Maverick," I said.

She might have replied, but I was a little too busy staring at her and trying to understand how I could have managed to find the one person in the world who was exactly like me. What were the odds that I would end up meeting someone completely perfect for me thanks to a guy like Steve Evans, who was basically my opposite? I was pretty sure they were low. Very low. Like I'd won the lottery.

No one could have predicted this.

"Brennon, are you okay?"

I blinked, focusing on her again. "What?"

Her frown was only half a frown, like she was more confused than worried. "You're not really yourself today."

How would you know who I am? "I'm fine."

"You said that already."

"Technically I said my day was fine." I winced, clenching my jaw as she tensed up a little at my sharp comment. I shouldn't have grumbled like that. "I'm sorry. It's been a long week."

She narrowed her eyes. It wasn't suspicion, just scrutiny, but I didn't like it. Did people feel like that when I did the same thing? I felt like my every little move and expression was being judged, and I felt so exposed. "You've said that already too," she said. "Do you want to talk about it?"

Absolutely not. "Talk about what?"

"Whatever's bothering you. You don't have to, but I just thought maybe—"

"I really am fine. My condo flooded the other day, so—"

"Wait, what?" Katie put her hand on my arm across the table, and when I flinched, she frowned and slowly moved her hand. "That's kind of a big deal, Brennon. I'm not going to pretend I know what's best for you, but maybe I could—"

"I really don't want to talk, Katie."

But that was a lie. I *needed* to talk.

And before I could stop myself, all of the words spilled out: "I just don't understand why people can't be predictable sometimes," I said. "Why do they have to be one thing for so long and then turn around and be something else without warning? Like, if you're going to spend your entire marriage being the perfect husband, don't start lying to your wife and doing things behind her back when you *know* she's had her life controlled for her for most of it and needs you to be perfectly honest with her. Don't walk into my office one day and ask me why I haven't gotten the promotion I've wanted for years because you're the one who should have given me that promotion instead of pretending like I'm not valuable to the company. Why *wouldn't* I want to be promoted? That's the whole point of staying in a job for more than a couple of years, isn't it? To get promoted and climb that ladder people are always talking about? And don't act like secrets are commonplace when you can absolutely tell they're hurting one of the best women I know because it's making the people around you doubt everything they know about you."

I stuffed my hands into my hair, fully aware that Katie was staring at me but not even caring because all of this was way too much for me to deal with inside of me anymore. It had to come out. "Don't make me think you're in love with me when you know you're going to disappear," I whispered. "And don't come back after fifteen years pretending nothing changed. Don't pretend *I* haven't changed. *Stop making me live again.*"

Oh boy.

That was not the kind of thing a guy wanted to admit to himself or anyone else.

Grimacing, I met Katie's gaze. She was looking at me like I might explode, and I didn't blame her even a little bit. I knew it wouldn't help much, but I quickly straightened my tie and attempted to fix my messed-up hair before she realized just how much I had totally lost it.

"I don't mean you," I muttered, knowing that didn't make things any better.

To my absolute bewilderment, she smiled. "I figured that part out on my own. So, I'm not going to pretend I have any experience in something like this," she said gently, as if afraid I might jump right back into my little rant if she spoke too loudly. "I've pretty much been the same my entire life, and I like that about myself. But something tells me the guy I met while speed dating, as great as he is, is not the guy you need to be." She rose to her feet, her fingers wrapped around the straps of her purse as always, and bowed her head a little as she watched me sit there in a complete mess. "And I'm pretty sure I'm not the person you need right now. I don't think this is something I can help you with, so you really shouldn't be with me. You should be with Molly."

I nearly collapsed into a pile beneath my chair, my heart pounding in my chest. "What? How did you…" I had only said her name once. Days ago.

"I'm an accountant, Brennon," she replied, and she was warmer than I'd ever known her. "I'm good at adding up the little details. And I know we don't really know each other—or maybe we really do—but can I give you a little advice?"

I nodded. Barely. Trying to make sense of what had just happened. It wasn't like I hadn't been thinking all of those things for the last few days, but something about saying them out loud—saying anything out loud—made it more real.

Smiling a little, Katie spoke quietly: "I have no idea who Molly is, but if you find someone who makes you feel as strongly as she is making you feel, don't let her go. There's a benefit to letting someone push you to be better. To be you. To be real."

I watched her climb into her car and drive off, feeling like I would never be able to breathe again as the last fifteen years of my life played out in front of me, backed by a terrible '80s love ballad saxophone. What had I been doing with my life?

Absolutely nothing.

Suddenly I understood what Steve was talking about on Sunday when he brought up our conversation in the hospital a year and a half ago.

"You've gotta see what's right in front of you," he'd said. "I was always focused on the next big thing, the next adventure, the next trip, and this week I've realized how dangerous that is. How much I could lose by not opening my eyes once in a while." He'd been talking about Lissa and how he had been ignoring so many signs that were pointing to exactly what he needed. He hadn't admitted it then—both of us had lied about our feelings for Lissa—but he'd been absolutely head over heels by then.

I'd still been thinking about Molly and the way she used to make me look at the world.

My phone was in my hand before I had even taken a moment to think about what I was doing, and for the first time in a long time, I didn't care. "Molly," I said when she answered. "I'll do it."

"You'll do what?"

"I'll get down to the bottom of what's happening with the Davenports. I need to know the truth."

"That's great, Brennon." I wasn't sure she really thought so, with how long it took her to answer, but her hesitation only made me want to get to the truth of things even more. If there wasn't something happening, Molly wouldn't be worried by it.

I took a deep breath then sat up straight. I had no idea if Katie was right—in fact, I seriously doubted it—but I decided to take her advice. This wasn't something I could do by myself.

"I need you to come with me, Molly," I said.

Whether or not she was good for me, I knew I would never be able to find peace without her by my side, pushing me to do more.

She was silent for a long time, but I knew she was still there. I didn't know how I knew, but I did, and I knew what her answer would be before she even spoke: "Okay."

CHAPTER THIRTEEN

I'd never been to a birthday party for a one-year-old, but I had seen enough unsolicited pictures from coworkers to have an idea of what to expect. They were intimate affairs, involving mainly family, since the kid wouldn't be aware of the day's significance, so it was mostly a way for the adults to get together and catch up while eating basic finger foods. There would be a simple little cake for the kid to make a mess of, and for the most part there wouldn't be much to it. Especially because Lanna and Adam weren't big socialites, I figured the party wouldn't be all that long or extravagant.

I was wrong.

That was probably because Lanna's mother planned the event, though. Lyra Davenport, in the few times I'd encountered her, was by far the most constant person I had ever met. When I imagined a millionaire growing up in Beverly Hills before marrying into another wealthy family, I pictured her. Gorgeous blonde hair, manicured nails, a stunning figure, and the best of the best wardrobe were her staples. She was perfect, in every sense of the word according to media standards, and therefore anything she planned had to be perfect as well.

When I stepped out of the guest room (after a few hours in my car with blaring music to calm me down enough to function again) with the intent of seeing if I could help with any of the party preparation, I found the entire house steeped in chaos, Lyra at the center of it in the front room.

"Those flowers are much too wilted," she was saying to a florist who looked on the verge of tears. "I did not pay for limp dahlias. Excuse me!" She snapped her fingers at a man carrying a bundle of lights. "I told you to go through the garage. Does this look like the garage? Where the heavens is that caterer? If she's not here in the next ten minutes…"

"Mom," said Lanna forcefully, appearing from the direction of the kitchen. "Diana got here twenty minutes ago. Relax. Those are beautiful," she added to the flustered florist. "Go ahead and set them up on the patio." Lyra opened her mouth to argue, but Lanna cut her off. "Please don't do what you did for Benny's first birthday and scare off all my vendors. It doesn't have to be perfect."

"But—"

"I'm going to oversee the last of the decorating," said Lanna and literally pushed her mother down onto the couch. "Take a breath, okay?" She gave me a quick smile as she passed, but she moved too quickly for me to ask how I could help.

I figured if I followed her out to the patio, I might stumble across something to keep me occupied until Molly arrived, but Lyra spoke before I took a step.

"You're that Ashworth fellow who dated Lissa, aren't you?"

I honestly couldn't tell if she considered Lissa beneath her or if she was disappointed I hadn't kept dating her. But what could I say to a question like that? I was far too busy dealing with some other issues, but I sorted through my options: *We didn't date. Yes, unfortunately. I'm just Catherine's neighbor.* "I'm Steve's best friend," I settled on, and then I thought about how little time I had really spent with my best friend over the last year. I was a *terrible* friend, and I honestly had no idea why Steve had kept me around.

"You work in stocks, don't you?"

How did she know that? I felt awkward standing in the hallway, so I stepped into the front room and sat in the chair opposite the couch where she watched me. "I do."

Her face seemed to be in a permanent scowl. If she ever smiled, she would have looked a lot like her daughter, though their personalities were pretty much opposites. "My children seem to like you," she said and crossed her ankles in the most proper manner imaginable.

Self-conscious, I sat up a little straighter. "I like them too." *That sounded ridiculous.* "They're great people, and I owe them a lot."

Her expression didn't change as she shifted the topic. "Matthew says you have some impressive clients. Anyone I might know?"

Lyra Davenport knew no one but the elite, of which there were many in the Bay Area, and though I didn't approve of her prejudice against anyone who wasn't a millionaire, at least I could honestly name a few she would undoubtedly know. I wasn't sought after as a broker because I made people poor. *Geez, Brennon, when did you get such an ego?* "I work with Chandler Wixcomb," I said. "John Foster. Colin Donovan."

"Donovan?" Lyra leaned forward with interest. "That's a new name, but a name I know well."

"He's a good friend," I said. *Why did I say that?* I didn't care what she thought about my friends. Honestly, I wasn't sure I could even call him a friend now that I was rethinking my entire adult life.

"He has a promising future," she replied. "And he's really making a name for himself with his charity work."

That was true, though the report Jake had done involved putting a decent chunk of money into a failing summer camp, which wasn't the smartest decision. But, as I'd learned while talking to Donovan this morning on the phone, it was a non-negotiable donation despite the little chance of any return. At least the guy could afford it. I was well enough off, but people like Lyra Davenport and Colin Donovan put my cushy life to shame.

"He certainly doesn't have much to worry about," I said. *At least in terms of money.* The guy had plenty going on in his work and home life to still be stressed out, which was half the reason I tried so hard to make sure he didn't have to worry about his money too. "I should go see if Lanna needs help with anything," I muttered and got to my feet.

"She works too hard," Lyra replied, and I paused. She suddenly looked weary as she sat there, not nearly as glamorously flawless as she rubbed her temples and sank into a slouch. I didn't like it. Lyra Davenport was one of the few people I could truly count on to be exactly what I expected her to be. "I think she gets that from me."

Was it too rude to just walk away and pretend I hadn't heard her? Did I even care about being rude?

Giving me a tired smile—*that's terrifying*—she sighed. "Matthew is like that too, but Indiana has been good for him. Slows him down so he doesn't work himself to the bone like he used to. But Lanna tries so hard to be everything the world expects her to be, and it wears her down."

"At least she's got Adam," I said, since I really didn't know what to say about Lanna that wouldn't sound like I was arguing against the woman who raised her.

Lyra's smile grew warmer. "I've always liked Adam Munroe," she said. "I knew from the beginning he and my princess were meant for each other. He gives her courage and stability, things I can't give her myself."

Well, he used to.

I glanced down the hall, still standing just in front of my seat because I neither knew what to say nor had a good way to make my exit.

"You know," said Lyra, "you remind me a lot of my eldest."

I blinked, heat blossoming in my face. I knew very little about Lanna's oldest brother aside from the fact that he died young and Benny was named after him. But the way Lyra was looking at me, I sincerely hoped she meant that as a compliment. "Oh?"

Nodding, she rose onto her stilettoed feet and slid her arm through mine, which I figured was a signal to lead her to the patio now that she'd taken a few minutes to relax. "He was always a quiet boy," she said softly, "but he was smart. And kind. He cared more about the people around him than he did about himself."

There was something in her tone of voice that made me pause just in front of the back door. "Isn't that a good thing?" I asked.

She smiled and patted my arm. "Sometimes. I think he often forgot about himself, and no one can live properly when they're only living for others. Oh, heavens no, you are not putting that cheese platter out

looking like that!" And just like that she was off, chasing down a terrified waiter as he headed to the food table outside.

Twice in one day a practical stranger had me questioning the way I
lived. Or didn't live. And I couldn't decide if that was a good thing or
a bad thing.

Molly arrived just as the party, which involved a couple hundred guests
and an entire string octet, was beginning. She found me standing awk-
wardly in a corner of the lawn trying to avoid making eye contact with
anyone, especially Lanna's mom, who seemed to have taken an interest
in me. And while I was about to tell her how I wasn't sure I had the
energy to do any real digging tonight, my words stuck in my throat
when I saw her.

Molly's general attire as an adult was much like it had been in high
school: jeans, t-shirt, the same ratty canvas shoes that would never be
their original color again because they'd gotten too dirty. She usually
kept her curly hair in a ponytail because, as she put it, it wouldn't do
what she told it to even if she tried. But in the last fifteen years, she
had learned to dress up when she needed to, and I was suddenly reminded, almost painfully, of our senior prom and the picture that had
sat on my nightstand but was now tucked underneath my pillow for
safe keeping.

She was beautiful. Her flowery white dress was as classy as Catherine's (which was saying something), and her hair, shorter than it was in
high school, hung loose and framed her face. And her face... I wasn't
sure if I hadn't noticed it before or if I hadn't cared, but she was radiant
in a way a teenager never could be, and her brilliant smile was enough
to make the world spin. Was it really possible she could have gotten
more beautiful over the years?

Of course it was. This was Molly Piper.

She slipped her hand into mine, which felt like the most natural
thing in the world tonight. "Is this normally how millionaires celebrate
first birthday parties?" she asked as she took in the ridiculously fancy
gathering with wide eyes and pink cheeks.

I shrugged because I didn't know. Plus, I'd been singing the same happy birthday song in my head for the last twenty minutes, and it was really starting to get on my nerves. "Welcome to the world of the Davenports," I said.

"Rich people are so weird."

"Not all of them. Some of us are pretty normal."

"Are you telling me you're rich, Brennon Ashworth?" Anyone else would have asked that question with interest, but Molly said it as if she'd never heard anything funnier. "You used to hate rich people."

There were a few too many of those "rich people" surrounding us at the moment, and I could feel their attention shifting our direction, as if they knew we weren't part of their exclusive little social club. I had spent plenty of time in this elite world to know how to be one of them if I needed to—the wealthy liked to invite everyone to their parties, including stock brokers and plastic surgeons—but I had never considered myself one of them. Money wasn't everything.

I smiled and pulled her closer as we made our way through the milling crowd. "That was before I realized how nice it was to have money," I said with a wink. "The things you can do…"

"You can do a lot without it," she countered playfully. "I have exactly no money, and I'm just fine." As her fingers wrapped a little tighter around mine, it felt like she was telling me something with her hold. Some secret she wanted me to know as she paused near the unlit fire pit on the patio and met my gaze.

What was she trying to tell me? I had a feeling it was important, and I just wanted her to come right out and say it. She'd never held back before.

"Molly?" I said and leaned closer.

"Have you heard anything new in the, uh, secrets department?" she replied, and her carefully placed mask slipped, revealing a nervousness she could no longer hide. There was something more going on.

For as long as I had known her, Molly had always been fearless and laughed in the face of danger. But when she got into trouble she couldn't get out of again, I had been the one to step in and help. A week ago, I would have left her to her own problems, but my whole body seemed to be pushing me to step in and protect this girl as my heart pounded faster.

"Molly, what's going on?"

She shook her head and tried to smirk. "That's what we're here to find out."

"No, what's going on with *you*?"

"This is about the Davenports, Brennon."

The Davenports were fine. Adam was at Lanna's side, where he should be, his baby in his arms and a smile on his face. Seth was chatting with Lanna's father over by the champagne tower, probably revisiting their recent encounter with the black sheep of the family, Milton. Matthew was...where was Matthew?

It wasn't like I couldn't easily lose him in a crowd this big, but I had seen him over by the food table only moments before Molly arrived, where he happily told me I "wasn't looking sharp" because I'd put on a t-shirt instead of a button-up. He'd been helping Benny load up his plate, but now the kid was sitting at a table next to Indie, and Matthew was nowhere in sight.

Steve was missing too, and Lissa didn't look happy about it, her eyes roaming the crowd with suspicion as she sat on Indie's other side.

I didn't like it.

"Well that's a look," said Molly, pulling my attention back to her.

She seemed more than willing to change the subject, and I wasn't complaining. Not when this involved my friend.

"I can't find Steve," I replied.

She laughed a little, clearly not understanding why that would be an issue. "I'm sure he's fine," she said.

"He's blind, Mol."

"And he's surrounded by friends and family."

That wasn't as reassuring as she probably meant it, and I kept scanning the crowd, desperately hoping he was with Matthew and not wandering around on his own. It wasn't all that dark outside yet, but dusk was quickly approaching, which meant his sight would get steadily worse as the night went on.

"There he is," Molly said, pointing, and I relaxed.

But only for a second. He and Matthew were deep in conversation as they approached the table where their wives sat, and the moment they got close enough to potentially be overheard, Matthew gave Steve a nudge to the ribs and they both shut their mouths.

A quick glance at Adam told me he had noticed the pair of them as well and was already handing his son over to Lanna so he could head their way.

"Let's get closer," Molly said and took my hand again.

I didn't resist.

"Adam!" Matthew greeted the moment he saw his brother-in-law, and Molly and I took seats at the next table over, trying not to be noticed. "I was just about to look for you. I've got a question about your, uh, car."

Indie gave him a confused look. "Since when do you care about cars?" she asked. "You avoid Adam's garage like the plague."

As he seemed to turn a little pale in the dusk light, Matthew waved her question away and put his hand on Adam's shoulder to steer him away to a far enough distance to not be overheard.

"What were you guys talking about?" Lissa asked Steve as he sat next to her.

He kissed her cheek then stole a shrimp off her plate. "Nothing important. Lyra really outdid herself with this party, didn't she?"

Lissa frowned, her expression tying a knot in my gut. "Steve," she said, quieter this time, "what's going on? You've been acting weird for days. Indie and I were—"

"What kind of party do you want for your birthday next month, Benny?" Steve asked across the table. "A big party like this?"

Benny shook his head as he picked at a piece of cake. "I wanna go to the zoo," he said.

"That's a fantastic idea. What's your favorite animal?"

I kept my eyes on Lissa, who looked either on the verge of tears or anger, I couldn't tell which. Indie had taken her hand, but the pair of them hardly looked equipped to comfort each other when they were clearly experiencing the same thing. At least Indie was leaning more toward the irritated side of things, as far as I could figure, and even if she was many months pregnant, she had enough fight in her to go up against her husband.

I wished there was something I could do for them, some clarity to offer, but I still had no idea what was going on. The one thing I did know was I wasn't sure how much longer I could witness Lissa's misery and discomfort before I punched Steve in the face. She deserved to smile and be unencumbered with unnecessary worry. They all did.

"Oh my gosh," Molly whispered beside me. "You're in love with Lissa Evans."

"No," I said without looking away from Lissa's pained face. "I'm really not."

"You absolutely are. I can see it on your face."

This wasn't exactly a conversation I wanted to have when we were sitting a table away from the woman in question. Keeping a firm hold on Molly's hand, I pulled her away from the tables and closer to the musicians so they could help cover up our words before someone heard something they shouldn't.

"I don't believe in love," I told her. The words tasted sour.

Molly rolled her eyes. "Brennon, I've known you basically my whole life. I think I can recognize when you're in lo—"

"Are you sure you want to finish that sentence?" I asked, folding my arms.

She immediately shut her mouth.

"That's what I thought."

My eyes involuntarily returned to Lissa's table, but Steve was rising, his phone to his ear and a nervous expression on his face. "Come on," I said and pulled Molly with me again, following Steve as he carefully made his way to a secluded corner of the garden. Thanks to his blindness, he had no idea we were there as we crept along the rose bushes until we were close enough to hear what he was saying.

The problem was he was saying it in French.

"Do you speak French?" I whispered.

Molly shook her head. "I barely passed high school Spanish. You know that."

Whatever Steve was saying, he wasn't all that thrilled to be saying it, and the longer his conversation went, the more frustrated he became. He started to pace, one hand in his pocket while he spoke so fluently that I had to wonder why I'd never heard him speak French before now. And then, just as I was about to pull out my phone and see if I could get it to translate for me, Steve switched to English.

"And if my wife finds out about this," he practically snarled, "you know what happens when Seth Hastings gets angry." He listened for a second. "No, Jean-Marc, you'll only wish you were dead. Get it done."

He hung up, let out a frustrated sigh, and then he put on a smile and headed back to the tables.

I was pretty sure I was about to pass out.

Molly must have noticed me swaying on the spot, because she grabbed hold of my arm and said, "Are you okay, Bren?" Her voice echoed in my ears.

"My best friend is doing something illegal," I whispered. Saying it out loud didn't make me feel any better. I should have known that would only make things worse after what happened at lunch today. Saying things out loud made them real.

Stroking my arm, she guided me to a chair that seemed to come out of nowhere. "We don't know that," she said.

"Did that sound legal to you?"

"Shh." Her soft hands brushed through my hair. "Bren, you need to get the whole story before you start jumping to conclusions."

"How?" I moaned and dropped my face into my hands. "They're all part of this, and I highly doubt they'll just let me in on the secret." What if it was something dangerous? Seth could do a lot of things, but he couldn't be in three places at once to protect all of them. "Why did they have to drag Steve into this?"

Molly took hold of my hands and pulled them away, and she was only a couple of inches from me as she gave me a sympathetic smile. "We still don't know what's going on," she said, and her voice was oddly soothing considering she looked more nervous than I felt. "Think for a second, Bean. Where can we find more information? Maybe Adam has something on his computer?"

I stared at her, and I couldn't help but think how dissonant the gentle string music was against the pounding of my heart. This was a tragedy, not a celebration. "Are you suggesting I break into Adam's computer?"

Shrugging, Molly glanced over the party. "Maybe you can find a way to get Steve out of it, at least. Unless you want to just let him ruin his life. And Lissa's."

I looked at Lissa. She seemed a little happier now that Steve was back at her side, but it didn't hide her underlying anger and hurt. Indie looked pretty much livid now, and if Lanna wasn't putting on a smile for the people who had come to celebrate her child, I had a feeling she would be right there with them. Even Catherine, who was pretty infallible, watched Seth join in with Adam and Matthew, her eyes slightly narrowed as if she was starting to figure out something was definitely up.

This needed to stop. Whatever it was.

Groaning a little, I took Molly's hand again and pulled her toward the house, dodging elites who gave us looks of disdain as we hurried through the party, like our presence alone was enough to ruin their night.

The house itself seemed dark and empty, which was eerie for the Munroe house. The silence was almost suffocating as we tiptoed to Adam's office, and a sudden sense of foreboding hit me. I stopped Molly before she could open the office door, and I took a moment to consider what I was about to do.

"Maybe we shouldn't," I said, though I knew Molly would argue.

"You said it yourself," she said. "Something is going on."

"But snooping around on someone's personal computer? Mol, that's just…"

She let out a sigh that was more of a huff of frustration. "Do you want to help Steve and Lissa or not? And what about Catherine, who has been through enough in her life? Or Indie, who is clearly being lied to? Or Lanna, who—"

"Fine," I growled and pushed the door open, dragging Molly in with me.

Adam's computer was still on and, to both my relief and annoyance, unlocked. Though Molly seemed excited, she let me take the helm, for which I was grateful. We only needed to find some proof of money being where it shouldn't, and I could imagine many things on this computer that Molly—and I—didn't need to see.

"There," Molly said and pointed to a folder on the desktop labeled 'Finances.'

I liked the guy, but sometimes Adam was a little too trusting. Opening the folder, I glanced through the first spreadsheet quickly. All of it was art dealing and likely prepared for him by his accountant. Nothing sketchy there. The next file contained Adam's will; I clicked out of that one quickly before either of us could read something that was absolutely personal. Below that I found a spreadsheet labeled 'France' and felt my heartbeat kick up a notch.

"That has to be it," Molly whispered.

I took a moment to read through some massively large payments going both in and out of an account that was with a bank separate from the one I knew Adam and Lanna used, and I quickly realized this was exactly what I was looking for. The money had been moved pretty regularly, all within the last couple of weeks, and though I would have to look into it at work the next day to be sure, I was almost convinced the transactions involved a shell company.

"Adam, what have you gotten yourself into?" I whispered.

"What is it?" Molly asked.

But a muffled voice outside the room made me jump, and I looked around quickly, searching for a place to hide.

Molly pulled me to the sliding door and shoved it open, pushing me out onto the tiny balcony then slipping out after me. She closed the door not a second too soon, and we stood motionless as the office door opened and bathed the room in light from the hallway.

I desperately prayed the thin curtains hid us from view, particularly because it wasn't Adam who came into the room. It was Seth.

Giant and menacing, he rummaged through the desk drawers until he found whatever it was he was looking for. He was halfway back to the hallway when he paused and turned his head, his face silhouetted in the darkness, so I had no idea where he was looking. Had he seen us? My heart felt like it was pounding so fast it would burst out of my chest, but at least I could say that if Seth was going to kill me, he would do it quickly. Small comfort, but a comfort nonetheless.

After a moment, during which I thought I might faint because I was holding my breath so tight, he continued on and shut the door behind him.

Molly immediately let out a laugh of relief, wrapping her arms around me and dropping her head against my chest. "That was terrifying," she breathed. As if I didn't already know. "Does he realize how intimidating he is?"

"Yes, he does." I looked away from the room and down at Molly, suddenly startled by how close she was. And how much I didn't mind. And while I knew the best thing for us to do was get out of there and back to the party, I remained motionless and said something that seemed to come out of nowhere: "Do you remember that final football game our senior year?"

As she lifted her head to match my gaze, Molly's eyes seemed to sparkle in the lights of the party below. "You mean the away game when you snuck into my room at the hotel?"

I grinned at the memory. "Only I timed it wrong, so Mrs. Angerbauer hadn't come to check your room yet."

Molly looked enchanting in the glow of the party lights. "You climbed up onto the balcony and got stuck out there because stupid Suzy Lancer would have told on you if you came into the room," she said. "And you figured you would just wait until she fell asleep."

"Only, Suzy Lancer is an insomniac," I said and pulled her just a bit closer, since the balcony where we stood was rather small. I didn't want her to be at risk of falling. Not that we were all that high, but still.

"So I came out onto the balcony with you," Molly said, barely above a whisper. "And we stayed up and watched the sunrise."

"You fell asleep in my lap," I reminded her. My voice got stuck in my throat, and I tried to swallow the thickness away. It didn't work.

"But you woke me up for the sunrise."

"You knew I would."

Molly was so close now that I could almost taste her. We had never been this close before. Not like this. "That was the best sunrise of my life," she whispered and touched her hand to my cheek.

I had spent the last fifteen years of my life making choices based on how they would affect other people. I had always considered myself selfless, told myself that I changed my responses because I wanted the people around me to be happy and comfortable. I had always known that was a lie, but I had never felt the burden of my life quite as acutely as I did at this moment. A week ago, I probably would have frozen in this moment, looking down at Molly and trying to figure out what she wanted from me.

For the first time in fifteen years, maybe even my whole life, I didn't care what Molly wanted. I cared about what *I* wanted. I needed to start *living* again before I forgot how. "Let's go for a walk," I said.

It was time to have a talk. A real talk, one that I'd been having in my head for the last fifteen years. If Molly was disappointed, she didn't show it, and she simply took my hand and brought me back through the house and out the front door.

CHAPTER FOURTEEN

W e walked until we found the coast. I had no idea what time it was, just that it was dark. We both seemed drawn in the same direction, following the crispness of the ocean air and the sound of the surf hitting the rocks. Though we didn't say anything for at least two hours while we walked, that was nothing new. Sometimes our walks would last all night without a single word passing between us because some problems couldn't be solved with words. Some things simply needed another person to share in the silence as they worked themselves out. For now, this was one of those, and I was perfectly okay with that.

It gave me time to think. Time to make myself strong.

By the time we hit the ocean, the moon was bright above us. It gilded the water with silver and gave the night a sense of possibility that I hadn't felt in years. Walking onto the tiny, familiar beach we'd found, my hand tight around Molly's, I felt like myself for the first time in a decade and a half. I was desperate to hold onto that feeling.

Something about reminiscing on that balcony had pulled me fully back into the past, into the person I had been before I left it all behind. No, not something. Molly had brought out the old Brennon, and I knew I had to keep him around, at least for tonight. It was important, and I would never be able to get on with my life without him. I had spent so much of my life being whatever the people around me needed to be, and I had forgotten how it felt to exist solely as me.

Suddenly I could breathe again.

"This is beautiful," Molly said when we reached the end of the beach. She sat in the sand and looked out over the dark water.

I sat beside her, my eyes fixed on her. "Yeah," I said.

She was absolutely perfect as she buried her toes in the sand, and more beautiful than she'd ever been. More than the curve of her cheek and the curls of her hair, her beauty radiated from inside. She was pushy, and forward, and way too curiously determined, but she was perfect. Always had been. She pushed me to be better. She wasn't afraid to make a move and take a stand. And she knew nothing was more important than the truth.

"Do you remember that walk we took when it rained?" she whispered.

We had taken so many walks that there were several times it had rained on us. But the way she said it told me everything I needed to know exactly which day she meant. I had missed being able to read her like this, in a way I'd never been able to do with anyone else. Maybe Molly was unpredictable, but she was never that way when it mattered.

"That was the day your mom died," I said.

She dropped her head onto my shoulder and sighed. She had really never known her mother, since Molly had been too young when she left, but the news had still hit her hard when her dad told her. "Do you remember what you said to me?"

Honestly, I had no idea. There were so many conversations, so many words shared between us. And I had spent enough of my life trying to forget all of them that I had succeeded.

"You said she would have loved me if she had been brave enough to know me," Molly said. "You said some people just aren't strong enough to share themselves with other people because they're too scared of losing who they are if they give up even a part of themselves." When she turned to face me, her eyes shone with tears, but I knew she wasn't crying. Not yet. "I've missed you, Bren," she whispered. "You always made life so much easier to bear."

It would be easy to go back to the guy I had been for the last fifteen years. The guy who worried that everything he said would come out wrong, that someone would take offense or see right through it or think there was something wrong with him. It would be easy to lie and tell her that I didn't miss her because if I missed her, it meant I still cared for her. And that required me to feel something, to feel pain and joy and everything in between. To risk losing a part of myself to her. It would be easy to keep myself hidden from the world and pretend I didn't ache to be a part of it again.

But sitting here with Molly, I didn't want to be that guy. I wanted to be me. Honestly, unapologetically me. "

Mol," I said, and I sounded stronger than I felt. I could ruin everything. "I've never stopped loving you."

She touched her fingers to my cheek. "I know."

"Why did you leave?" Once out in the air, the question seemed to have brought out of me a weight I hadn't known I carried until just now. But until I got an honest answer, it would always be right there in front of me, never completely gone. "Molly, why did you leave?"

She pulled her knees up to her chest and hugged them, once again focused on the ocean in front of us. "I was scared," she said after a long moment.

"Of me?"

"Of course not, Brennon."

"Then what?"

She didn't answer, and a wave of frustration shot through me. Didn't I deserve at least a response, however small, after everything I had gone through with this girl? If I could risk losing myself in her, she could do the same.

"Molly, please," I said and took hold of her hand, desperate to get her to look at me again. "It's been fifteen years. I'm sure whatever it was is gone now."

"I was scared of not being with you."

I fell motionless as she bit her lip, trying to understand what her expression meant. She looked frightened and sad and hopeful all at once.

"What?"

"I knew I couldn't follow you to greatness, and that terrified me." She sounded small, like everything that she was had suddenly disappeared with the last wave.

"I don't understand," I said, and it felt like that night, the last night I had seen her, was replaying right in front of me. It was right after our graduation, and we'd come to this beach. We had gone up to the lighthouse to celebrate. And I hadn't been able to hold it in anymore. "I told you I was in love with you," I said. "That I had been in love with you for years. And you said…"

"I said there was no future for us," she finished for me. "I told you I didn't love you and never would." She turned tearful eyes to me and took my hand. "I lied, Brennon."

My whole chest seemed to turn to a solid lump inside me, so heavy that I wanted to scream. Molly never lied. "Why?"

Molly took a shaky breath. "Because there was no future, just like I said. I couldn't afford Stanford."

"You said you got a scholarship," I argued. "Like I did."

Shaking her head, she returned her attention to the waves. "I lied. I didn't even get accepted."

But I saw her letter, same as mine. We had celebrated by going bowling. "Mol, I don't understand."

"You were so excited," she whispered. "Going to Stanford was your dream, and you were so good a friend that I knew you would give it up if I couldn't go with you."

I wanted to argue, but I couldn't. I would have given up everything for her. But that didn't make this any easier to hear. "So you left because of me?"

She leaned in close, taking my hands and holding them tight against her chest. "I left *for* you, Brennon," she said. "You deserved to go to your dream school and get your dream job and become this amazing man you are now. I would have just gotten in the way."

My mouth was so dry that I worried I wouldn't be able to keep talking, but I did anyway. "You broke my heart, Mol."

"I know."

And the most important question I could ever ask her was right there on the tip of my tongue, waiting to be said. Once I said it, her answer would seal our fate. There would be no going back from here:

"Are you going to break it again?"

She looked at me, her eyes glistening in the moonlight, and one of her hands slid up to my cheek. Running her thumb over my lips, she drew in so close that I couldn't breathe anymore. "I never want to hurt you, Brennon."

And then she kissed me.

I had wanted to kiss Molly Piper since I was fifteen years old. I'd imagined it, longed for it, and I'd thought nothing could compare to how I'd built it up inside my head. I was wrong. Kissing Molly was taking my first breath of fresh air after a lifetime of suffocating. It was sailing through the sky on wings. It was sitting beneath the stars and seeing the enormity of the universe but knowing there was nothing more important than her and me and the two of us together.

It was lightning. A flash of light so intense that it seemed to set the sky on fire.

And I had never felt more whole than I did at that moment.

Sitting on the beach and talking to Molly felt like the most normal thing I had done in years, and I didn't want it to end. We talked about our families. We talked about how our favorite foods had changed and how we both still listened to the same music that we had in high school. We talked about how much we missed living next door to each other. Molly told me exciting stories of photos she had taken and dangerous situations she had gotten herself into. I told her less exciting stories of correctly predicting stock market trends.

We reminisced about old times. Old friends. Old heartaches.

Talking to Molly felt like breathing life back into the world. Like healing.

Eventually we stopped talking, and that was almost better. I could just sit there on the beach in silence—no songs, no unspoken thoughts—and hold her as the night seemed to stretch on forever, giving me this chance to have something good in my life for once. To believe that I could open myself up again and belong to the world like I had when I was younger.

I didn't need a fancy condo in downtown San Francisco. I didn't need to become a partner at a stock brokerage I had never stopped to wonder if I actually liked. I didn't need money, or clout, or fancy suits. I just needed Molly, the one person in the world who truly knew me. The *only* person who knew Brennon Ashworth and wouldn't let me hide in the personalities of the people around me like some human chameleon.

And I knew Molly, so when she pulled herself out of my arms and jumped up without warning, I knew exactly what had just gone through her head as she grinned down at me.

"No," I said immediately. Emphatically. "I'm not breaking into the lighthouse again." I had been noticing the building on the other end of the beach all night, but I had been actively ignoring it just in case Molly read my thoughts and decided they meant I was interested.

"Come on," she urged, a sparkle in her eye as she gently tugged my hand. "Be that guy I fell for when I was in high school, the one who wasn't afraid to let loose and be happy."

Happy. I hadn't realized how completely I had forgotten what that felt like, but Molly made it easy to remember. We were near opposites, but that made us so well suited for each other that even as my brain told me it was a bad idea, my heart said I had been denying myself happiness for long enough.

"Okay," I said, and Molly's smile warmed me to my very center.

Instead of pulling me toward the lighthouse, she moved closer to me and slipped her palms onto my cheeks. "I can't pretend to understand exactly what I did to you," she said, "but I see you, Brennon Ashworth. You're so afraid to be something special, and you let those fears hold you back. Will you promise me you'll stop living with one foot still inside the door? Please?"

I would promise her the world if she asked it. "I'm not afraid when I'm with you," I said. When she was next to me, I felt like I could be anything.

But to my surprise, she shook her head. "You don't need me to be brave. You've always been special, Bren, and I've had nothing to do with it. You have a career and a life and a family, and none of that was because of me."

A darkness settled over me as she spoke, like some omen lingering just out of sight. The shadow that follows lightning. "You're not going somewhere?" I asked, slightly horrified at the idea of her leaving again.

It had been bad enough the first time; would I make it through a second?

She pressed her lips to mine. "I told you," she said, though her kiss left me with a slight ringing in my ears so I barely heard her. "I don't want to hurt you."

That wasn't exactly answering the question, but I believed her. She wouldn't lie about something like that.

"Come on," I said and gave her a smile. "At this rate we'll never get to the top of the lighthouse."

When we got to the lighthouse, logic caught up to me a bit, and I realized we probably wouldn't be able to get inside. It wasn't like buildings like this were open to the public, especially in the middle of the night. But I wasn't about to just give up, not with Molly standing right behind me, so I put my hand on the doorknob, took a deep breath, and pushed.

It opened with a happy little click.

"When did you learn to pick locks?" Molly asked in surprise when I pushed the door open the rest of the way.

I badly wanted to say it was something I'd taught myself when I had to get myself out of a sticky situation, but I figured honesty was the best policy, especially if I wanted her to be honest with me. "It was unlocked," I said and winced.

Molly laughed. "Oh, Bean," she sighed. "One of these days I'm going to have to teach you when to lie."

She led the way up the stairs eagerly, and I followed like the unwitting sidekick to her butt-kicking heroine and was simply there to make her look better by comparison. I had to smile at that. It had been like that our whole lives, and it felt completely normal to be Molly's shadow. She was always the adventurous one, and she would always be a step ahead of me.

That was okay with me. I had never considered myself a leading man, and if the awesome girl settled for me in the end, I would be perfectly content with my lot in life. I had no problems holding her spotlight steady to make sure she shone like the star she was.

"There are a lot more stairs than it looked like from the outside!" Molly whispered as we continued to climb. She didn't seem keen to slow down, however.

"Maybe if you weren't so old it wouldn't be so hard," I said, and I was definitely more out of breath than she was.

"Brennon Ashworth, I am exactly four months and two weeks older than you. Don't even think about going there, old man."

We finally reached the top of the staircase, and Molly pushed through the door with impressive flair as the cool salty air blasted the pair of us like a wave. She went immediately to the railing and peered over the edge with wonder in her expression, and I couldn't help but smile as I watched her.

How could I have been so unfair to her and mistrust everything she said? This was still Molly. She hadn't changed, and being suspicious of her all this time had only made everything harder.

"You're intoxicating," I said.

She grinned back at me. "You sound like you're straight from a chick flick," she replied. "Who talks like that?"

I wrapped her in my arms and closed my eyes, letting myself memorize how it felt to hold her like this. Not as a friend but as a man who was irrevocably lost to her. "I talk like that," I said, fighting the urge to start humming that song from Titanic. "Apparently."

The only other time I'd ever come close to saying things like that had been when I first met Lissa, and looking back on those moments made me feel ridiculous. I liked Lissa, but I had never fallen in love with her.

I'd lost my heart to Molly when I was fifteen and had never gotten it back.

"Do you know what I wish?" Molly asked in a whisper, leaning into me.

"What?"

"Hey!" The door opened, bringing with it a blinding light and a jumpstart to my system as adrenaline burst through me. "You're not supposed to be up here!" What was clearly a security guard appeared from behind that light and had his flashlight pointed right at us, along with what I was pretty sure was a taser.

"Run," my mouth said before my brain could catch up.

Molly listened, but she tried to drag me with her. There was no way we could get past the man by running straight at him, so I tore myself free of her grip and bolted to the side, drawing the guy away from the doorway. By some miracle he followed me, and I chanced a glance behind me to make sure Molly took the opportunity I gave her to dash back down the stairs.

Good.

I got halfway around the top of the house then stopped, knowing I needed to give her more time. "I give up!" I said quickly and held my hands in the air, praying he didn't tase me.

"How'd you get up here?" the guard asked. His voice shook, which meant he probably didn't have many people interrupting his quiet nights. I hadn't gotten a good enough look at him after being blinded to hazard a guess at his age, but he sounded pretty old.

You failed at your job. You're a terrible security guard. Don't say that, Brennon. "The door was unlocked," I said. "We just wanted to get a good view of the bay."

"Likely," he growled. "On your knees."

I was pretty sure he didn't have the authority to arrest me, but I wasn't about to test that theory. I slowly knelt, keeping my hands in the air so I wouldn't startle him. "I'm very sorry for causing you any trouble." *Maybe you should be better about locking your doors.*

The guard came around to face me, probably because he wasn't keen on the idea of not seeing my face and being able to anticipate what I might do, and I was perfectly okay with being able to see him too. For the very same reason. He was definitely old, probably pushing seventy, and I had the horrifying feeling that he looked familiar. Could he have possibly been the same security guard who found us the last time? That time he had given us a warning—probably because Molly had burst into tears after she broke my heart and I was an absolute mess—but I was pretty sure he wouldn't be as lenient this time.

"What was your plan?" he asked roughly. "Smash the light like usual?"

I'm not a teenage boy. If I wanted to get out of this, I couldn't just kneel here and stay silent, so I frantically searched for something to say. It had been a long time since I had had to talk Molly out of trouble, and I wasn't sure I would be able to do it anymore. Keeping someone happy was far different from convincing them of something I knew they wouldn't believe, particularly when it was my own neck on the line.

I cleared my throat. This was going to be horrendous, and I was going to get myself tased for sure. But I couldn't see another option.

"I really am sorry," I repeated. "My girlfriend and I were walking along the beach. Ya know, taking a moonlit stroll. Like you do. And, I mean, I've been wanting to propose for weeks now, but I hadn't found the right moment because she's, like, the best thing to ever happen to me, and I wanted everything to be perfect. And then *bam*, suddenly this lighthouse appears out of nowhere, and I'm standing there thinking to myself how perfect it would be if I could propose at the top. You can't get much more romantic than that! This is like California's Eiffel Tower."

The guard stood so tense I was worried he was going to pull the trigger on his taser gun just by holding it a little too tight.

I kept talking, and it felt like I was saying more than I'd said in the last ten years put together. I'd also developed some weird Brooklyn accent I must have picked up from Steve back when we were first roommates. "And I figured," I said, "even if there's not a light on at the top, there's gotta be someone up here I can talk to because light-houses are a nighttime thing, right? So I tried the door, and since it was unlocked, I figured that was a good sign, but I couldn't say anything about my plan to my girlfriend because naturally that would ruin the surprise, which is kinda the whole point, so she had no idea what was going on and was just excited to look out over the water and the city and all that. And yeah, okay, so when we got up here there was no one to give me permission, but I figured that since we were there anyway, and we were alone, and I had the ring all ready to go, that maybe I should just drop down on one knee and pop the question before I got too nervous because, like I said, she's the best thing to ever happen to me, and—"

"Where's the ring?" the guard interrupted.

I froze. "What?"

"You said you had the ring ready, so where is it?"

My pockets were completely empty, and he could clearly see it. "The ring?" I said, and my voice seemed to stick in my throat again. "I…I dropped it. When you found us." And I probably shouldn't have sounded so unbothered by that thought. Cringing, I made one slight movement as if to go back near the stairs to look for it, and I realized too late my mistake.

The guard fired his taser, and my whole body went rigid with pain as I collapsed onto the floor and thought to myself, *Yeah, I probably deserve that.*

CHAPTER FIFTEEN

The two police officers who showed up at the lighthouse twenty minutes later were incredibly kind and seemed to believe me when I told them I had not entered the lighthouse with the intent to do damage. It probably helped that I told them the truth in full detail. Though the security guard put up a fuss and wanted me sent to prison for a decade, Officer Ramone and his partner must have taken pity on me the moment they saw me zip-tied and slumped against the rail, and they only talked to me for a few minutes before they said they'd take me to the hospital, just to make sure I hadn't gotten any injuries during the incident.

They were having a slow night, Officer Ramone told me.

The urgent care nurse who checked on me had the same pitying look in her eyes as she did her examination, and I had to wonder what about my appearance made them think something was wrong. Nothing was wrong. Sure, I was absolutely exhausted after getting tased, but I was happier than I had been in a long time, and I couldn't wait to catch up with Molly and laugh with her about the whole thing. She would want all the details, and I would happily give them to her because it would mean another long conversation with my best friend.

I had fifteen years of those to make up for.

"You got someone you can call?" Officer Ramone asked me after I'd been cleared by the nurse—and given a sticker and a lollipop. "I'd offer to give you a ride, but we've got our rounds to get back to."

I was pretty sure he was about to reach for his wallet to give me money for a cab, and that was a little too much. A man still needed to keep a little dignity. "Yeah, I'll be good. Thanks, though."

Though he still hesitated for a moment, Officer Ramone patted me on the shoulder then followed his partner out to their squad car, leaving me in the quiet urgent care lobby. A nurse offered to let me use the desk phone, and I lifted up the receiver and was halfway to dialing when I realized I didn't even know who to call.

I wasn't smart enough to have memorized any phone numbers, least of all Molly's, whose number had been in my phone for all of a few days. I knew my office number, which wouldn't help me this early in the morning, and I knew my parents', though they could both sleep through a tsunami and wake up in the morning wondering why their things were floating out to sea. It would probably be better to call someone who could get me home before I had a chance to count the tiles on the floor.

"Steve," I decided, partly because he was my best friend and partly because his was the only other number I actually knew. I wouldn't blame him for hating me for calling him so early, but what choice did I have? "Sorry, buddy," I said then dialed his phone.

It rang three times, and to my horror it was Lissa who answered. "Hello?" she asked, her voice gravelly.

I was never going to hear the end of this. "Lissa, it's Brennon. I, uh, need your help."

Lissa showed up at the clinic almost an hour later. I heard her voice, a bit muffled through the door of the empty examination room I'd taken refuge in so I could lie down, and I couldn't help but reflect on how lucky I was she hadn't questioned me when I gave her a recap of the events. Sitting up, I stayed where I was because I knew the over-helpful nurses would point her in the right direction, and I tried to decide how she would react when she saw me.

More important, how should I react? I could be my usual impassive self, the one she'd gotten used to over the last year and a half, but my lighthouse escapade kinda negated the validity of that personality. It was strange, as I stood there, considering that the person I'd been for such a large chunk of my life wasn't me at all. After going to the beach with Molly and getting all of my depressing past out in the open, I wasn't sure my masks would even fit anymore.

I never would have thought a person could change so suddenly, but it was like I couldn't even remember what post-high school Brennon was like. I was just me, the guy who would follow Molly to the ends of the earth and always take the fall for her because she was never meant to be in a cage.

Hopefully she would be waiting for me outside the Munroe mansion so she could help me laugh about this, and I could almost picture her pacing back and forth as she drew up her battle plan to rescue me.

The door to the exam room opened, and I braced myself for whatever expression Lissa might have for me.

But it was Steve who stood in the doorway, his eyes almost eerily fixed right on me and a look on his face that said, "You and I need to have a little talk."

Leaving the door open, he sat next to me, and for several minutes, the only sound in the room was the crinkle of the paper beneath us. He may not have been looking at me, but I could see his expression shift multiple times as we sat there in silence, a healthy combination of anger and worry. Had I looked like that back when I was constantly afraid he wasn't taking care of himself? It was probably a good thing he hadn't been able to see me, or things would have been ridiculously tense between us for a year and beyond.

"So," Steve said finally.

"So," I repeated.

"You got arrested."

I smiled, glad he couldn't see my expression well enough to understand it. "Not technically," I said. Yes, I'd sort of gotten arrested, but overall, the night had given me so much freedom over my life that I was almost glad it had happened.

"I'm guessing it was Molly's idea to break into the lighthouse?" His voice carried an undercurrent of something low that sounded an awful lot like hatred.

"I don't know what you're talking about," I said, even though he was absolutely right. I just didn't want to have this conversation, not when I needed to get back to Molly and make sure she was okay. "We should go so you can get back to bed."

But Steve grabbed my arm before I could stand. "No, I think we need to talk about this."

Sighing, I tried to see this from his perspective before I said anything. If my best friend called me in the middle of the night, needing a ride from the hospital after getting tased, maybe I would be a little concerned too.

Who was I kidding? That had been my entire relationship with Steve. One eventful night couldn't even compare to fifteen years of worrying over the guy who loved adrenaline as much as I loved my suits.

"There's nothing to talk about, Steve," I said. "Really. It was just a misunderstanding, and—"

"So where is Molly then? Why isn't she here?"

This coming from the guy who had told me just a couple of days ago that he liked how I acted when I was around Molly? *Make up your mind.* Either he liked Molly's influence or he didn't, and I didn't have time to try to understand which it was.

"Steve," I said, pulling myself out of his grip and getting to my feet. "I'm tired, okay? I just want to get to bed." *And find the girl I'm hopelessly in love with.*

Steve stood too, planting himself in between me and the door. He wasn't nearly the size of his brother-in-law, but he wasn't small either. Even blind, he could easily hold me back if he tried.

"We're going to talk about this, Brennon," he said, his voice low. "Whether you want to or not."

Well this was just getting ridiculous. "I don't need you pretending to be my dad," I growled back. "I already have one of those."

He cocked his head, his frown growing deeper. "What is wrong with you?"

"Nothing's wrong with me."

I tried to step around him, but he managed to keep my path blocked. The room was too dark for him to be able to see me well, and yet he somehow knew where he needed to be to stay in my way.

"Steve," I growled, "let me through."

"No," he replied. "Not until you tell me what's going on with you. And don't tell me you're fine, because this is not the Brennon I've known since Stanford."

"Maybe that's a good thing."

"Getting arrested is a good thing?"

"I told you, I didn't get arrested."

"Brennon, just talk to me."

I groaned and tried again to get past him, but this time he grabbed my wrist.

I was halfway to throwing my fist into his face before I realized I was doing it.

When my knuckles collided with his jaw, the jarring pain in my hand disappeared beneath my absolute horror as Steve stumbled sideways and collided with the examination table. He barely managed to catch himself, and I stared with my mouth hanging open and my right hand gripped in my left as if my fist had done all of that on its own.

"Steve!" I gasped and took a step away from him. "I didn't... I'm..." *Brennon, you absolute idiot!*

Steve laughed.

Straightening up and massaging his jaw, he kept laughing as he tried to pick me out from the rest of the dark room, and he only just managed to get the words out as he said, "How long have you been wanting to do that?"

I had no reply.

"You seriously pack a punch for a little guy," he continued, leaning one elbow on the exam table. "How's your hand?"

I glanced down at my knuckles. They throbbed a little, but it was not nearly as bad as I would have expected. "Fine," I muttered. All of the adrenaline that had made me punch him in the first place was dissipating, leaving me absolutely exhausted. "How's your face?"

He grinned. "Well, that hurt a lot less than getting tased."

"Wait," I said, "have you been tased before?"

His grin said, "Yes," but his words said, "I don't know what you're talking about. Now, can we talk about whatever you're going through? Please?"

I really didn't want to waste any more time, and even if I felt bad for punching him, I could apologize later. "Steve, I'll tell you all about it later, but—"

"You've been acting weird ever since—"

"Oh, don't go pretending you're perfect," I grumbled. It was rich, getting chastised by a man who had made his wife cry multiple times in the last several days. "I know about what you've gotten yourself into with the Davenports, and you—"

"How do you know about the Paris house?" he asked in alarm then flinched and barely held back a curse. "Sh—please tell me she didn't hear that."

I stared at him, trying to understand. Almost automatically, I glanced out the open door, where Lissa was chatting with the nurses, probably about me. "What Paris house?" I asked.

Steve frowned, clearly just as confused as I was. "Wait, what were you talking about? Did you think we…" His eyes going wide, he grinned and fought back another laugh. "Bren, you idiot. Did you think the likes of Adam Munroe would get himself into something *illegal?* Do you know the guy at all?"

"Apparently not," I mumbled. "So what *are* you guys up to?"

Still grinning, Steve stepped close so Lissa would be even less likely to overhear as he whispered, "We're buying a house in Paris for our wives to share, but we wanted it to be a surprise. And you have no idea how hard it is to lie to these women who know us better than we know ourselves."

My mind was spinning fast enough that I was tempted to lie down again. All of this illumination in the last twenty-four hours was not good for me. *That* was what all the secrecy was about?

"I'm so lost right now," I muttered and dropped into the doctor's chair so I could rest my face in my hands. Was it possible for a man to survive so many conflicting emotions throughout a day? Probably not.

Chuckling, Steve put his arm around me. "I think we need to get our delinquent friend to bed," he said as a shadow blocked the light coming through the doorway, which meant he was probably talking to Lissa now.

How could I have suspected the Davenports? I wanted to say it was Molly's fault for planting the idea, but I hadn't tried to argue it very hard. I'd agreed to look on Adam's computer. I'd thought the worst of my best friend simply because he had acted out of the ordinary, which was such a characteristically human thing that my chest ached to know I had ever forgotten otherwise. Wasn't that exactly why I tried so hard to understand people? Because they were unpredictable?

I'd thought I was figuring out who I was again, but clearly I was far from put together. I was just a mess of shattered pieces, everything I had pretended to be for the last fifteen years poorly glued together in a kindergarten collage that looked nothing like it was supposed to.

"Steve," I said, choking on his name.

He lifted me up to my feet. "Dude," he replied, "you look exhausted, and I can't even see you. Let's take you home, okay?"

He was right. I *was* exhausted. And it wasn't just from being up all night or because of the 50,000 volts that ran through me an hour ago. "I don't have a home," I said.

"Your apartment will be fixed soon enough," Lissa replied, and she latched onto my other side to help guide both Steve and me to the car.

That wasn't what I meant, I wanted to say, but I couldn't bring myself to admit it out loud.

Lissa and Steve dropped me off outside the Munroe mansion and both suggested I take the day off and get some sleep. I was inclined to agree, but the moment I caught sight of the guest bed I had been using, I had no desire to sleep. It may have been nearing six in the morning, but the night wasn't over yet. I had to make sure Molly was okay.

Finding my phone on the nightstand where I'd left it before the party, I fought against the worry that sparked to life inside me when I realized I had no missed calls, emails, or even texts. Had something happened? I pulled up her number and called without letting myself think the worst.

"We're sorry," said a cheerful voice before the line had even rung once. "You have reached a number that has been disconnected or is no longer in service."

My blood turned to ice. That phone number had been perfectly active less than twenty-four hours earlier. I had seen Molly less than three hours ago. And I could barely think straight enough to wonder if she'd tossed her phone before or after our little beach excursion.

I sank onto the bed, but I stood up almost immediately because I couldn't just sit there and let my panic rise. Sitting felt like defeat. "It isn't what it seems like," I told myself and headed for the front door again. "There's a reasonable explanation."

I said the same thing over and over again as I climbed into my car and stepped on the gas, driving a whole lot faster than I usually did because the drive into the city was way too long and I didn't want to sit still any longer than I had to.

"It was probably a temporary number," I told myself, wishing I had a song—any song—in my head because the silence was unnerving. Turning on the radio felt like an omen. Like she was gone. "She was only in town temporarily, so there was little point in getting a permanent phone."

Then why give out the number when it was only going to be disconnected a few days later?

I had to find her. She probably saw me get stuck with the cops and went back home so she could figure out what to do, and…

As I entered downtown San Francisco, the whole world seemed to slow down until everything moved at a crawl. I didn't even know where Molly was staying. She'd been in town for nearly a week, and I had no idea where to even find her. She always found me. Where could I possibly go in a city this large and expect to just run into a girl who never stayed in one place for long?

I didn't have an answer, but I just kept driving. I refused to believe she had disappeared again.

She wouldn't do that to me. Not after last night.

But I had nowhere to look, nowhere to start, and eventually I pulled to a stop outside my apartment building. I knew I wouldn't find anything good inside, but I turned the car off anyway. She had shown up there once before, and maybe…

I reached the second floor landing and felt like a stranger in my own home, my eyes fixed on my closed door as I tried to work up the courage to see what I would find on the other side. Probably just the guts of the building. Frames. Beams. Drywall. There might even still be a hole in the ceiling above. What had happened to my neighbor who had caused all of my problems? Had he come back from vacation yet only to find his possessions mingled with mine?

I had taken two steps toward my door, my key at the ready, when I froze, my gaze falling on the sheet of paper that had been stuck to the door. I couldn't read it from this distance, not when I was this tired, but I slowly moved closer as if I knew exactly what it said.

I definitely knew who it was from.

Brennon, it said, in a handwriting I knew as well as my own.

> *I'm sorry. You don't deserve what I've done to you, and you'll never understand, but I'm sorry. I hope your apartment is fixed soon, but it was the only way to make sure you stayed close to the Davenport family, and I wouldn't have done it if I didn't have to. I wish I could tell you why, and I wish I didn't have to leave, but I have to disappear before things get worse. Take care of yourself, Bean, and don't be afraid anymore. Talk to your boss. Let yourself fall in love. Be the amazing Brennon I know is in there. You deserve every good thing in life. I love you.*
> *-Mol*

My hand shook as I pulled the note from the door and held it delicately, as if it would fall apart if I held it too tight. And without understanding any of it, I unlocked my door and pushed it open so I could see what used to be my life, now in crumbled pieces that would likely never be restored and whole again.

CHAPTER SIXTEEN

"Well this is worse than I imagined."

Yesterday, I would have jumped out of my skin at the sound of Seth suddenly right behind me. Today, I was too numb to feel anything. "They'll fix it," I said. I'd been sitting just inside the door for at least an hour, staring at the empty nightmare of my condo, and I only turned to look at Seth because it gave me a good reason to stop looking at my despair.

He leaned against the doorframe, as giant and perfect as ever, and he raised one eyebrow that spoke clearly his disappointment. "I wasn't talking about the condo," he said. "Evans called me when he realized you weren't at the Munroes' and said you might be in need of a friend, and while I try not to listen to anything my brother-in-law says, he made sure he was hard to ignore this time."

"I'm fine," I said automatically.

Seth crouched down to my level, and I imagined he was looking at me the same way he had looked at IEDs and other threats while in the Special Forces. Expecting me to explode at any moment. "I hate to say it," he muttered, "but I think he was right. And you're a lot worse than I expected, which probably means something happened between your little crime spree and Steve's less-than-welcome early phone call."

I could see him eyeing Molly's note where it sat on my lap, and there was little point in trying to keep it a secret. "She's gone," I croaked and held it out to him.

Seth read the note quickly, and his eyes grew steadily darker as he did so. "So if I'm reading this right," he said as he sat on the floor with me, "she's the one who did the whole flooding thing upstairs? To get you into one of our houses?"

I nodded, and I didn't even care that his anger was building. She clearly deserved his distrust and had from the beginning.

"I mean…" He frowned and looked up at the hole in the ceiling. "Her plan worked, but she could have killed you."

I was well aware of that and had been thinking about it for most of the last hour. How could she have thought flooding my house would be a good idea?

"She must have been after your money," I said with a sigh. "Why else would she want to get in with the family?"

Seth didn't answer for a while, and I couldn't bring myself to look at him in case he had that murderous expression that was so terrifying. I couldn't bear to have his glare focused on me.

"With all due respect to your intellect," he said finally, "if she was after our money, she would have gone straight to Adam this morning, asking him to help get you out of jail. He wouldn't have asked questions, and he probably would have written her a blank check and sent her on her way before he found out you weren't arrested."

Maybe. "But why else would she use me to get to your family?" I turned to him and desperately hoped he had an answer so I could understand at least some part of all of this.

Seth's frown tightened. "I guess that's what we need to find out," he said. Rising to his feet, he gave me an excited smile and held out his hand to help me up. "Lucky for you," he continued when I was up, "I happen to be married to the world's most terrifying FBI intern, which means the two of us are, in my humble opinion, an extremely powerful couple. How about some breakfast?" He held his arm out toward his own condo, and I knew better than to argue.

Catherine listened to my story only long enough to learn Molly had vanished into the wind and was involved in some kind of scheme, and then she had her phone in her hand. "Miles? Remember last winter when I did that thing for you and you said you owed me one? Time to pay up."

I leaned over to Seth as we both sat in the front room and watched her work. "What did she do for Miles?"

Seth shrugged one shoulder. "One thing I dearly miss about my old job is being in the know when it comes to government affairs. Adam doesn't exactly require national secrets to operate. The FBI, however..."

Catherine was now chatting with someone else entirely and pacing the living room in front of us. I couldn't guess at what she was saying because I didn't even know what language she was speaking.

"Catherine isn't a big fan of secrets," Seth continued, "but that's the job."

I looked at him. Now that I knew all the secrecy was about a house in Paris, the whole thing seemed so trivial. "Speaking of secrets..."

His eyes lit up in a way I wouldn't have expected from a guy like him. "Steve said you've learned a thing or two. It's not my favorite way to operate, but I think the end result will be worth it."

"*Hvala vam*, Tomislav," Catherine said, and she hung up the phone looking a lot more excited than I would have guessed after ten minutes of talking to people on the phone. "Almost there," she said. "Where's breakfast?"

A knock on the door interrupted whatever Seth might have said in reply, and we all turned as Matthew came into the condo with a bag of what smelled like fried heaven.

"Special delivery," he said happily. "I grabbed all the bear claws before Indie could put them in the donut case, so you'd better start eating before she gets mad at me. She likes you guys more than she likes me."

Catherine's phone rang, and this time she went into the kitchen to answer it, probably because she couldn't hide the conversation behind an unknown language. "Talk to me, Miles," she said before the door closed behind her.

"So the secret's out?" Matthew asked and tossed me a still-warm donut.

"Only to Brennon," Seth replied.

Matthew dropped into a seat and kept his eyes toward the kitchen as he said, "The sooner we get this done, the better. I've been on the verge of blabbing for a week."

"Try living with that one," Seth replied, jerking his head toward the kitchen. "She can see through pretty much anything."

"And Adam's about to crack," Matthew added. "I'm honestly surprised he's held out this long."

I didn't like sitting there silent, which by itself was a strange feeling on top of everything else happening. I generally avoided talking when I could. But something had changed in me, and I missed being a part of things.

So I took a deep breath and asked, "What is left to do?"

Matthew literally paled a bit, the first sign of true fear I'd ever seen in him. "Well," he said and dropped his voice, just in case, "one of us really needs to go to Paris and sign the actual contract. Because we've been doing this under the radar, the seller is a little concerned we're just a scam."

"So you need a reason to go to Paris without your wives suspecting you," I concluded, and both men nodded. I had never been to Paris, and my clients almost entirely stuck to the US market. I wanted to help them so they could stop lying, but any of these men were more likely to have a reason to travel to the other side of the world.

"Paris," Catherine said, appearing at the kitchen door.

All of us froze.

"Sorry?" Seth muttered.

Catherine glanced between us as if concerned something was wrong with us. I didn't blame her, seeing as Matthew and Seth both looked like they'd been caught breaking into the cookie jar and I was probably just a mess all around, half a sticky donut pinched between my fingers.

Catherine raised an eyebrow. "Molly. You know, the whole reason I'm here instead of at work. She's heading to Paris."

I felt Seth and Matthew staring at me, but I kept my eyes on Catherine. "Are you sure?" I asked.

She grinned. "Well, unless my contacts are getting paid their ridiculous salaries to be bad at their jobs, your *amour* has gone and booked herself a flight, which is on its way to Paris. And, though I don't know the full details yet, she's being blackmailed, which explains her sudden disappearance."

"Blackmailed?" Matthew and I said at once.

Catherine matched the smile Seth was giving her then reached her hand out for a donut, which Matthew gave her. "She's pretty much broke, and it seems her blackmailer found a way to still gain something from her even after her funds ran out."

Was that what Molly was trying to tell me at the party? But how was I supposed to figure out something like that?

"Something to do with our family," Seth guessed. "Though if whoever he is wasn't after our money, I'm not sure what else he could hope to gain."

The conversation lulled as we tried to think of a reason, and I sat there without a clue how to process this information. She was being blackmailed? But did that mean everything she had done, everything she'd said, had been under duress? If I could just know what was real...

"Sounds like we need to go to Paris," Matthew said, and there was a hint of laughter in his voice. Of all the places she could have gone, it turned out to be exactly where the Davenports needed to go.

Seth sat up a little straighter. "That's exactly what it sounds like," he replied.

Both men gave each other a look that must have said more than what I got out of it, because they nodded before Matthew said, "We should probably bring Adam with us. He's the only voice of reason we've got among us."

"Bring him where?" asked a new voice, and Steve stepped into the condo with Lissa at his heels. "Please tell me Brennon is here," he added, his worry clear in his thin voice.

I frowned. "I'm here," I said, though I had no idea why *he* was.

Steve looked legitimately angry as he sought out Seth in the room, something he accomplished when Lissa subtly pointed him in the right direction. "You were supposed to tell me if you found him," he growled.

From the looks of things, Seth tried very hard not to roll his eyes as he calmly said, "I sent you a text. Didn't you see it?"

Steve did *not* like the joke, and he practically snarled his words. "Hastings, I swear to—"

"Can we focus?" Catherine snapped before the pair of them got any more annoyed with each other. "We have Molly to rescue."

Steve immediately shifted gears, his anger transforming into interest. "Rescue? What's going on?"

"Molly's being blackmailed," Matthew replied. "And you're coming with us to Paris to go find her."

Seth grabbed a computer from the end table next to him then looked up at his wife, studying her for a moment before he said, "Cat, my love, you're going to be late for work."

Catherine narrowed her eyes. "But I can help," she said, as if she knew there was more to Seth's comment than a simple reminder. He probably wanted her gone so they could talk about the house freely, and she probably knew it.

Steve caught on to Seth's plan and turned to Lissa. "I think this is going to be a boy's trip," he said and kissed her cheek. "No point in you standing around being bored."

Narrowing her eyes, Lissa looked like she was about to launch into a similar argument as the one brewing in Catherine's eyes, and that was only going to make all of this harder.

"We've got this," I said and looked right at Lissa.

She had always thought she knew me and understood me, and she had always tried to use that to her advantage. I couldn't blame her for that when I did the exact same thing with everyone. But something had woken inside of me, some long lost part of me who stood up for himself and didn't care what someone else might think of me.

It was time I took a stand and stopped living in the past.

"You and Catherine can leave," I said, as gently as I could so they wouldn't think I was just tossing them aside. "We'll be fine."

Glancing at Lissa, who didn't seem to like the idea any more than *she* had a moment ago, Catherine let out a sigh then stepped over to kiss Seth's forehead. "Be careful," she told him.

"Always," he replied and smiled as she disappeared deeper into the condo.

Lissa was not as easily persuaded, and she held tight to Steve's hand even as he tried to join Seth on the couch. "I don't know why you need to go," she said quietly. "Seth and Matthew can handle it."

Steve smirked. "I'm sure they could. But they need someone who speaks French."

"Seth speaks French."

Seth only half held back his groan before he grumbled, "Not as well as your husband," as if admitting Steve was actually good at something literally caused him pain. "Besides, he's the only one who has actually been to Paris."

"That would be helpful," Matthew said, lifting his phone to his ear. "Adam! Good morning, my favorite brother-in-law. Since you're richer than the rest of us combined, what do you say to buying a few plane tickets to France?"

"What if it's dangerous?" Lissa asked Steve.

"Because Brennon has lost his Molly," Matthew told Adam.

"I'll be fine," Steve said. "Seth will make sure I don't step into traffic."

Lissa frowned. "That's not funny."

I agreed. I didn't need my best friend getting hit by *another* car.

"Today, if we can," Matthew said to a question Adam must have asked him, though he was watching Steve and Lissa with interest and probably not paying too much attention to his phone call. But then he frowned at whatever Adam said. "I know last-minute flights are expensive. What's the point of having all that money if you're not going to spend it?" Then he rolled his eyes. "Because I spent most of mine refurbishing a coffee shop. And you have more miles than I do."

"Okay," Lissa said quietly, though she definitely didn't like the idea of sending her husband off to Paris where she couldn't keep an eye out for him. "You promise you'll be safe? I don't want to lose you."

"I promise," Steve said, and he touched his forehead to hers. "You are the best thing to ever happen to me, Lissa Evans."

"Hang on, Adam," Matthew said, his eyes still on the pair of them. "Hey Lissa?"

She reluctantly pulled away from Steve to look at him. "Yeah?"

"Look after Indie for me, and I promise I'll make sure Steve gets home safe and sound. He's my family too." He said it with so much conviction and absolutely no hint of jesting that it would have been impossible not to believe him.

Finally smiling, Lissa nodded, gave Steve a quick kiss, then headed out the front door.

"One down," Seth muttered, his eyes sliding over to the door Catherine had disappeared through. "Not a word about the house until she's gone," he warned, though that was hardly necessary.

All of them knew as well as I did that Catherine was not someone to take lightly.

"Yes, I'm still here," Matthew said into his phone. "And yes, you're coming with us. Like I said, you're the filthy rich one." He paused. "Adam Munroe, you don't have a choice in the matter."

I didn't see why Adam coming was strictly necessary, unless his presence was the only way they would be able to finish the sale on the house, and I hardly wanted to force him to come on my rescue mission if he didn't want to.

"Hand me one of those donuts," Seth said and started typing away at his computer. "I'll get the tickets. I've got Adam's credit card memorized."

"Oh, calm down, Mr. Grumpy Pants," Matthew said as he held out the donut bag. "Seth can memorize anything. You're coming, and that's final." And he hung up before Adam could argue.

"Window seat, Davenport?" Seth asked.

"Obviously."

"Evans can sit in the middle."

"Middle?" Steve scowled as he plopped himself down on the couch right next to Seth, though he ended up a little too close and bumped into him. "You'd better be buying first class, Hastings. We're not peasants."

Seth shoved him aside. "*We're* not peasants," he growled. "No clue what you are. Alright, four first-class tickets to Paris leaving in two hours."

Two hours wasn't a long time, but we could make it. It wasn't like we were packing for a vacation, and... I frowned. *Four* tickets? I had been sitting in silence for the last several minutes and trying not to panic—trying not to react at all because I was likely to explode—so it took me a second to figure out why that sounded off. Seth, Matthew,

Steve, Adam… I counted their names on my fingers while Seth and Steve started bickering, just to be sure I wasn't counting wrong.

"Hang on," I said. "What about me?" *Wake up, Brennon!*

All three of them paused and looked at me in surprise, as if they'd already forgotten I was sitting there.

Seth gave me an amused look that made me feel completely useless. "We've got this covered, Ashworth," he said as he returned to his laptop. "You can sit this one out."

"No I can't." How could I possibly let them go without me?

As Seth paused again, Matthew gave me a pitying grimace and said, "No offense, Brennon, but you've been dealing with a lot the last few days and could really use a break. We'll find her, I promise."

"It doesn't matter if you find her," I said as I got to my feet, "because I'm the only one who can bring her home."

When Steve rose as well, I knew my tenuous confidence had not been strong enough to convince them I had to go with them to Paris. He approached cautiously, like I was a wild animal, and put his hand on my arm as soon as he was close enough.

"Hey man," he said, speaking low enough that only I could hear him. "We're not going to let anything happen to her no matter what. But do you really want to do this? I may not know much about this girl, but I'm pretty sure she's left you twice now. Then and now. Who's to say she won't do it again after you rescue her? Let us handle this, and you don't have to get hurt again."

What kind of a stupid idea was that? "Let you handle it?" I said and pulled away from his touch. I could feel Matthew and Seth's gazes on me, but I didn't care. "Who was the one who helped her climb down from that tree when she got too high? I was. Who taught her how to ride a bike with no hands when Garrett down the street made fun of her for not being able to? I did. Who spent a week in detention so she didn't get expelled after she beat up the bully who was terrorizing the freshman girl in a wheelchair? Who let her cry on his shoulder when her dad remarried? Who talked to her for hours until she was brave enough to go to her mom's funeral? *I did*. Molly is afraid of only two things in life: losing her freedom and losing the ones she loves, so unless you know how to convince her she doesn't have to be afraid of this thing that is threatening both, you are *never* going to be able to bring her home."

No matter how hard the Davenports tried to convince her she was safe, Molly would keep running unless I found a way to prove to her she didn't have to.

I was pretty sure she'd been running since the day she left at eighteen.

"Say what you will about Molly," said Matthew, who seemed on the verge of laughing as he looked over at me, "but she certainly brought out a different Brennon from the one I've known the last year. And she's *way* better than Katie."

Had that been up for debate? Of course it had. I half wondered if these guys had placed bets on who I would end up with. Disconcerting as that was, I hoped they had at least laid down decent money.

"Is that a good thing or a bad thing?" I asked.

I definitely felt different from the man I'd been the last fifteen years, but I didn't feel like the kid I'd been in high school either. That Brennon had broken down when Molly left the first time, and I wasn't about to let that happen again. This person that I was becoming was someone new, and I had no idea what to do with that.

I just hoped this version of me was the one who could get Molly home.

"Definitely a good thing," Steve said as he wrapped an arm around my shoulders. "Even if that means I might get punched sometimes."

"Oh, is that what happened to your face?" Matthew asked. "Nicely done, Brennon!" He lifted his hand for a high five.

I kept my hands at my sides.

"Well that settles it," said Seth, clicking away at his computer, though he grinned as he probably imagined his brother-in-law getting punched. "*Five* tickets to Paris. Let the rescuing commence."

CHAPTER SEVENTEEN

"I'm not sure how I ended up driving us to the airport," Adam grumbled from the front seat.

Matthew was munching on a plastic bag of Cheerios, which he must have found in the back seat, since it had only recently been cleared of car seats. "I fully plan to be a good and mature adult when I become a father," he said, "but not until I actually have the part, my friend. So you get to do all the dadly things until then. It was Seth's idea," he added when he caught sight of Adam's raised eyebrow in the mirror. "And I'm smart enough to listen to the likes of Seth Hastings."

"I would have offered to drive," Steve said from the front seat, "but I forgot to renew my driver's license last year."

Seth, who had been scowling ever since Steve called "dibs" on the front seat, was wedged in between Matthew and me and hugging his knees because he barely fit, and he took a very deliberate breath that was probably meant to keep him from reaching forward and strangling Steve from behind.

He grumbled something to himself, and it sounded a whole lot like, "Why does Ashworth get to punch him and I can't?"

I forced myself not to grin.

"I don't see why we couldn't have hired a car and avoided parking," Adam continued.

"Clearly you've never experienced the beauty of a road trip," Matthew replied with a mouth full of cereal.

"We are literally driving twenty minutes," Adam said. "I'm not sure driving to the airport qualifies as a road trip."

"Molly and I once drove from San Leandro to Golden Gate Park," I remembered out loud. "Got snacks, made a mixtape, all the things. It's not really the distance that makes a road trip a road trip."

"The man has spoken," Matthew said, which apparently ended the argument.

Adam still seemed off-put when we arrived at the airport, and he pulled his bag onto his shoulder with such a sour expression that I had to wonder why he agreed to come at all. If his mood was going to make me feel like I had dragged him into my problems, this was going to be an exhausting journey.

"Follow me!" Steve said cheerily once we'd passed through the airport doors.

Seth, who was right behind me, literally growled and clenched the strap of his duffel. He was holding it so tight that I worried it would fall to pieces beneath his fingers.

"He's just messing with you," I said warily. "You know that, right?"

More than concerned for Seth's mood, I was worried about Steve's safety. He clearly loved annoying his brother-in-law, but Seth wasn't someone I personally wanted to cross, not when he was more than half a foot taller than me and at least fifty pounds of muscle heavier. Probably more. Steve, however, didn't seem afraid of the ex-soldier in the least, and I had no idea how.

Luckily for my friend, Matthew wrapped an arm around Steve and turned him in the right direction, and the rest of us followed the pair of them through the busy building.

"I know he isn't an idiot," Seth said after we'd gone through security. He had his eyes on Steve, who laughed about something with Matthew as they walked, and he couldn't seem to decide if he should be angry or not. His scowl was only half there.

For the first time since meeting Seth Hastings, I wanted to know what made the man tick. "So why do you let him bother you?" I asked. "You've known him more than a year now."

Seth shrugged one shoulder. "I guess it's because I know I can't intimidate him, and that means he's perfect for Lissa. Which drives me crazy."

"Wouldn't someone being perfect be a good thing?" I asked.

Chuckling, he looked ahead of us, where Matthew, Adam, and Steve walked together toward our gate looking like movie stars going down a red carpet because they were all so impressive. "I had hoped no one would be good enough for my little sister because she deserves so much, and then she went and found him by accident."

"With all due respect," I said, "isn't that how you met Catherine?"

They had been trapped together in a cabin by a blizzard, but I knew there was a lot more to it than that, including something about a near-death experience. I'd never been brave enough to ask. All I knew was their circumstances of meeting had been absolutely one in a million. I didn't know if they believed in fate, but coincidence couldn't explain everything.

It certainly couldn't explain how I had met Molly twenty-five years ago.

Seth immediately smiled, and he didn't have to say anything to tell me that he wouldn't have had his life go any other way.

"Well," said Matthew when we joined up with them at the gate, "since Seth is clearly the king of choosing flights we barely have time to make, they're boarding first class already. So if any of you want to back out of this adventure, now would be the time to do it."

Adam looked ready to take Matthew up on that offer and go straight back to the parking lot, and suddenly I was desperate to make sure he stayed, no matter how grumpy he might have been. I needed someone calm and collected, someone who didn't intimidate me and make me feel completely inadequate. Adam fit that role well.

So before he could say anything, I opened my mouth and said, "I really need all of you on this one."

Thank goodness the entire family was made up of people too good of heart to deny a request like that. Outside of the dreaded Uncle Milton, of course… After checking with his family to make sure none of them backed out, Matthew slung an arm around my shoulders and started leading me toward the gate. The others all followed suit without a word.

Somehow, I would figure out how to thank them for dropping everything to come to my aid, but for some reason, the Davenport family was big on giving but not so much on receiving. I would find a way to pay them back for their kindness, in a way they wouldn't be able to refuse, but for now, I would accept that they were just good people.

"So," Steve said once I'd helped him settle into the seat across from mine.

I had never flown first class before, and it was almost so overwhelming that I couldn't focus on him. Everything was so comfortable and spacious and everything economy class wasn't. Still, I tried to ignore the fact that I could lean my seat back *all the way down* and actually get some sleep during the eleven-hour flight, and I turned to face my friend.

"Why did you never tell me about Molly?" he asked then flinched, as if I might punch him again.

I had been waiting for that question pretty much since the day he met Molly outside my condo, and I was surprised it had taken him this long to ask it. I had met Steve only a few months after things ended with Molly, and we had been friends ever since. The topic of past loves had come up many times, but I had managed to keep Molly a secret.

Pretty impressive, I thought to myself, though that wasn't important at the moment.

"There's one thing you have to understand," I said. "I was in love with Molly for years. And when I finally worked up the courage to tell her after graduation, she told me she had never and would never feel the same way. She completely gutted me."

Steve gave me a commiserating wince but said nothing.

"I know it's not like when Amelia left you," I said, "and I should have been better, but I felt like I couldn't go on living the life I had been."

"No," he agreed, rolling his eyes, "it's not like when Amelia left me. My fiancée left because I was a jerk and refused to let her stay in my life when I clearly needed her, and now she's blissfully happy in her new marriage. What Molly did to you was a million times worse because you didn't deserve it. But do you really think she's happy because she left?"

I sighed. I didn't know what to think, and Steve didn't know Molly enough to ask questions like that. There was a lot to my backstory to explain, and though we had several hours of this flight to kill, my body was starting to shut down. I had been awake for over twenty-four hours and had been tased this morning, and I wasn't sure how much longer I could last. Especially now that things were in motion, there was nothing I could do to change our current path. I would end up in Paris whether I wanted to or not.

"I don't know," I said. "But when she left the first time, I didn't feel like I could be the same person anymore. That version of Brennon was gone, murdered by her rejection, and I had to become someone new. And the only way to do that was to leave behind my old life. All of it."

"I always wondered why you were so vague when you talked about life before Stanford," Steve said, and he smiled a little. "I figured you just wanted to keep yourself mysterious so the girls would be more interested."

"Until you realized I never went out with any of them," I said.

"Well, I had other theories about that one."

I grabbed my pillow and threw it at him, hitting him right in the face.

Laughing, he settled back into his seat as the plane thrummed to life and began moving slowly toward the runway. "For the record," he said, "I'm not saying the Brennon I've known the last fifteen years isn't worth knowing, but I like this new Brennon more. The real Brennon. Fists and all. You seem happier, all things considered. Free. No matter what happens in Paris, maybe Molly showing back up in your life isn't the end of the world."

I really hoped he was right.

Our taxi arrived in Paris in blazing sunshine on a lovely summer morning, which would have been great if I wasn't completely jetlagged with a pounding headache. Reclining seat or no, I hadn't slept much on the plane because I was too busy dreaming up a million different scenarios of what would happen if we actually found Molly.

Some of them had been rather pleasant, like the one where I saw her standing on a corner dressed like Audrey Hepburn and looking absolutely radiant before she caught sight of me and rushed into my waiting arms. Some of them had been less so, like the one where I was standing in the rain, looking into a fancy restaurant where she sat opposite some faceless foreign prince who had already done my rescuing for me.

As we gathered up our things from the taxi outside the hotel, Adam immediately pulled out his phone and lifted it to his ear. He'd been too far away for me to talk to him during the flight, but it didn't look like his mood had improved much. He seemed just as reluctant to be here as ever, which dampened my already dwindling spirits. I knew he probably felt obligated to help alongside his family, but I wouldn't have judged him if he'd stayed behind. He had already offered his house and his closet to me, and I couldn't expect anything more than that, no matter how much I wanted it.

As if he knew I was losing what little hope I had, Steve put his arm around my shoulders and took in an exaggerated deep breath. "I've missed this city," he said. "The sounds, the smells…"

All I heard were people shouting and cars rumbling past, and Paris smelled of nothing but cigarette smoke. "Are we in the same city?" I muttered.

Laughing, he shook his head. "It's not the greatest place on the surface level," he admitted. "Too many tourists. But it's the little things. You'll learn to appreciate them over time."

"Let's get ourselves checked in," said Matthew, though Adam had wandered a bit away to have his phone call. "And maybe get some food. I'm starving."

At those words, I suddenly felt like I hadn't eaten in days. And then I realized that was almost true, mainly because, first class or no, the airplane meal hadn't been all that large. "I'm pretty sure I could eat an entire menu," I said as my stomach growled at me, incredibly angry. "Maybe if Steve hadn't eaten my food on the plane…"

"You've got that backwards, buddy," Steve said, still holding onto my shoulders. "Now, if you could kindly direct me in the way of the door, I would be most grateful. Or maybe I'll just follow that hulking giant," he added, nodding toward Seth. "The guy's huge."

"Huge and hungry," said Seth, and he held the door open for us. "So maybe don't push your luck this morning, Evans."

I'd never considered the idea of teasing Seth Hastings—I cared about my life too much—but suddenly I wanted to know what Steve found so entertaining about it. It was probably the sleep deprivation talking. Seth was heading for the front desk, and I had a feeling he would find it particularly annoying if he didn't get the chance to show off his language skills and prove he was just as good as Steve.

"Seth is heading for the concierge straight ahead," I muttered to Steve, whose expression brightened almost immediately.

Separating himself from me, he hurried forward and almost tripped over Seth in his hurry to get past him and beat him to the desk. "*Bonjour!*" he said in the worst French accent I had ever heard, making Seth drop his face into his palm. And then, without missing a beat, he busted into what sounded like the most perfect French ever spoken by a foreigner, though I had no idea how true that was.

I knew all of four words in French: *Bonjour. Merci. Bon appetit.*

I figured the woman behind the desk spoke excellent English, but she lit up as she chatted with Steve. With a hotel this fancy, I figured she didn't often get to speak her native language with guests, particularly charming American ones.

"So now there are two of you?" Seth said suddenly, making me jump. I hadn't noticed him slink back to where I stood with Matthew, and I had no idea how a guy as big as him could be so sneaky.

"What?" I said, though my voice cracked a little. "I'm not scared of you," I added. "Just tired." And then I clenched my jaw before I said anything else. I probably shouldn't push my luck.

Seth narrowed his eyes and folded his arms, which made him more intimidating than he had a right to be. Seriously, how did a guy manage to win all the lotteries? Looks, money, size—he had it all, and it was little wonder Catherine had fallen in love with him.

"You're not scared of me, huh?" he asked and took a step closer.

I forced myself to stand my ground, though instinct told me to keep my distance. Run. I wasn't *really* afraid of Seth because I'd never given him a real reason to threaten me, but that didn't make him any less frightening. Still, Matthew was fighting back a laugh as he watched the two of us in anticipation, and I had the weirdest urge to push any buttons I could find. Steve did it for a reason, didn't he?

Spending any amount of time around Seth Hastings while running on very little sleep was definitely a horrible combination.

"No," I said and tried to stand a little taller, though my six-foot-even frame didn't compare to his. I so seldom felt short that I nearly winced as he leaned closer. Honestly, I couldn't remember the last time I'd actually gone to the gym I paid for every month, and Seth would take me down in an instant. "I'm not scared of you."

Steve had stopped talking to the concierge, and both of them were riveted on the pair of us. The woman couldn't seem to decide if she should reach for her phone and call the police or smile at the ridiculousness of what was happening.

Steve seemed to know what was about to happen and waited with bated breath.

I had no idea what I was doing or why it even mattered, but I stuck to my guns because I was tired of assuming I knew what people would say or how they would act. Hadn't I seen enough over the last few days for me to realize that I had no control over the actions of other people? I could only make my own choices, and it didn't matter how people might think of me.

I was me no matter what.

"Do you want to know why I'm not afraid of you?" I asked, and I tried to give Seth the most confident grin I could manage.

A smile tugged at the corner of his mouth. He was curious, but I sensed a bit of wariness there too. Did he know what I was about to say?

"Hey Steve," I said, "do you remember that night a few months ago when you heard a crash out in the hallway, and I went to go investigate?"

Seth's eyes went wide, his smile dropping. "Don't you dare, Ashworth."

Grinning, Steve stepped a little closer. "You said What's-His-Name down the hall dropped something when he was moving in."

"I did say that," I agreed, and I couldn't help but match Steve's smile. "But that might not have been the truth."

"I did think it was weird that someone would be moving in at eleven o'clock at night," Steve replied.

Seth dropped his arms to his sides. "Brennon."

"The power was out that night," I continued.

"Which I wouldn't know about," Steve said. "It's always pretty much completely dark at night."

"And that hallway doesn't have windows."

Steve's smile grew, and I was pretty sure he knew exactly where this story was going. "I didn't know that."

"So it was really dark."

"That can make things dangerous," Steve remarked.

"Ashworth," Seth growled, while Matthew burst into laughter behind him.

"Seth was coming up the stairs," I said. "Not sure why he was out so late."

"He was at an event with me," another voice chimed in. Adam had come in the door behind me, and he looked infinitely happier than he had before his phone call. He also seemed to know where the story was going and gave me a look that clearly said to finish what I was saying.

"Anyway," I said, "he had missed the last step and tripped."

"Please tell me he went straight through the wall," Steve said, as if nothing in the world could make him happier.

I couldn't help but laugh, and soon the rest of them joined in while Seth turned a surprising shade of red.

Maybe it was because he didn't want me to exaggerate, but Seth let out a sigh and finished the story for me: "My shoulder put a hole through the drywall," he said in resignation. "The super had to bring in a guy to fix it."

Almost gasping with laughter, Steve reached his arm out and moved closer until he caught hold of Seth's arm. "It's okay," he said, though he couldn't quite get the sympathetic tone he was trying for. "Not everyone is talented enough to navigate the void."

"And that," I finished, "is why I'm not afraid of you, Seth Hastings, because until that night, I had never seen a man who was so scared of the dark that he fought a wall when it touched him."

Matthew was laughing so hard he had to sit down on a nearby chaise, and Steve looked like Christmas had come early, even as Seth shrugged his hand away. And Adam?

Adam put a hand on my shoulder and smiled at me. "I like you, Brennon," he said quietly. "Sorry if I haven't been in the best of moods. I haven't been away from my family in more than two years, and it is remarkably hard to go a day without seeing them. A day without Lanna and my boys feels like a day without the sun."

I had to say it, no matter how much he wouldn't like it: "Thank you, Adam. For everything."

"Can we please just dump our stuff and go get some food?" Seth asked, though it was hard to hear him over Matthew's laughter.

"Happily," Steve replied, grabbing Matthew's arm and helped him to his feet. "I'll lead the way."

As Seth followed the pair of them with a groan, Adam touched my arm again and held me back. "You might not think it," he said, "but you deserve thanks too."

I stared at him. Why in the world would he have a reason to thank me? I'd been nothing but a burden, pretty much since the day we met. I'd moved into his house and exposed his family to someone who was being blackmailed, which was potentially more dangerous than any of us realized, and I couldn't think of a single thing I'd done that might have helped them.

Adam must have seen my confusion, because he smiled and nodded his head toward the three others. "I have *never* seen Matthew laugh like that," he said, and there was a weight to his words. "Not in the nine years I've known him. Since he met Indie, he's been happier than I've ever seen him, especially with that baby of his coming, but he still struggles. His life hasn't been easy, and he's lost so many people that I think he forgets *how* to be happy. He puts on a happy face, but sometimes I see that darkness of his creeping back in when he thinks no one is looking."

Matthew had always been Steve's friend, so I didn't know much about him. It was hard to imagine him not being his cheerful, light-hearted self, but I wasn't about to question Adam with something like this. Adam generally didn't take things lightly, particularly when it involved those he loved.

"Unfortunately, I think I'm out of stories," I muttered, though it wasn't a great response to something as heavy as that. This whole time I had known him, I'd thought Matthew could never be serious. Apparently it was the opposite.

Adam smiled and nudged me toward the elevators where the others were waiting. "I have a feeling we're only just getting started with your stories," he said, and then he looked up and raised an eyebrow. "Are any of you losers going to push the button, or are we just going to stand here and hope the elevator comes on its own?"

Soft-spoken Adam calling his family losers? Jokester Matthew being depressed? Super-soldier Seth being self-conscious of his size? Clearly, I had not spent enough time with the Davenport family, and as I watched them fight over who got to push the button as if they were all five years old, I realized how excited I was to actually get to know them.

Stranger still, I realized how much I wanted them to know who I was. Who I really was. Maybe Adam was right. Maybe I did have more stories to tell them. A lifetime of them.

CHAPTER EIGHTEEN

I was so anxious to get out and start the search for Molly that I barely took the time to rinse off in the shower, and then I was back down to the lobby to wait for the others. Everything looked so bright and cheery that it all looked wrong, and I couldn't help but pace the length of the room despite the concierge's eyes following me. The longer we took to get started, the harder Molly would be to find, and we were already several hours behind her. What if we couldn't find her? What if she had booked the flight to throw people off her true location? What if...

I paused when I realized someone else was in the glittering lobby with me, sitting in a somewhat shadowed corner by the luxury fountain on the opposite end from the front desk.

Matthew?

He had changed into fresh clothes, but he'd taken even less time to freshen up than I had. Not like that was a big deal, but the look on his face told me there was probably a good reason for that. He looked... Pensive. Worried. *Sad.*

Adam's words repeated in my head as I slowly approached, because if he hadn't been completely serious when he told me how hard it was for Matthew to be happy, I might have thought this expression Matthew wore now was something different. Matthew Davenport was never sad.

So I'd thought.

When I got close enough to be noticed, Matthew blinked and glanced over, and he didn't even attempt a smile. "Hey," he said.

I sat near enough to hear him but far enough that he wouldn't think I was trying to invade his space. This felt like one of those situations where I needed to be cautious, not because Matthew was dangerous but because the emotions just beneath the surface might be. Real feelings. Something told me Matthew liked those as much as I had the last fifteen years.

"So you've never been to Paris?" I said, hoping the easy topic would be a good way to ease into whatever conversation Matthew probably needed to have.

People like Matthew didn't generally sit in hotel lobbies, staring at fountains, because they liked the atmosphere.

He smiled gratefully, but only for a moment. "I'm not really big on vacations," he said. "I think you and I have that in common."

He wasn't wrong. "It's been fifteen years since I really did something for myself," I replied. "Sounds like we both need to work on that."

"Maybe."

If I could just know what was bothering him, I could find a way to help him talk about it. Molly was right when she reminded me that people needed to talk about things sometimes, but I was pretty sure Matthew didn't easily open up to people. If I had to guess, he hid behind the jokes and the smiles because it numbed the harder stuff, the stuff that could really get to a guy if left to fester.

If I had learned anything from Molly coming back, it was the fact that keeping your emotions and thoughts bottled up did nothing but make you miserable.

"Matthew?" I said, since I wasn't going to get any headway in this conversation if I didn't just ask.

He turned to me and spoke before I could say anything else: "Not that I don't think you're capable, but why didn't you trust us to be able to bring Molly home?"

I wasn't sure how to answer that beyond what I'd said this morning.

Likely realizing this, Matthew shook his head and tried again. "I know you think you're the only one who really gets her, and you're probably right. But you could have told us what to say to her or given us a note to give her, and you could have stayed where it was safe. My family… We're pretty persuasive, and we're good at helping people. Most of the time," he added with a slight quirk of his lips.

"It's not that I don't trust you," I said slowly. How could I even explain it when I didn't know the answer myself? "It's not just about what you guys are capable of, either, and…" I groaned. Of all the times to not know what I needed to say, it had to be now? This conversation felt important! "Molly is… She and I… I couldn't just…"

"You need to be a part of this." It wasn't a question, and something seemed to have clicked in Matthew's brain as he looked at me. Like he suddenly understood me.

I nodded. "I can't just sit on the sidelines when there's the chance I could lose her forever."

"You love her."

I thought I'd already established that. "Yes, I love her," I said. "But it's so much more than that."

Was it? I had no idea. But it seemed my mouth knew better than my head—that had been happening a lot lately—because I just kept talking, as if I'd known all along.

"I love her," I said, "but I haven't told her why. I haven't told her *anything*. And she needs to know how amazing she is. That she's worth saving. That even if we don't end up together, there's so much good in the world she can do, and I'm not going to let her sacrifice her future just because I didn't have the courage to get over myself and recognize she was in trouble."

Why was talking so exhausting? Sure, I hadn't slept for what felt like days, and jet lag was a serious energy killer even for the best man. But all of this self-discovery that kept happening was going to be the end of me, and I slumped in my seat a bit as I thought my own words over.

After everything, I hadn't even told her what she truly meant to me. Of course she'd run away.

Though Matthew smiled like he had the last time I'd spewed a bunch of words, he still had that underlying misery in his eyes, and he took a slow, careful breath. "I wish I'd been as brave as you," he said.

Was this him trusting me with his own vulnerability? I had no idea what he meant by it, but I knew he wasn't done.

He closed his eyes and seemed to be talking himself into speaking, and when he did speak, it was quiet. Low. "People have been rescuing me my whole life," he said to his knees. "And I'm not always sure I've deserved it. But I wish I… I've learned the hard way you've got to tell people what they mean to you before you no longer have the chance."

He's lost so many people that I think he forgets how to be happy, Adam had said.

I knew about Matthew's brother, Benjamin, but there had to be more to it than that. Who else had this man lost?

More importantly, what was I supposed to say to that? How could anything about my life's experiences help this man come to terms with the life he'd been given and the people he'd lost?

"Matt, you down here?"

A shout from Steve across the lobby saved me from fumbling through a poorly conceived pep talk, and I was pretty sure Matthew was as grateful for that as I was as he turned to greet Steve.

"What's up, Evans?" Matthew asked, loud enough to direct Steve our way.

Steve had his "bad idea" grin as he stumbled over to us. "Seth's just a few minutes behind me," he said. "Any idea how to hotwire an elevator?"

A grin spread across Matthew's face, which was a far better sight than the constant frown I'd gotten the last several minutes. But now was not the time for pranks.

Coughing, I shook my head and said, "Can we focus, please? Molly."

"Right," Matthew said, though he glanced over at the elevator with a bit of wistful longing as the doors chimed and opened for Seth and Adam. I was pretty sure he muttered, "Next time," to himself as he rose and put an arm around Steve's shoulders.

Those two were going to be the death of someone. Whether that someone was Seth or themselves, I had no idea.

"Cat just called," Seth told us when he got close. "She's got someone following a lead that could be promising, so I suggest we go get some food while we wait."

Food. Somehow, I had forgotten just how hungry I was, and I was glad I had these friends with me to keep things logical. Otherwise I would have been completely lost. My heart had taken charge, and despite the complications that came with that, I was one hundred percent okay with it.

Or I would be, as soon as I got myself some breakfast.

I wasn't kidding when I said I could eat half the menu, and I had to stop myself from ordering three different entrees at the cafe down the street because they all sounded so amazing that it was impossible to choose. I ended up asking Steve what he thought would be best, since he had been to Paris many times, and he suggested the crêpes.

"Can't go wrong with crêpes," he said then ordered in French something that didn't sound anything like crêpes.

Once our food arrived—Steve only got a croissant with jam on the side—I ate so fast that I almost didn't have the chance to really savor the food, though it was quite possibly the best thing I'd ever tasted. But eating so quickly left me sitting there growing more anxious by the second while I waited for the others to finish. Once breakfast was over, it would be time to move onto our next task: find Molly.

"Bren," Steve said after maybe five minutes of me sitting in silence, "you need to relax, buddy." He nudged his leg into mine, and I realized I'd been bouncing it.

"Sorry," I muttered, but the idea of relaxing was almost laughable. The seriousness of the situation was quickly building a suffocating weight over the top of me again. "I just wish I knew what I was doing," I admitted. "And I know Molly. If she's being blackmailed, it probably means she won't be easy to find. Maybe you guys don't understand, but when you don't have a lot, you learn to survive."

Seth cocked his head. "Meaning?"

How did I even put it into words that made sense? "Molly and I… We're not like you guys. We didn't grow up rich."

"Dude," Steve said with a scowl, reminding me that he had worked for everything he had.

Adam snorted a small laugh. "Before the art thing, I was as poor as they come."

"Homeless," Matthew said cheerfully, raising his hand.

"It's not as easy as it sounds," Seth added.

There were way too many things to unpack from those responses, particularly Matthew's, but I couldn't focus on that when I was so close to the end of this ride. As soon as we found Molly—with this family on my side, I knew it wouldn't take long—it would be up to her to decide what happened next. No matter what I said, it would ultimately be her choice to stay or go.

And that unknown decision did nothing to help my nerves.

"It's not just that," I muttered. "I don't have the confidence all you—"

Their laughter cut me off, and when Matthew grinned along with the rest of them, I couldn't be too embarrassed. Not if it helped him.

"Brennon," Matthew said and put a hand on my shoulder.

It was strange interacting with him like this, even knowing what I knew about him now. But I was pretty sure he trusted me now, and that brought me some much-needed faith in this whole rescue thing actually working.

"I know you've got this thing where you're convinced you understand people," he continued, "but I'm pretty sure you've got your own mask, just like the rest of us."

I definitely had a mask, and the thought of dropping it hadn't gotten any easier since coming to Paris. It was terrifying even if I knew I had nothing to fear from this family. After living with that mask for fifteen years, I couldn't just flip a switch and go without it. I was trying, but it wasn't easy to just let myself say the things I wanted to say.

Seth leaned forward, his smile less smug than I was used to. Hopefully that wasn't because he was still humiliated from my story at the hotel. "Look," he said, and his voice was softer too. "Take it from a guy who can barely sleep without his wife breathing next to him: no one is as confident as he might look on the outside. We've all got our demons."

I understood they had their problems, but it was hard to consider it the same thing. Fifteen years of living beneath the rock Molly's rejection had pushed me under would take a long time to recover from. Despite what I was learning about the Davenports, I knew they were all too strong to lose their battles.

"I still get nervous when I have to talk to strangers," Adam said, and he gave me a knowing smile when I looked at him in surprise. His whole job as an art dealer was talking to strangers, and he had practically built an empire around it. "I think of a million different ways to say something, and I'm always terrified I'm going to make a fool of myself and people will realize I have no idea what I'm doing."

"I'm going to be a dad in just a few months," Matthew said. "And I have never been more scared in my life because I have no idea if I can be good enough for my kid. I barely feel worthy to be Indie's husband, and throwing a baby into the mix?" He laughed a little. "That's terrifying."

"The point," said Steve, his gaze as fixed on me as it could possibly be, "is that you don't have to have all the answers. You don't have to fix things on your own. But you do have to trust that no matter what, if you just keep trying, things will work out."

"Especially if you let your family help you out," Matthew added.

I stared at them all, trying to understand how they could possibly talk like this, even after everything Molly had done and all of the lies I'd told, mostly about myself. I still didn't fully believe I deserved their friendliness.

"I'm not your family," I mumbled. *No matter how much I wish that were true.*

Steve let out a sigh so loud that a few other people in the cafe looked up. "Brennon," he said, "if you haven't realized by now you're like a brother to me, then I'm a little worried about your mental capacity."

"And that makes you my brother by default," said Seth.

"And my cousin," said Matthew.

"And mine," said Adam.

Steve grinned. "So basically you're stuck with us for the rest of your life, pal. Deal with it."

If I wasn't sitting in a French bistro surrounded by people, I might have broken down and sobbed because it felt like so much weight had suddenly disappeared from my shoulders. I could breathe again, and I didn't feel like I was drowning anymore. The Davenport family hadn't just given me a hand up to the surface; they were driving a speedboat and had pulled me onboard.

"Well," said Seth, rising to his feet, "now that we've got that all settled, how about we go find ourselves a runaway, huh?"

"Do you really think we can find her?" I asked. This was Molly we were talking about, and she had more street smarts than anyone I knew. She wasn't going to make this easy. "What if she doesn't *want* to be found? I'll just be getting in her way, and—"

"That woman loves you, Brennon," Steve said firmly. "She wouldn't have left if she didn't. Of course she wants you to find her."

Matthew was the last to stand, which made his words feel extra important when he said, "Don't be like me, Brennon. Unsaid words are a heavy thing to carry with you."

I shut my mouth before another ridiculous excuse slipped out. He was right. No matter what Molly decided, I would forever regret not telling her the things she needed to hear if I didn't suck it up and be brave, like she wanted me to be.

It was just like Jake had said when I was trying to figure out that whole thing with Jefferson at work. Wow, that felt like a long time ago… *Initiative*, he had said. If I wanted something, I had to open my mouth and say so. Otherwise, I could only blame myself when I didn't get the promotion or the newer model of car instead of the one I was sold or the love of my life telling me she loved me too.

Besides, Molly needed to know how important she was. Not just to me but to the world. And I was the only one who could make her understand that.

"Okay," I said and took a deep breath. "How do we find her?"

It was almost two in the morning back in California, but Catherine answered Seth's call immediately. He barely said anything, mostly just listened, but the longer the call went on, the tenser he became. By the time he hung up, he looked ready to shatter his phone like he had the glass at dinner on Sunday.

"That's a good news face," Matthew said warily, and he'd grown more serious too. Seeing him stand in the same stance as Seth reminded me again that he'd been a soldier too, and he was surprisingly intimidating when he wanted to be. "What did Kitty learn?"

Seth shook his head, and we all leaned a little closer, knowing he would be talking quietly. We stood in a huddle in a little square down a side street, where it was quieter, but Seth still glanced around us to make sure we wouldn't be overheard by anyone walking past.

"So it turns out Molly is literally my guardian angel," he said with a frown.

My stomach flipped. "Uh, what?"

"Back when I was…" His eyes darkened, and he shook his head again. "Laos," he said and looked at Matthew.

Matthew nodded. "Seth was captured by a terrorist group six years ago," he explained to Steve and me, and I could tell Steve was just as thrown by the news as I was. This information wasn't something small. "The People's Liberation Army. He managed to escape to California, but one of the terrorists followed him and was the one who kidnapped Catherine in Tahoe. We were lucky we found him before he did more damage than he did."

Catherine had been kidnapped? What else didn't I know about this family?

"The rest of the group would have come after me," Seth said, and his voice shook a little. He either didn't notice or didn't care. "But a photographer had collected enough intel on the group to get them indicted. Said photographer's identity was never disclosed, but…"

My stomach didn't just flip this time; it seemed to twist itself into so many knots that I felt sick. "Molly," I whispered. She had mentioned Laos at dinner, and that was when Seth broke the glass. It all made sense now.

Seth nodded. "Unless Catherine's wrong," he said, "and she's never wrong, the blackmailer is using her identity as leverage. There's a chance they didn't capture the whole organization, so there might be someone out there who could get to Molly and anyone she cares about if the blackmailer chooses to inform them."

That was why she ran. If she had stayed, that would have put me in danger too.

"I have to find her," I said, and I had never needed to do anything more. Looking at each man in turn, I silently begged them to help me.

"*Le Regent Montmartre*," Seth said, which must have been the name of a hotel.

"Are you sure?" I asked. If there was even the slightest chance a terrorist group was after Molly, I couldn't afford to waste time checking random hotels.

Seth shrugged one shoulder, his hands stuffed in his pockets. "Cat is never wrong," he said again.

We arrived at the hotel twenty minutes later. I practically shoved my way out of the taxi and rushed inside, but as soon as my feet hit the lobby floor, I froze. I stopped so suddenly that Seth bumped into me and nearly knocked me over, but he balanced the both of us and muttered an apology.

"I'll figure out which room she's in," he said.

I grabbed his arm. "Wait."

Matthew and Adam, both with confused expressions, seemed to think Seth was the best option for getting information. To my relief, Steve gave me a reassuring smile that meant he was waiting for my explanation before he offered his opinion. I just had to figure out my explanation.

"She'll have safeguarded against you," I said. When Seth frowned, I shook my head. "Not you specifically," I clarified. "I mean, she'll have warned the front desk about anyone coming in and demanding to know where she's staying. She did it once when we were fourteen, and she decided it was a great idea to run away and join the circus. She told the front desk she was hiding from an ex-boyfriend, and they didn't ask questions, just lied and said they hadn't seen her when her dad went looking for her."

Thankfully, she'd given up on the circus dream the moment she remembered there were clowns in the circus, or I might never have had the chance to realize I'd fallen in love with her. Never in a million years would I have thought I would be grateful for a clown, but there I was.

"Let me talk to the desk," Steve said.

But I shook my head. "No, this is my fight now," I said, almost to myself. The Davenports had gotten me this far, but I had to find Molly on my own. "You guys look terrifying all standing in a group like that. Go wait outside or something."

Matthew grinned, Adam blushed, and Seth and Steve glanced at each other as if trying to decide who was more terrifying out of the two of them.

"We'll be across the street," Adam said just as Seth opened his mouth to say something. "Call if you need us."

As soon as they were gone, I swallowed and approached the desk, searching desperately in my database of personalities for the best thing to use in this situation. Most likely the guy behind the front desk didn't even speak English, but if he did, how could I possibly convince him that I wasn't here to endanger Molly? I had to make sure he understood that I was only here to protect.

"Uh, *bonjour*," I said and cringed because I couldn't have sounded more American if I'd tried. I probably should have had Steve teach me some phrases on the plane ride over. "I'm, uh, I'm looking for my friend."

"*Oui?*" The guy was younger than I would have expected in a Parisian hotel, but what did I know about Paris? Pretty much nothing. "*Quelle pièce, monsieur?*" I had no idea what that meant, and thankfully he repeated himself in thickly accented English: "Which room?"

How could I possibly get this across?

"Look," I said, stuffing my hands into my pockets because I thought that might be the least threatening stance I could take. "I know she probably told you that someone might come after her and that you can't tell anyone that she's here, but I have to find her. Please. She's about five and a half feet tall, and I have no idea what that is in centimeters, but she has curly blonde hair and the face of someone who can brighten even the darkest of days and I can't go another day without her in my life because she's the whole reason I am who I am. She's the reason I can be myself even if I can't be me around anyone else, and she makes me feel brave, and honest, and like the world can't push me down because as long as I have her by my side it doesn't matter what happens because we can get through it together. She makes me better. And I have to find her. I have to tell her that she doesn't have to run anymore because I will always be right there by her side like she always was for me. I will *always* love her."

I took a breath and realized that the desk attendant had shifted back several inches, and he was probably terrified by the wave of English I'd just thrown at him.

"You probably have no idea what I'm saying, do you?" I asked, wilting. I reached into my back pocket and pulled out the photograph I had stuffed in there this morning. It had seen better days, but the sight of it brought a smile to my face before I showed it to the desk attendant. "Do you understand?" I whispered.

"You talk much," he said, nodding, "but I understand. *L'amour?*"

I nodded back, only partially convinced that meant love. "The woman I love," I agreed. "Please help me find her."

He still seemed hesitant, but I prayed he could sense my sincerity. "Wheat," he said finally.

I stared at him.

"Uh." He thought for a moment then held up eight fingers.

"Room eight," I breathed, understanding. "Thank you. *Merci.*" I clasped his hand for a second then ran, taking the stairs two at a time to the second floor. Passing a maid's cart, I found number eight and tried opening the door, though that was idiotic because of course it was locked, and then I knocked as loudly as I could.

"Molly!" I shouted. "Molly, it's Brennon. Open the door! Please."

Two other doors opened, and I gave their occupants quick glances just to make sure they weren't Molly. Knowing her, she might have convinced another guest to switch rooms with her.

AS LONG AS YOU LOVE ME

"Molly, I know you're in there!"

Something shattered inside the room, and I froze, listening hard for any other sounds. It hadn't sounded like anything large, but I had definitely heard something break on the other side of the door. I glanced around the hallway and spotted a ring of keys sitting on the maid's cart. I could barely believe I could be so lucky, but I snatched it and stuffed it into the lock, begging the universe to send me something good. The third key I tried turned, the lock clicked, and I tossed the keys back toward the cart and slipped inside before the maid came out of whichever room she was currently cleaning.

Molly's room was empty, the curtains drawn and the lights off. But a glass sat broken in the sink, a couple pieces of ice slowly sliding along the edge of the sink toward the basin. My heart racing, I pulled open the closet and checked every corner, and then I turned toward the window.

I have a bad feeling about this.

Nudging the curtain aside, I found the glass door open onto the little balcony outside, but the balcony was empty. We were too high up for her to have jumped to the street level below, and my hands started to shake. I took one step out onto the balcony and turned.

"Molly," I gasped.

She had pulled herself onto a tiny ledge on the wall, probably to try to get to the next room over, but she hadn't gotten very far. She stared back at me with terror in her eyes, her whole body trembling as she gripped a thin outcropping that ran the length of the wall level with her chin. "Bren," she whispered.

She was too far for me to grab, though that didn't stop me from trying. I leaned as far as I could and reached.

"Grab my hand, Molly," I said weakly.

Her fingers were white from gripping the brick. "You shouldn't be here."

"Molly, take my hand. Please."

"It's not safe."

"Mol. Let me help you."

She shook her head. "I don't deserve it," she said. She glanced down and paled as she realized just how high up she was. "You shouldn't be here."

She was slipping. I knew she was. "I am not going to watch you fall," I growled. "Take my hand before I climb out after you."

Though her eyes went wide, she nodded a little and took a couple of quick breaths as she readied herself. But then she grew still again. "I can't," she said. "Brennon, I can't."

I reached out farther, hooking my feet onto the railing to steady myself. "It's okay," I told her, though it was hard to believe my own words. If she fell... "You're going to be fine. Just take my hand, okay?"

She gripped the brick tighter, her fingers going white. "I can't do it."

I could barely breathe, but I forced myself not to imagine the worst. I had to focus on the now, on what I could control. "Jump," I said. "I'll catch you."

"I can't." Tears slid down her face, and her arms were shaking so badly that I worried she didn't have enough strength to jump.

I was *not* going to lose her again.

"Molly, jump!"

She did, pushing herself sideways toward me with a shriek.

I caught her arm and pulled, leaning back into the hotel room, and she crashed into me, knocking me into the curtains and tearing them from the rod as we fell to the floor in a heap. I ignored the sharp pain in my shoulder from landing on it and hugged her against me. We lay there, tangled in curtains, and I almost couldn't let myself believe we'd made it. That she was okay.

Molly sobbed into my chest, and I held her tighter, refusing to let go. "You're safe," I whispered, though I wasn't sure I would survive much longer with my heart pounding as fast as it was.

"No, I'm not," she whispered back. Against my silent protests, she pulled herself free and crawled away from the window and toward the little bed, falling against it as she continued to cry. "I'm never going to be safe. I didn't do what he wanted, and now he's..."

Now that she was no longer hanging off the side of a building, I could breathe again, and I sat up and took her in. She looked awful, exhausted and dirty and wearing what looked like stuff she'd found in tourist shops or at the airport. She was scared, and I wished I could make her understand that I would never let anything happen to her. I could say the words, but she would never believe me. I had to prove it to her somehow.

"How did you find me?" she asked after a moment.

I swallowed. "The Davenports."

Turning even more pale than she already was, Molly hugged her arms around herself. "You shouldn't be here, Bren."

"I know you're being blackmailed."

"What?"

I sat up a little straighter. "Mol, we're not going to let him get to you."

Whoever he was, I was going to spend every ounce of energy I had to keep this girl safe.

"He knows too much," she moaned and curled up in a tighter ball. "He threatened my dad, so I couldn't… He's powerful, Brennon, and you shouldn't be here. You need to leave, because if your friends can find me, so can he."

"I am not letting you push me away again." My words came out rough, which surprised both of us, but I let them hang in the air between us so she would understand that I meant them. "Mol, you left me. Again. You said you wouldn't hurt me, and you left."

Tears spilled down her cheeks as she looked at me. "I said I never *wanted* to hurt you," she corrected. "I never said I wouldn't. I could have killed you, Brennon. Your apartment. It wasn't supposed to—"

"Who's threatening you, Molly?"

She shook her head. "It's better if you don't know," she said. "You need to leave before he finds me. I won't let anything happen to you, and if he finds out you—"

"Who is he?"

"Bren."

"Molly."

She shook her head, but she'd lost any force behind the movement. She wanted to tell me, I knew she did, and I wanted her to trust me. After all these years, didn't she realize I would always get her out of the trouble she couldn't get out of herself?

"Molly, let me help you," I begged.

She bit her lip. "Milton Davenport."

I froze as I took in that name because it was so far from what I expected that I was almost convinced I'd heard her wrong. There was a weird buzzing in my ears, and though Molly still looked terrified, I suddenly felt like laughing.

"Milton Davenport," I repeated. "As in Catherine's dad?"

Nodding, she wiped her cheeks as she realized that I wasn't nearly as worried as she was. "He said he would tell the People's Liberation Army that I was the one who exposed them if I didn't ruin the rest of his family. That's why I was so desperate to figure out what they were hiding. But I couldn't do it. Not after I met them and realized how much they mean to you."

Milton wanted to see his family fall to ruin just like he had. That was all this was, and it felt like the universe had finally given me a chance to make things right between us. My whole body relaxed, leaving me a lump of exhausted limbs on the floor.

"They're buying a house in Paris," I said and couldn't help but grin. "Mol, they don't have a sinister bone in their bodies. It would take a whole lot more than a little secret to ruin that family."

"So I'm doomed," she replied, dropping her head onto the bed.

"No," I replied and crawled over to her so I could take her hand. "Mol, you're fine."

"How can you be so sure?" she asked.

My smile grew wider. "Because downstairs is the one guy Milton is truly terrified of." She looked confused, so I pulled her up to her feet and took her other hand before I said, "I'm guessing you've never seen Seth Hastings when he catches sight of his father-in-law. Davenport isn't going to go anywhere near you when he finds out who's on your side."

To my utter relief, Molly agreed to go down and meet up with the Davenport men so we could make a plan, though she still seemed to think she was in danger.

I may have only seen the guy a couple of times, but despite being a despicable human, Milton Davenport was pretty harmless. Whether he actually had contact with terrorists, I didn't know, but I did know that as soon as Seth found out his father-in-law was behind the blackmail, it was game over for Milton.

He had already set fire to the bridges, but there was no way he would get anywhere close to his family after pulling a stunt like this.

I kept my hand tight around Molly's as we took the stairs down to the lobby. There was still the chance she would try to run, and this time I was determined to make sure she didn't. However safe she thought she was keeping me by staying away, there was nowhere I would rather be than by her side. I just had to hope she felt the same way about me, or things were going to get interesting really soon.

I wasn't going to let her go so easily this time.

"They're in that cafe," I said when we reached the sidewalk outside. I pointed across the street and gave her a reassuring smile. "Everything's going to be okay, Mol. I promise."

She didn't look convinced, but she gave my hand a little squeeze. I hoped that meant she at least wanted to believe me.

"Come on," I said and pulled her across the street.

Just as we reached the other side, something slammed me into the wall. I hit the stone hard and stumbled, my hand slipping free of Molly's.

She screamed, and though I was disoriented, I followed the sound and felt my heart stop for a second when she disappeared into an alley.

"Molly!"

I burst into a run and turned the corner, and without knowing what I was doing, I tackled the unfamiliar man who had grabbed her. We hit the ground and I rolled over top of him, but he ignored me and went after Molly again. I leapt and grabbed his legs. He kicked, catching my cheek with his boot, but I ignored the stinging pain and used his leg to pull myself up on top of him again, trying to keep him down. He rolled and pinned me, and I flinched as he raised his fist.

"Try it and you're dead," said a low voice over our heads.

I should have been glad to see Seth and Matthew with their guns. They had probably just saved my life, but the sight of Molly wrapped in Adam's arms and Steve talking in rapid French to whom I hoped were the police on the phone made my blood burn hot. As Matthew gestured for the assailant to stand up against the wall, I scrambled up to my feet and tried not to scowl at my friends.

"I had him," I grumbled. I knew that was a lie, but I didn't like knowing I hadn't been able to save Molly on my own. If I couldn't protect her against a man who was clearly just a hired thug, since he didn't resist when Matthew shoved his face into the wall, how could I possibly convince Molly I could keep her safe?

"I know you did," Seth said. His gun was still trained on the thug, but his focus was on me. "You okay, Ashworth?"

I was about to mumble a response when a flurry of blonde hair slammed into me, almost knocking me to the ground again.

"You saved me," Molly whispered into my neck. And then she leaned up and kissed me, which was quite possibly the only form of gratitude I would accept from her ever again.

I momentarily forgot about anything else in the alley.

CHAPTER NINETEEN

The Paris police took care of the thug, who was an American muscle man sent over by Davenport to scare Molly into returning to her task. As soon as they drove off with him, Seth grabbed his phone and moved to the other end of the alley so we wouldn't hear what he said. By the look on his face, however, I was pretty sure he was making sure Milton Davenport knew he had no power over Molly or anyone else he might choose to threaten.

"I almost feel bad for my uncle," Matthew said as we all watched Seth make his threats.

Adam raised an eyebrow. "Seriously?"

"I said almost." A little smile on his face, Matthew folded his arms and explained, "If he had just figured out that we Davenports are all about being decent human beings now, maybe he could have become part of the family again. But no, now he's all alone because his third wife was smart enough to realize no amount of money is worth being married to a turd like that. I hope she took everything he had left in the divorce. If he even had anything left at that point."

"Molly?" I whispered. She was shaking in my arms, her face buried in my neck, and she'd been silent for over twenty minutes.

"You should take her inside," Steve suggested. "They have some fantastic tea, and I would guess she'd like to sit down."

I looked down at her, a question in my gaze, and she nodded. I gently led her into the cafe where the Davenports had been waiting for us, and we took seats in the most secluded corner. Molly stayed pressed up against my side, and I wasn't complaining, but she did look horribly pale.

"Are you okay?" I asked her after we ordered some hot chocolate. "What can I do?"

"Is it really over?"

"It's really over."

She dropped her head onto my shoulder, probably completely exhausted. "Your family is amazing, Brennon," she sighed.

They're not my family. But I stopped myself from saying that because it wasn't true. Not anymore. "Yeah," I said as I wrapped my arm around her. "They are." And in a strange way, I might not have realized it if she hadn't given me a reason to run off to Paris on a whim.

How was it Molly made my life better even when it seemed she was making it worse?

"You're amazing too," Molly said.

I smiled. "I don't know about that."

"Brennon." Pulling out of my hold, she turned to face me and put her hands on either side of my face. "I told you already. You need to stop thinking you're not worth being your whole self. The world needs Brennon Ashworth."

As much as I felt extremely bolstered by her words—as much as they were probably true—I didn't care about the world. "But do you need me?" I asked.

I really didn't like the expression on her face. Why would she feel sad when we were coming to our happy ending?

"Brennon," she said.

"Well," Seth announced loudly, leading the rest of the Davenports through the door and coming to a stop in front of our table. "I never thought I'd say this, but I am happy to be the son of Gordon Hastings. Like I suspected, threatening to divulge government secrets— like the identity of a certain photojournalist—to a known terrorist group, whether or not one has contact with an actual member of said group, falls under Homeland Security. And my dear dad is more than happy to take care of your little problem, Molly."

She sat up, her eyes wide as she stared at him. "I'm safe?" she asked. Seth's smile was warm. "You're safe."

It was more painful than I wanted to admit that she hadn't believed it when I told her that, but I couldn't fault her for trusting Seth's opinion.

"Also," Seth continued, leaning his elbows on the table so he wasn't hulking over us, "I have to say thank you, Miss Piper. Your bravery saved my life, and Catherine's. And we'll never know how many more."

As Molly started to cry again, Steve nudged Seth's arm. "Jean-Marc has the deed ready for us," he said quietly. "How about we drop Bren and Molly off at the hotel because they both look ready to fall asleep, and we can go finish this nightmare before our wives kill us."

"An excellent idea," Matthew said. "You may be blind, my friend, but you certainly see clearly."

"And then we can get them home," Adam added, giving me a warm smile.

Molly stiffened, and though she wasn't even looking at me, I could tell exactly what she was about to say, and I cut her off.

"No," I growled, and both Steve and Adam jumped because I was louder than I'd meant to be. "Molly, you have a home."

She frowned. "How did you—"

"I don't care if you feel like you're on your own, because you're wrong." Sitting didn't feel powerful enough. Forcing myself to my feet, I pushed Seth out of the way so I could stand directly across the table from her.

She looked at me with wide, teary eyes, her curly hair in disarray and her mouth hanging open because she probably hadn't expected anger from me either.

Despite all of that, she was the most beautiful person I'd ever seen.

"Let me be your home," I said.

The Davenports all froze around me, but I kept my focus on Molly, leaning my hands on the table so she would know I was absolutely serious.

She pulled her eyebrows together. "Brennon, I'm no good for you."

This from the woman who refused to let me hide the real me? "You're perfect for me."

Frowning, she tried another excuse. "I barely stay in one place for more than a couple of weeks."

"I don't care."

"You love San Francisco."

"I do," I admitted.

"And I love traveling the world."

"I haven't seen much of the world."

"What about your job? The promotion? Helping Jake become a broker?"

There were a lot of things in there, primarily how she knew my assistant's aspirations, but I ignored the fact that she had probably had many a chat with Jake and had likely pushed him to help me get promoted. There were more important things at stake.

"Molly," I said, making sure I had her full attention. "I need you to listen to me, okay? You think you're no good for me, but you help me grow in ways I can't by myself or with anyone else. You make me better. And contrary to popular belief, I am perfectly capable of spending time alone now and then." I threw a scowl to Steve, who pretended he had no idea I was glaring at him even as he grinned a little. "I actually enjoy it. You and I have always worked better as a duo, and you know it, and I *know* you could never be happy living your whole life alone."

And now for the most important part.

"You spend so much time helping everyone else see their potential and worth, but you don't realize you need someone on your side cheering you on too. You were worth rescuing when we were kids, and you're worth rescuing now, and I will rescue you for the rest of your life if you'll let me. Marry me, Molly. Marry me, and I will tell you every day for eternity how much I love you and want you at my side."

The words came out without me planning them. Without me even really thinking them. And yet, as I stood there, my shocked brothers behind me and an even more shocked Molly in front of me, I had no regrets about any of those words.

I meant each and every one of them.

CHAPTER TWENTY

"**M**r. Ashworth? There's a Colin Donovan here to see you."
I looked up at Sierra as she stood in the doorway. She'd been my assistant for two months now, and I hadn't been able to convince her to call me Brennon. She was too terrified of doing something wrong, and maybe that was my own fault for hiring a twenty-two-year-old. Still, when she'd applied at Bay Bridge Investments, Elliot Hatch down the hall from me had been about to claim her, and there was no way I was letting him near the girl. Not this soon after his divorce, anyway.

I had told her I had a better opportunity for her, and thankfully she had taken it.

"Go ahead and show him in," I said and smiled at her.

At least she smiled back. "Right this way, Mr. Donovan," she said, holding the door open for my friend.

I stood to greet him but forgot to hold out my hand for him to shake when I saw him. I wasn't entirely sure what it was, but he looked different. I'd seen him just a few months earlier, but now that he was back from his summer vacation with his daughter, something had definitely changed.

Perhaps it was the scenery, which Donovan took in with a quick and keen eye. Always the tech CEO, Colin Donovan. He was not one for wasting time.

"I liked your old office more," he said with a slight frown. "You had a better view."

I grinned. "I don't think Bay Bridge would have taken kindly to me setting up my own firm in their building," I replied. "It was hard enough to convince them to let me quit."

I gestured for Donovan to sit then did the same.

"Jake didn't want to come with you?"

"Jake was too good to be an assistant. He took my job when I left."

In fact, I had spent three days on the phone convincing a reluctant Jefferson to promote Jake, and within a week my old assistant had blown the other brokers out of the water, outperforming all of them.

Donovan nodded and took another look around my little office, which wasn't like him. He was generally a calm and collected guy, but he sat tense in his chair and seemed distracted. Something was bothering him, and I very much hoped it didn't have to do with his money.

"You didn't have to follow me and leave Bay Bridge, you know," I told him. It still blew my mind that several other clients had done the same as him and dropped my old firm to come hire me as soon as they heard I'd gone freelance. "You could have had Jake be your broker, and he would have—"

"I don't care about the company," he said without hesitation. "My loyalty was never to Bay Bridge Investments. I'm just glad you're still brokering, because I would have hated to lose *you* too."

Lose *me* too? There was definitely something bothering him. I hadn't thought anything could bother the unshakeable Colin Donovan, who was probably one of the most influential people in San Francisco right now and had the world at his fingertips, but he was entirely on edge and barely made eye contact with me. That alone told me he probably needed to talk.

"You don't seem very much like yourself today," I said. "What happened over the summer?"

He looked up, and an array of emotions crossed his face. "That's a long story," he said with a sigh. The guy looked exhausted, like he had been through the gamut of summertime catastrophes and needed a vacation after his vacation.

"I have plenty of time," I told him.

But he shook his head and got to his feet. "I don't," he said. "I really just stopped by to say congratulations."

I followed his gesture to my left hand, where my silver wedding band sat so comfortably that I honestly forgot it was even there. Molly had put it there a month after Paris, and I would never grow tired of seeing it.

"Thanks," I said, knowing I was probably smiling like an idiot.

"I must admit, though," he said. "I was surprised when I heard the news. I didn't think you were dating anyone."

He had a very telling frown on his lips, and I wasn't sure he was aware of it. Maybe I was wrong, but I had a feeling his current woes were not unlike what mine had been a couple of months ago.

"Trust me," I said, still grinning. "I'm surprised as well. So you really don't have time to talk? You might need it."

He shook his head, but then he matched my smile. He didn't do that often, smiling, and it was good to see. "Maybe I'll tell you my story sometime, though," he said. "Then you can introduce me to your partner in crime."

He left with a distracted wave, and I pulled out my phone so I could look at the picture Molly had sent me that morning. She was somewhere in the Amazon covering a story on some illegal burning of the forest, but the picture of her with a sloth on her shoulders told me she was keeping her distance from the conflict and staying safe.

In the month and a half since our wedding, Molly had only been home for a few weeks as she followed story after story, but I wasn't worried. We talked every day, and she constantly told me how much she loved me as if she was afraid I might forget her while she was away. I missed her, but no matter how far away she went, I knew she would always come back home.

As my stomach rumbled, signaling the arrival of lunchtime, I tried not to dwell on how much I also missed Jake and his ability to keep me fed at all times, and called through the open door. "Hey Sierra?"

She didn't respond, and I frowned. She was always so quick to answer, as if afraid she'd be let go if she wasn't absolutely perfect. Was something wrong? I headed for the door to check on her, but as soon as I got into the front room, I stopped dead.

My assistant was there, perfectly fine, but she was standing next to her desk and talking to—

"Molly," I gasped then grinned when she sent me one of her stunning smiles. "But I thought you were—"

"I came back early."

"But—"

"Just kiss me, you idiot."

She didn't have to tell me twice. As Sierra busied herself at her desk, I pulled Molly into my office and closed the door so I could wrap her up in my arms without wondering what my assistant might think. I had gotten so much better since Molly came back into my life, but sometimes I still forgot there was a power in recognizing just how little someone else's opinion mattered.

I had to remind myself that I could kiss my wife however much I wanted.

"Looks like you missed me," Molly whispered against my mouth, and I kissed her again before she could say anything else.

Was it just me, or had she gotten even more beautiful?

Eventually I let her go, and she looked around my little office with her smile wide and warm. "You've added more pictures," she said and grinned when she caught sight of one when we were twelve and had spent a summer pretending we were pirates. I had lived in that massive hat, and she had committed to continually wearing the eye patch until her dad worried she would damage her eyesight.

"I'm trying to remember it all," I said.

She paused at a Halloween photo taken the year we'd decided to be ninjas, and she started humming as she smiled at it. It only took a few seconds before "Everybody Was Kung Fu Fighting" started playing at full volume in my head, and I smacked her.

"I hate you," I groaned, because I could already tell that song would be stuck in my head for hours, exactly as she hoped.

Laughing, she slipped her arms around my neck and grinned up at me. "You make it too easy," she replied. "Let's go get some lunch. You're probably starving."

How was I supposed to resist an invitation like that?

Oh, how I loved this woman who knew me better than anyone, and I told her so with a kiss that felt like it contained the world. With the way Molly kissed me back, it probably did.

The End

Special sneak peek of Book 6 in the Simple Love Series,

Dear Dalia

EXCERPT FROM *DEAR DALIA*

Just as I was about the lead the girls off to our cabin, a wave from the flagpole caught my eye. Linda gestured me over, looking flustered. Man, she was really starting to cramp my style.

"Hey Julia," I said quickly, "lead the way, will you? I'll be right behind you."

Julia stood straight and proud, her grin infectious. "Aye aye, Captain!" she said with a flourished salute. "This way to Cabin Three, you scalawags!" And she marched off, a trail of girls following close behind.

I watched Macy Donovan for just a moment as she took up the rear, but only a few seconds after the march began, Kristy Kane took her by the arm and started chatting with her as they went.

Good girl.

Linda had gone into the rec room, which meant she was probably in her office. As girls around me said their last goodbyes to parents and hurried off after their counselors, I slipped across the field and hurried inside, determined to make this chat last as short a time as possible so I didn't miss too much of the start of summer bonding between my girls. It was one of my favorite parts of the year!

I started talking before I stepped through Linda's door, deciding I had best remind her how much I loved the first day of camp. "You really need to stop killing my buzz, Linda, or I swear I will toss you into the lake and—"

Linda coughed her *very important* cough, killing my threat immediately, and then she nodded her head to the chair in the corner behind me.

I was almost too afraid to look. The last time we'd had someone in that chair, it had been a police officer here to tell us there was a fugitive on the loose in the nearby forest. It was the *bad news* chair and always complicated things. The fact that someone sat in that chair on the very first day of camp had to be a bad omen.

Turning slowly, I saw the cell phone first, pressed to his ear as if he were in the middle of a conversation on it and had only stopped because of my interruption. I saw his suit next, well-tailored and the blackest of blacks. It fit over a slim but strong body, the kind I'd expect to see on someone who went to the gym often but didn't live there. His shoes were the shiniest I'd ever seen, though there was already a patch of dust on the left one. I had a feeling he hadn't noticed yet. I looked at his face last, not on purpose, but it seemed appropriate when I took in features that most definitely equaled Ryan Reynolds's. He had a sharp jaw, sharp haircut, sharp gaze. Handsome though he was, everything about him was sharp, as if he thought smooth edges were a weakness.

"Colin Donovan," I guessed. "Macy's dad." That last part I wasn't sure about, mostly because he neither looked old enough to have a nine-year-old nor had the countenance of a father who would personally bring his daughter to a summer camp in Northern California. He looked like the sort to stuff her into a car and send her on her way, glad to be rid of her for the summer. Plenty of parents dropped their girls off every June, but none of them looked a thing like this guy.

Realizing he still held his phone, Mr. Donovan glanced at the screen then decided to hang up, though I heard a voice on the other end start asking if he was still there. He kept the phone in his hand, ready to jump right back to it when he'd finished conducting his business.

"Her?" That one word filled the air with his disgust and disapproval.

I'm sorry, what? I knew the question was for Linda, but I stepped in between her and this guy who was starting to get on my every nerve. I had campers to go welcome, his daughter among them, and I did not need some high and mighty bigwig thinking me incompetent. "I'm Beck Alvarez," I said and held out my hand, though I would have rather hit him with it than let him shake it. "One of the head counselors here at Camp Rockwood. Is there a concern I can help you resolve while I'm here?"

He didn't even consider reaching for my hand, instead leaning around me to fix Linda with a stare that, honestly, I was glad wasn't for me. "I thought I made myself clear in my emails, Mrs. Young."

Behind me, Linda sputtered a little, which was uncharacteristic. Organized as she was, she always had the perfect responses for irate parents, no matter their grievances. "Of course, Mr. Donovan. I assure you, I was incredibly diligent in choosing which cabin your daughter should spend her stay here at—"

"My concern is not for the cabin," Donovan said, and he fixed that stare on me.

I wasn't usually intimidated, but jeez, the guy knew how to scowl. I felt myself withering, which was not a feeling I enjoyed experiencing. What right did this jerk have to step into my world and assume he knew everything? How could he possibly think a couple of sentences— spoken in jest, no less—were enough to gauge my entire character?

"Beck," Linda said, her voice thick with warning. She knew me well. "I called you in here so we could discuss expectations for the next two months. If you could take a seat." It was not a request.

This is fine, I told myself as I sank into the chair closer to Linda's desk. *We'll just have a little chat, he'll leave, and I can get back to my girls.* Sitting there with my back to Colin Donovan, though, I was finding it hard to focus on positivity. I could practically feel his disapproval searing the back of my head.

"Like I started telling you this morning," Linda said to me, "Mr. Donovan's daughter will be attending our camp this year. Macy. I've put her in your cabin because I feel you're one of our best counselors, and—"

Mr. Donovan cleared his throat. "And I happen to disagree with her choice," he said.

Linda tensed, but I pretended I didn't notice and turned instead to face the guy behind me. There were a lot of things I thought about saying to him, but I kept my words civil. For now. He thought he had some kind of power here? He didn't, and I would make sure he knew that.

"I'm sorry you feel that way," I said calmly.

His jaw tightened.

"I truly believe Rebecka here is our best counselor," Linda added, and I had to turn and give her a warm smile because I knew she wouldn't say it if she didn't mean it. There was no room in that organized head of hers for lies. "I understand your concerns, Mr. Donovan, but there really is no way for us to change things now that camp has begun."

He narrowed his eyes, and his hand seemed to tighten around his phone. "Just switch her with another girl," he suggested. "How hard can that be?"

I snorted a laugh before I could hold it back, and his surprise made it all too easy for me to ask, "Do you understand girls at all, Mr. Donovan?"

"Excuse me?"

"Beck," Linda sighed, but she had sat down in her chair, knowing full well it was dangerous to step between me and a challenge.

And Mr. Donovan was certainly a challenge. Whatever he thought of me, he seemed to think he could make whatever changes he wanted without any consequences, and I had to make sure he understood exactly why he couldn't do that. I had to protect my girls. *All* of them, whether in my cabin or not.

"Mr. Donovan," I said and stood to face him, "we're twenty minutes into the first day of camp."

"Which should make a change like this easy," he said. Jeez, did he know any expressions outside of that scowl of his? And he kept his voice so smooth and controlled that I wondered if he even had any emotion behind that thick skin of his.

"You mistake my meaning," I replied. "Two minutes, maybe, but by now those girls have picked their bunks, chosen their best friends, decided on their enemies, and elected a leader to follow. You try to upset that, and you'll have eighty girls out for blood. Yours, specifically."

Donovan tilted his head to the side a little, a bit of a wrinkle marring that smooth forehead of his. "You make them sound like a savage civilization with no law and order, Miss Alvarez."

"She's not wrong," Linda said, probably not as under her breath as she might have planned.

"My point," I continued, "is we can't have you upsetting the whole order of things just because you're a little worried. Mr. Donovan, I promise I will be looking after your daughter all summer."

He got to his feet, folding his arms as he towered above me. He was tall, but it was his powerful energy that made him loom over me like he did. "But you're not looking after her at the moment," he said.

"Yes, because I'm busy talking to you."

"Rebecka." Linda's voice was as sharp as Donovan's skinny black tie as she stood and put on her *I mean business* face. "Could I speak to you in private for a moment? Mr. Donovan, if you don't mind," and she gestured toward the door.

I couldn't decide if his expression meant he wanted to storm out or shout at me until his voice went hoarse, but he thankfully agreed to Linda's request and slipped out of the office, closing the door behind him.

I didn't waste a second. "Don't try to tell me I'm overreacting. That is classic control freak behavior, and honestly I bet his daughter's relieved to be here at camp where he can't get to her because a man like that couldn't possibly be fun to have for a dad when he can't even step away for a few minutes let alone a few months, and I'm surprised you haven't sent him packing now that the girls are settling in and—"

"Beck," Linda said.

I dropped into my chair, staring at her. I'd never heard her sound like that, like the world was on her shoulders and she wasn't sure she could hold it up any longer.

"We can't afford to anger Mr. Donovan."

"Can't afford—"

"He has made a generous donation—extremely generous—to Camp Rockwood, and without it, we wouldn't..."

I swallowed, though it felt like my throat was stuck shut. "What are you saying, Linda?" Camp Rockwood had been open for fifty years, and never once had there been any money problems. At least, not that I knew of. Linda would have told me if... Wouldn't she?

Collapsing into her chair, Linda let her breath out in a steady stream and deflated. "The city has decided to sell the land, Beck. Some developer wants to come in and create a high-end resort, and we don't have enough stored up to... Without Colin Donovan, we'll lose this place. We'll lose everything."

"Sell the land?" The words tasted bitter, like when Chuck put too much cilantro in the salad. "I thought we owned the land."

Linda shook her head. "We've been lucky for so many years," she sighed. "The city has allowed us to use this plot, since we take on the girls from Hargrave School every summer and give the foster families a bit of a break. But with this economy, they're hard pressed to sell while it still gets a good price."

"And Colin Donovan's money can buy it," I surmised. "But only if he stays happy and doesn't pull his donation." My heart ached at the thought, sitting heavy in my chest as my ears rang a bit. Lose Camp Rockwood? I couldn't even imagine the idea. I'd been coming to this camp since I was six years old, and I'd been a counselor since I turned eighteen. For the last twenty-two years, this place had been my home every summer. If all that went away...

Linda uttered a word I'd never heard her use here at Rockwood, and I raised my eyebrows. But she waved my reaction away and said, "I'm sorry to spring all this on you, Beck. I should have told you sooner, but I was hoping to find a way around it before I worried anyone. But you of all people... You deserved to know, and I'm sorry."

It'll be fine. I didn't believe that. *We can make it work.* That sounded better. *We'll find a way.* Reasonable. "I can be nice," I assured Linda, though the idea of facing Mr. Donovan again, especially now that my energy seemed to have been sucked out of my chest with a plunger, was making me a little nauseous. "I promise."

If Linda believed me, it didn't show on her face. She had been head of Camp Rockwood for six summers now, so she and I knew each other as well as we knew our own families. She could read me easily, but I could also read her.

"What?" I asked warily.

"I'm not sure you can last that long," she admitted.

I didn't realize she had such little faith in me. "It'll only be a few minutes," I reasoned. "An hour at most, and then he'll be gone."

Linda's face turned as white as the marshmallows we had prepped for tonight's campfire. "About that..."

ABOUT THE AUTHOR

Dana LeCheminant has been telling stories since she was old enough to know what stories were. After spending most of her childhood reading everything she could get her hands on, she eventually realized she could write her own books too, and since then she always has plots brewing and characters clamoring to be next to have their stories told. A lover of all things outdoors, she finds inspiration while hiking the remote Utah backcountry and cruising down rivers. Until her endless imagination runs dry, she will always have another story to tell.

Made in the USA
Monee, IL
22 March 2022

93314859R00152